AUTHOR'S NOTE

This series is dark. Like, really dark. If you've read my other books and are thinking, "No big deal, I can handle this…" I assure you, this is darker than anything I've ever written before.

So, if you have any issues or triggers with dub-con, forced marriage, humiliation, or a dark ménage that will end in a MFM relationship, then turn back now.

If you just read all of this and you're not triggered, then read on and I promise you'll love what happens ahead.

THE FERAL PRINCESS - BOOK 2

Madeline,
Dang girl, are
you a werewolf?
Because I'm lycan
what I see.

defiled

ANN DENTON

LE RUE PUBLISHING

Haha
Hope you like
the book better
than the lame
werewolf joke I
told. Thank you
so much! ♥
Ann Denton

Cover by Covers by Aura

Le Rue
Publishing

Le Rue Publishing
320 South Boston Avenue, Suite 1030
Tulsa, OK 74103
www.LeRuePublishing.com
ISBN: 978-1-951714-26-0

Dedicated to the moon goddess and my amazing beta readers. I love you as much as Jonah.

1

ELENA

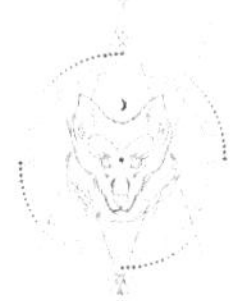

My life is as insane as a movie right now, I think as I twist the skirt of my candy-red dress with my fingers and listen to the shrill whine of the catering van's wheels beneath me as we speed down the freeway. Jonah and I are making a wild, crazy bid for freedom in a van that rattles and seizes up if we try to go over seventy.

My heart still pounds wildly even though we've been on the road for an hour. It feels like I've been sprinting the entire time, as though I'm trying to dash a marathon, pushing with everything I've got. My entire chest aches from the effort. But my heart rate and reality are out of sync; I'm scared, but I'm not literally running. Instead, I'm running away from my problem … a huge, furious alpha male.

I crouch in the back of the van on an old black plastic floor mat that cracks and groans each time I move. I stare out the windshield at the moon goddess as Jonah drives, trying to focus on what's ahead, not what's behind us, but my neck keeps prickling—warning me. Black has to know we've left by now.

If he's still alive.

What if he didn't survive the fight with Stone?

My stomach gives a lurch at that thought but I blame it on a pothole because I don't care if the fucker is still alive. I don't. Black was literally ready to make my life a living hell full of sex and servitude.

I don't want to think about the glint shining in his dark brown eyes, don't want to know what he's thinking right now, because the very *idea* of him, much less the mental image of his massive nearly seven-foot-tall form, sends spiders skittering down my skin.

The only reaction I have to him is fear and loathing, I rebuke myself, but it almost feels like my mind is trying to coach my body into believing that truth. My body has all sorts of different reactions to him and his billboard-worthy abs, his Jason Momoa-style long hair, his dark eyes—reactions that are as dark and depraved as he is.

My body's a fool.

As we go up a curving ramp in a section of the city where highways weave around each other like friendship bracelets, I brace myself against the metal food racks on either side of the catering van—our grand escape vehicle. The old white van, with its cheesy cartoon elephant logo painted on the sides, is a far cry from anything in the *Fast and the Furious*. If anything, we're as embarrassingly uncool as *Scooby-Doo,* not that I give a shit.

The racks I'm clasping are filled with stacks of covered metal serving dishes that slosh with every turn we take. The scent of curry and masala sauce colors the space—apparently Black had Indian food catered for the fight, which is an odd choice, but whatever, at least the catering van's scent makes for the perfect cover for my own idiotic omega scent, which attracts wolves like bees to honey.

I turn and peer out the back window trying to see if we're being followed by anyone from the Lobo pack. My reflection gazes back at me—gray eyes and black hair both wild. I blink and focus beyond my dim reflection on the cars behind us but I don't see the sleek Audi that Black kidnapped me in. I don't see anything that looks like it would belong to that pretentious asshole. Just a few semi-trucks and some minivans. As far as I can tell, we aren't being shadowed.

Yet.

When I glance over at Jonah, his white-knuckled death grip on the wheel tells me all I need to know: He's just as tense as I am. His normally go-with-the-flow, good-natured beta posture is rigid as a board. Jonah's MMA-style arm muscles remain flexed—and not because I'm making him pose for nude pictures like I did two weeks ago. No, he's worried as fuck—I can see his head turning, eyes glancing at the side mirrors every few seconds.

He's looking for the exact same thing I just was. A tail. My sweet blond boy with his All-American looks and his soft smile is as scared as I am. Maybe even more, because if we get caught ... I'm pretty certain Black won't kill me.

But Jonah?

A steak knife pierces my naval and the sharp barbs jerk upward as I picture just what Black might do to my beta.

We won't get caught. I scold myself for even allowing negative thoughts to creep in. Both my track coach and my dad constantly pounded me with positive visualization crap. I put it to use as I try to focus on the road as we level back out, leaving the twisting pretzel of ramps and the glowing lights of the city behind us. The Colorado countryside comes into view, and I gaze at the silhouettes of the pine trees, the moonlight, and the soft glow the goddess casts on the asphalt. It looks almost as if she's lighting the path just for us. I wonder if she's trying to help us, if she saw everything and knows what we've been through.

"Moon Goddess, help us," I whisper softly.

Jonah hears and snorts but doesn't crack a joke.

Any other night, he might mock me; we might end up in one of our lengthy debates about belief—he doesn't think the moon goddess or any goddess is real. But he doesn't say anything tonight, because tonight *everything's* different.

One day.

What a difference a single day can make. Yesterday, we were passing dirty notes in class. Today, we're running for our lives.

My life, really.

Alpha Black claimed me and thought he could toss a ring on my finger and get a free pass to do whatever he wanted just because my wolf's an omega. Stupid fucking shifter magic.

I almost wish my wolf hadn't shown up at all. Everything went downhill the moment she did.

I search for her inside my head, that coal-black coat, and moon-colored eyes, but I can't find her. I give up and gaze down at the huge, sparkling ring from Black

—the one that would make me Mrs. Maddox—and yank it off, scratching myself a bit in the process. Part of me wants to hurl the hunk of rock away, but the realistic side of me knows we might need to pawn it.

We didn't run with money.

Fuck.

"Here. Check how many hours we have to go." Jonah holds his cell phone up so I can see it through the little sliding window that connects the cab and the back part of the van. I'm crouched in the back, which helped keep my flaming red dress and my scent hidden as we trundled slowly out of the gates at Black's estate. At this point, it's not worth stopping to change seats. Actually, even if we stopped, it's probably best if I stay in the back where my scent is cloaked. Who knows what shifter territory we're driving through. An omega's scent does wild things to alphas. I've seen it and it isn't pretty.

I shove the engagement ring into my strapless bra for safekeeping—even though it digs in uncomfortably—and carefully make my way to the little window. I reach through and grab the phone from Jonah's hand before lightly bopping him on the shoulder.

"You trying to top from the bottom?" I ask the beta shifter because he gave me an order instead of politely asking.

He gives me a tight grin and pretends to be eager. "Will that get me in trouble?"

I chuckle, but neither his grin nor my laugh is sincere; we're both putting on a show, trying to comfort the other with some sort of normalcy and banter. But I appreciate the fact that he saw me staring at that ring, about to spiral into a full-on freak-out, and yanked me out of it with a distraction. That's what's amazing about Jonah. He actually sees me, unlike that bastard Black, who just sees my omega status.

I scoot to the side of the sliding panel so that Jonah can still see me but I'm not blocking his view out the back window. I lean back against the racks, ignoring the way one of the drawers handles pokes uncomfortably into my ass as I pull the map up on his phone. My own phone was left behind because there was nowhere to hide it in this ridiculous dress with its low-cut top and all the slits in the skirt. It's high-class trash. I can't wait to throw it in the garbage—and these shoes too, with their stupid heels.

"Where are we going?" I ask.

"New York City."

I start to enter in the name but then I have a realization that makes me pause. "Wait. Won't they be able to track your phone?"

"No. I downloaded one of those VPN things. They hide your location and shit."

"Oh." I breathe a sigh of relief; Jonah seems to have thought of everything. Thank fucking goodness because without a phone we'd be dead in the water.

As soon as I think that though, a text comes through from an unknown number.

You're dead, Murky.

A shiver travels up my spine. Even though the number is unknown, I know it's Black. It has to be. He used Jonah's pack name, just like he did when he first brought him down to the basement to see me. Anger stacks up inside of me at the text. Fuck him for threatening Jonah.

I don't acknowledge the little corner of my stomach that unclenches, grateful that Black won his idiotic fight. That part of me is just happy to be dealing with the monster I know, instead of a big unknown. I can avoid the monster I know.

I plan to do just that.

I don't want Jonah worrying more than he already is, so I click on the message, and then find the option to delete the text. I briefly wish I could just delete Alpha Black from my mind, but technology is always easier and more efficient than real life.

I type with my thumbs and hear a faint clinking behind me, which causes me to stop and panic for a second at the unfamiliar sound before I realize that I'm just leaning on one of the drawers of cutlery. *Idiot,* I scold myself. Jumping at shadows. If we are in the damned Scooby van, I guess that makes me Shaggy.

I buckle down and focus on directions and driving time to our intended destination.

Jonah speaks, "Bright lights. Loud sounds. Awful smells leak out of the manhole covers, I'm told. Never been there. All-human city though. No wolf shifters in the Big Apple. I'll miss the forest, the trees, all my friends. But I'll take freedom over forest any day." His voice cracks a little because he's lying through his teeth. He's going to miss his friends and family like hell.

Goddess, I'm going to make everything up to this boy, I swear. I'm going to make it worth it. "Twenty-seven hours," I call out. "We can take shifts and drive straight through except for gas."

Jonah gives a nod, glancing at me in the rear-view mirror with those light, liquid blue eyes of his. He says nothing, which only makes me worry more. He's not the strong, silent type. Dirty banter and a dollop of whipped cream sweetness are more his style. My stomach twists uncomfortably as all the things we don't discuss whisper their worries into my ear. We don't discuss the difficulty that gas will be, considering we ran without any cash. If we use a credit card, I've no doubt that Black and the Lobos will track us instantly. We don't discuss housing when we get there. We don't discuss the fact that Jonah knows I slept with Black in an irrational moment of … of … of something.

My panic starts to creep slowly back, like ivy slipping its tendrils around another plant, going from innocuous to choking in what feels like the blink of an eye.

Shit. Did we make the wrong choice to leave tonight? Should we have waited, planned this out more? Twenty-seven hours feels like it will be a lifetime. How can my heart handle twenty-six more hours of this level of panic? A million what-ifs drift through my mind. But the fight was a good chance to escape. It was the only time so many alphas would be caught up in bloodshed and ignoring me and my stupid scent, which makes them frantic.

I glance back at the map, at the blood-red trail on the screen that we're supposed to follow to get out of these woods we're in. "Only a few hours until we get to Kansas," I say.

"There's no place like home," he retorts, still too stiff, his tone still too flat to pull off anything reminiscent of *Wizard of Oz*.

This time, I don't bother to play along because I'm just so damn grateful that we have somewhere to go that I nearly choke up. "Thank fuck there are places out there that shifters hate."

"Yeah. Thank goodness." His voice cracks.

Both of us apparently suck at this "cool under pressure" thing—we'd never be the badass characters in a movie. But that's alright. I don't need that. I just need him.

Jonah drives as I try to picture the two of us making it in the concrete jungle. New York City lacks the space and freedom to change forms and run. But I don't care about shifting. My wolf's been hiding ever since ... well actually, since Black appeared, I realize.

If that isn't a sign that we aren't supposed to be together, I don't know what is. I wish I'd said that to his stupid face. "My wolf hates you so much she won't come around, motherfucker!"

My mind flashes back to his face, then quickly flickers to the hot-as-hell sex, the rough pads of his calloused fingers, and that intense glow in his deep brown eyes as he hovered over me. No. Wait. Fuck. That's not what I meant to think about. I wanted to picture the angry look on his face. But his angry face and his sex face are nearly identical, goddammit. I shove that memory aside roughly, hoping it trips and falls flat on its face. Hot sex isn't the basis for a relationship.

Jonah's the exception to that rule because, though we started as a casual hook-up, he's become my best friend over the past year. My throat grows tight as I turn to stare at the back of his buzzed blond head through the tiny window. I wish I could sit up front with him. I wish we could hold hands through this. I wish I wasn't being toted off secretly like a convict escaping prison. Longing and wistfulness raise goosebumps on my arms and combine with a huge, massive fountain of gratitude. "What would I do without you?"

"Let's never find out," Jonah replies, hitting the gas harder as if flooring it will skip all the miles and hours of tension ahead of us.

"Deal," I say, and I have to blink back my tears as guilt seeps into the base of my stomach, writhing beneath the pit of eels already there.

I don't deserve him.

My mouth opens and I'm tempted to tell him how much he means to me, but this is not the fucking time or place. I don't want it to be a confession under duress. So, I shut my lips, realizing how dry my mouth is. I don't think I've had something to drink in a couple hours. I search around the back of the van for water, thankful when I find an open twenty-four pack with a few bottles remaining. I snag one for each of us and make my way forward to the little sliding window. I bend forward, bracing one hand on the bottom of the window so I don't fall if we hit a pothole.

I hand one bottle through to Jonah, saying, "Here. Water. We won't die of hunger or thirst at least."

Jonah cracks open his bottle and takes a quick swig as I stare out at the fields all around us before I look back at the side of his chiseled face. I'm certain he's thinking of the million other ways we could die. I know I am. My own mind drifts back to the way that Black half-shifted into his wolf when he fought off Pluto, another pack alpha. They'd looked like monsters with wolf heads and massive werewolf-like torsos. Those claws …

I can almost feel one dragging gently down my spine and making me shiver. I have to distract myself, so I clear my throat and say, "Road trip game. It's called 'My Cow.' Ever played?"

"Nope."

"Whoever spots any cows first gets to yell out 'My Cow' and then count up all the cows they see. Those are your points. If we pass a graveyard, you yell, 'My graveyard!' and that kills the other person's cows."

Jonah snorts derisively. "Who comes up with these games?"

I shrug as I open my own water and take a sparing sip —I want to minimize bathroom stops. "My dad." Memories of Dad flood me then; his smile, the laugh he had that boomed through the entire car and seemed to shake the glass the first time I won My Cow when I was seven. A soft smile crests my lips and I glance up at the ceiling of the van, sending up a thought toward him, asking him to send Jonah and me good luck. I hope he's watching over us. I hope that even though he turned his back on life, he didn't turn it on me.

Fuck.

Those types of thoughts are going to make me break down. I blow out a breath. Instead of allowing myself to think, I stare out at the landscape, which is getting flatter and duller, willing a damned farm to appear. I shout prematurely, as we crest a small rise, "My cow!"

Jonah shakes his head. "There are no fucking—"

I point, vindicated when a tiny farm with a few cows comes into view. "My-cow-one-two-three-four!"

"You cheated!" Jonah exclaims, but he chuckles as we drive past the farm with its three cows and solitary horse I mistakenly called a cow. He's not really upset and I'm just glad the mood in the van isn't somber as a grave site any longer.

"Yeah, I did. Get up on it, boy."

"If I cheated, you'd threaten to spank me."

"If you cheated, I *would* spank you," I retort. "Maybe I should do it anyway for you calling me out."

"Maybe you should." His smile in the rear-view mirror is real this time, and bright and beautiful as a sunflower. God, I just want to take his face between my hands and kiss every inch of his skin. He's so fucking precious I want to squeeze him to death.

"We're going to get to New York, and I'm going to find us a place and get a job, and then I'm going to spoil you rotten," I tell him. "I'm going to save up and buy you a new gaming system."

"What about a home gym?" Jonah asks with mock innocence. "I mean, if you want me to stay pretty and stuff for you."

I chuckle. "We'll probably have to live in a studio on the millionth floor of some high rise. Carrying groceries up the stairs should be enough of a workout."

"What about abs?"

"I can sit on your feet while you do sit-ups."

"Naked?"

"If that will motivate you."

Jonah's grin suddenly turns soft as he stares at me in the rear-view mirror. My breath catches and my heart thumps hard inside my bones as chills creep up over my neck. How is it possible that I stumbled onto a guy this perfect? And then I almost lost him. I have to swallow hard to vanquish the tender lump in my throat.

Heat trickles up my thighs like it normally does when I'm around him. But then it flares strangely, shooting up my spine, blazing across my cheeks, before falling back down again and pooling in my low belly. "Fuck!" I breathe, clenching Jonah's phone and my water bottle. The heat doesn't lessen. It intensifies like a fever, but a violent one. It whips me, lashes my arms and nipples, slides down my chest to my belly. In less than a minute, it has invaded like the Roman Empire—spreading across the continent, taking the fuck over everywhere. It ravages me, wildly.

Suddenly, I'm parched. I unscrew my water bottle and gulp a few sips, but that doesn't seem to help because my entire body is suddenly too hot. My clothes feel too tight, scratchy, uncomfortable.

I drop Jonah's phone through the partition window so that I have a free hand and can drag my nails deliciously over my skin. But the need isn't sated. The heat flashes back up to my face again.

I sink down to the ground, then lean over to the side to rest my cheek against the cool plastic wall that separates the cab from the rest of the van. Am I going to puke? Fuck. I feel lightheaded and *off.*

"What's wrong? Elena?" Jonah barks, sharp and panicked.

"I'm fine," I moan—though I feel anything but fine. My stomach doesn't twist but there's an inferno inside of me, and my blood starts pounding. Sweat beads on my neck and drips down to pool between my breasts, where my nipples suddenly pulse as if they've been pinched.

What the hell is going on? It's so hot, so warm, my eyes grow hooded as though I'm sleepy but I'm not—I'm panicking as I drop the water bottle, ignoring the fact that I didn't close the lid all the way. A line of water is flung across my skirt painting it with dark little droplets.

I press both my hands to the wall and hug it with my torso, trying to cool myself down. But the fire isn't on top of my skin, it's internal. It burns through me until it finds the perfect spot.

My pussy feels as hot as the sidewalk in July. The heat travels up and down along my slit, stroking it, invoking an involuntarily clench and my eyelids flutter shut as desperate *want* rips through me, burning away rational thought.

My hips start to gyrate where I sit and I feel my panties suddenly get soaked, though my hand hasn't even drifted down there. Want, craving, and that mindless yearning just before orgasm blasts through me and I quake for a moment—right on the cusp of falling over the precipice.

When I don't find immediate release, my body calms back down and the flames retreat a bit, but suddenly, bam! I'm on the edge of tears. I want to weep.

I want to cry because the smells in the van have gotten stronger and they're burning my nose—and because there's nothing soft or warm or safe about this space. My craving for touch shifts to a craving for safety, security, cuddles. Jonah.

Shit. Shit. Shit.

My mind claws its way through this fog of sensations as I slowly realize what's happening. "Jonah," I croak, "I think … I'm going into heat."

2

JONAH

Oh fuck.

Her heat's here?

I'm not qualified for this shit.

My wolf paces back and forth inside my head, his tail swishing side to side. My mind swings back and forth just like his tail. What the hell do we do? My instant reaction is fear. But then I catch a whiff of her scent—that lavender and white chocolate. Her exotic candy smell is laced with the salt of her sweat. My body reacts immediately, blood spiraling down my spine and gathering in my dick.

My wolf howls inside my head. I see him appear like an avatar in my line of vision, trotting across the black dashboard, his miniature gray head lifting until his nose points right at the moon. "Mate!" he proclaims.

I'd thought my hands were gripping the steering wheel as tight as they possibly could before. I was wrong. They tighten down on the leather until I can feel the hard edge of the metal ring underneath.

My wolf wants me to pull over on the side of the road and take care of Elena, who's moaning in pain or longing, or both. He can't fucking stand the fact that I'm doing something else right now. The survival requirement of driving does not register.

He flashes me vivid images of roughly fucking her and then gently spooning. In wolf form, of course.

I tell him to shut the hell up. *We're escaping right now.*

His gray ears flatten, and he fights the urge to bare his teeth at me, which for him, is practically as aggressive as another wolf's bite. He doesn't just roll over in my mind like usual but continues his annoying trot from side to side. We both grow frustrated with each other. But I don't really know what I can do right now.

I glance in the rear-view mirror to check on Elena; I can't see her, so I reach up and adjust the little rectangle, but she's hidden no matter how I angle it. She must be on the floor. That's no damn good. Does a heat hurt? I thought they were like ... sexy? Shit. I'm not sure what to do. If we stop, Black will find us. That's a guarantee.

Maybe Elena can grit it out. She's tough. Maybe if we don't encourage the heat, it will just fade away and come back a different day or something. Yeah right. I don't really hold out hope for that stupid thought. I just wish it was true.

I reach for the dash and fumble with the air conditioner. "How about some more A.C. Think that will help?" I grimace at how dumb I sound. But the only things I know about an omega's heat are that she literally gets warm and needs lots of alpha dick. I can't give her that.

"Yes. Water. A.C. Yes." Her voice is weak, like she's speaking through gritted teeth. But at least her answer is an affirmation. It's something I *can* do, as opposed to stopping.

I twist the little black knob and turn the air on full blast. Then I try to edge sideways in my lane because the semi-truck passing us is being an asshole and riding that center divider line. I don't have enough hands to flip him off, so I focus on my girl instead. I swivel all the vents in reach so that they point at that little window leading to the back.

"If you stand up, you should be able to feel the air," I say, squinting at a green road sign that tells me the next town is two hundred miles out. That's a long haul before we can stop for any supplies Elena might need.

What does an omega in heat need? Would a vibrator work?

I try really fucking hard not to picture her using one but fail miserably. It doesn't help that she stands up and presses her cleavage toward the little window as she pours a water bottle over her head. The droplets trace her cheeks, drizzle over her lips. They splash and skate along her skin and down her chest. Shit. It's like a damned beach porno or something.

I can't help but lick my lips before I realize I have to mash on the brakes because the semi who just passed me is cutting us off. Fuckwad. I flip him off because he nearly killed me and because he just ruined one of the greatest sights of all god-damned time.

There are some thumps and muttered curses as the quick braking sends Elena stumbling.

"Sorry!" I call out, cringing.

I don't know if she hears me because she doesn't immediately respond. But then Elena gives a long, shuddering moan that sounds almost orgasmic. My dick twitches and I can't resist adjusting the rear-view mirror again to check on her, hoping that moan doesn't mean she's actually hurt, and my stupid brain isn't just being a horny asshole.

Nope.

She's leaning back against one of the catering racks, her pale thighs jutting out of the slits in her red dress. Her eyes are glazed as she stares in my direction. What's more—they aren't even her normal gray right now. They glow gold and feral. Wolf's eyes.

Fucking hell. Is her wolf staring out at me?

That's so damned hot I can't even think.

Elena's lips part in lust and I watch her right shoulder, the one closest to me bob up and down, making any little droplets of water that still clung to her skin race down. My eyes travel south. Her nipples are hard under her sopping dress, which has turned from fire-engine red to scarlet in the wet patches. Her right hand has dipped inside one of those slits in her skirt and I'm pretty certain she's fingering herself right now. Oh my god.

I have to rip my eyes from the sight so that I don't crash this damn van. Instead, I stare ahead into the darkness, trying to count to distract myself and failing miserably. My breath comes out in short puffs as I struggle to focus on driving.

Without streetlights, the sky feels like a tunnel wrapping around us. My vision narrows. Sound becomes more intense. Every little whimper Elena makes and the soft *shlick* of her fingers moving down there gets louder until my ears are captivated. Dirty visuals of her soft pussy fill my head and my driving goes into autopilot for a minute.

But then Elena screams. I nearly jump out of my skin, my hands flying off the wheel. The narrow field of vision from my high beams changes from asphalt to weeds.

Fuck!

I have to grab back onto the wheel and swerve to straighten us out, my teeth clenched as we judder over the rumble strip on the side of the highway, the strip that warns you that you're about to careen off the road. I struggle not to yank the wheel and over-correct, sending us slamming into yet another semi passing this shit-for-acceleration van.

My heart spins as fast as our tires until I finally get us leveled out.

"Dammit Elena! What the hell was that?"

I glance in the mirror. Her face is pained, and her teeth are clenched. "I'm sorry! I need you!" She bursts into a sob, tears dripping down from her unnaturally golden eyes. A frown wrecks her gorgeous face as she stumbles toward the little wall dividing us and holds up a hand in the window.

Even in the shitty reflection of the rear-view mirror, I can see her fingers are sopping wet. "I can't come! I can't!" Her tears turn into deep sobs. Her entire chest quakes as she clutches that window and whimpers, "I tried. I tried to take care of it because I know right now is the worst time. I tried to make it go away. I can't."

That sopping hand, the one covered with her cum—no, wait, omegas have slick. That hand covered in slick reaches through the window towards me, glistening despite the darkness. I inhale, in both fear and anticipation, about to tell Elena to shut that window and back away. I need to focus on driving. But she's crying her eyes out. Elena doesn't cry. At least, not before Black, she didn't. Bastard.

I waver about what to do. I wish I could call someone and figure out the best way to help her. I—

The scent of her slick hits me. An omega's scent isn't supposed to affect betas. But Elena's has always driven me wild. Maybe because my wolf claimed her. Or because I did. Right now, her sugar-sweet smell is twice as potent. And there's something darker mixed with it. Normally, her scent brings to mind lightness and pale-yellow tones in my head, like mellowed sunshine. But now, there's anise mixed in with her white chocolate perfume.

Something about that dark smell feels desperate.

Wanton.

When her slippery fingers skim my neck … I'm a goner. My wolf senses growl. My eyes start to shift. I feel myself and my animal merge.

The darkness of the road suddenly brightens, and I can see all sorts of things I couldn't before. The tips of the tall grass around us separate from the sky. A cow wades through a wavering field near a tree line in the distance. Up ahead, a farmhouse peeks out of a dirt road cut right out of the side of the highway.

"Elena, we can't," I grit out, using the very last shred of my humanity to override my wolf, who wants to stop the fucking car and rut on the side of the road.

Her hands release my neck and she retreats while I avoid her eyes, not wanting to know what kind of reaction my rejection provokes. She's on edge right now.

Smash! She slams into the side metal trays and I flinch, my shoulders rising. The scent of masala sauce grows twice as prominent. Did she break the drawer? Yank it out? I can't tell, all I know is it smells like she spilled it all over the floor.

I can only imagine how overwhelming this is for her. I remember how badly the scents affected me during my first shift. And if her wolf has been hiding, she hasn't had a second to get used to anything. Wolf emotions, instincts, are different. They take getting used to … but throw a heat on top of it? Fucking bonkers.

I try to soften my tone, be more understanding. "Elena, honey, we can't—"

A wail that becomes a howl erupts from her throat and she smashes into the metal drawers again, a cacophony assaulting my ears. She goes full-on batshit.

I swallow hard, trying not to fucking yell at her when the van wobbles side to side during her freak out.

I need to be zen like Mom is, I tell myself. Calm. I try to breathe slowly in and out through my mouth to avoid the smell. My wolf—unhelpful fucker—keeps showing me damned wolf porn images while I try to play it cool and not drive off the frickin' road.

"Hey, we're almost there," I lie.

Elena collapses into another round of sobs, falling into a heap near the back doors of the van. I can just see the top of her black and white streaked hair in the rear-view mirror when she scratchily admits, "Jonah. I'm going crazy. I can't do this."

"Just a few more hours," I plead in a soothing voice. "Let's get further down the road to somewhere with lots of people to hide our scents." I really mean her scent, which is so potent right now, it's even overwhelming the masala smell. I look back in the mirror and see streaks of orange sauce sluicing down several drawer fronts, the drawers themselves dented. Elena's wildly yanking her hair, her hips gyrating into midair as she convulsively gasps.

"I can't Jonah. It hurts. I need you." She glances at the back door of the van and then back at me.

I hardly recognize her face. It's full of pain and teardrops, every ounce of her determination wiped away by torment. Her chest is shaking and her eyes are solid gold. Wolf eyes. Even when she was in Black's basement, she didn't look this bad. But right now, I swear ... she looks broken.

She gives off a whine that is somewhere between a human and wolf—high-pitched and pleading. It makes every part of me tremble.

Elena's sounds combined with my wolf's desperate images—he's convinced it's about to get worse, that she's about to leave us—make me grit my teeth.

Until I see Elena reach for the back doors of the van. She jerks the handle down, like she plans to jump out of a moving vehicle onto the highway.

My illusion of dragging this out, making it to the next town, pops and disintegrates.

My wolf's right. Mouse is right. Elena can't just push through this. She's so far gone that she's not thinking straight. She's going to find someone to take care of her heat. She'll kill herself to do it. *Fucking shit. We do not need this right fucking now,* I curse the universe.

I hit the wall. I snap. That farmhouse I saw in the distance is now a solid block to my right.

I jerk the wheel sharply toward the little road leading to what I'm sure is going to be the last mistake of our lives. But fuck it. I'm not letting Elena jump out of a van. I'm not letting some random stranger help with her heat. We ran together. We stick together. Until the end, however fucking soon that might be.

The van skids, tires smoking, because I've got too much heat for the ninety-degree turn I take and I'm forcing this fucking catering van to handle like a race car. "Hang on."

I can't slow down—a semi is on my tail—and I don't have time to check to see if Elena takes my warning seriously. All my focus stays on the dirt road as we streak off the highway. We bounce along a gravel path that feels like it hasn't been driven in forty years. Potholes are an understatement. There are craters. My knuckles tighten on the steering wheel and my knees sting as they ricochet off it repeatedly. Adrenaline sizzles inside my head.

My wolf gives a low growl as we're jostled. He hates this fucking car that runs slower than he could. He's pissed that I'm being so careless with our mate, letting her get thrown around every which way. He wants to take over. He thinks he knows what Elena needs.

NO! Fucker! I'm gonna give her what she needs, I think as I shove him roughly back, only leaving my eyes shifted because it's somewhat useful. He whines but doesn't fight, because he never fights. I ignore him. Other things require my focus. Driving. Scenting danger.

"You okay?" I call out.

"I survived if that's what you're asking." Her sarcasm is like a balm. That's the Elena I know. Not the weepy girl who begs with her eyes.

I blow out a breath, calming down and feeling better, trying to stay sharp. This van is not made for off-roading and I know if I take it too hard, this little grandmother of a car is going to fall and break some bones. I don't have the tools to fix her out in a place like this—Nowheresville, Kansas—so that *cannot* happen. "Come on, granny," I whisper under my breath as I navigate around a pothole that takes up a third of the road.

Sheaves of wheat and tall hay end up whacking the side of the van when I do that, but I ignore the angry sound, just focused on what I need to do. I need to take care of Elena.

I try not to think about the fact that I'm giving up our lead right now. I can't bear to think about the consequences if Black finds us.

Maybe he lost the fight.

I'd definitely have expected him to call me, to try to speak on the phone so he could use his alpha tone and order me to turn right back around. He hasn't. The phone hasn't rung once. But even if he lost, I'm pretty damn certain the alphas all figured out Elena was missing. And realizing that a single beta dude was also gone … it wouldn't have been hard to put two and two together.

I'm sure someone's after us. And knowing how Stone likes to punish his own wolves … Nope. Can't think about that.

I'm hoping that our head start plus the exhaust fumes stench from all the other cars on the road mean that all signs of our presence have been erased. I'm betting right now that everyone will think we're smart enough to stick to running, instead of stopping. Maybe, if we get lucky, the bastards will even think we headed for L.A. and go in the wrong direction.

We could use a bit of luck.

Even though I don't believe she's there, or gives a damn, I toss a quick look at the moon. I almost ask, but then Elena's slick-covered fingers pop out of nowhere and clench gently on my neck. She's reached through the window and is touching me. With a hand covered in her slick.

"Jonah," Elena whispers in a tone I've never heard from her before. It's higher, more girlishly beseeching. I chance a quick glance in the rear view at her tear-streaked face, which looks fierce right now, demanding. It's the face she gets whenever she's about to tell me to do something risky. Her eyes blaze like yellow fire and her grip on me tightens. My airway constricts.

"Almost there," I soothe, reaching up and gently prying away her fingers. I worry that if the heat hits her harder, she'll clench down on my throat. I don't mind a little choking in bed. On the road, it's a different story, especially with how this heat seems to have her swimming in and out of the deep end. Luckily, Elena relents easily, with just a needy whine.

Her hand retreats back through the window to her side of the vehicle. I try not to think about what she does with it because my job is to get her safely there before I *get her there*. There are still several steps I have to take. Step one: I need to figure out if I'm gonna have to fight anybody off.

If so—I hope to the fucking non-existent moon goddess it's a human.

I use my enhanced eyesight to scan the farmhouse as we approach. The building is a two-story, rundown clapboard building with blue trim and shutters. Someone cared about the landscaping at one point because there are a couple of rosebushes scattered here and there. But it has seen better days. Part of the roof has been covered in plywood, which juts up from the shingles like a square zit. Ugly as fuck. Okay, this family doesn't have a lot of money then. Still, we're in the Midwest, not Texas. The chances of them greeting us on their porch with a shotgun aimed in our direction are a bit lower. Kind of. I hope.

My eyes dart to the barn. The sliding door is shut. Nobody's over there. The barn's dark. A pond glistens behind the barn, but no one's around it. I come around a curve in the long drive, from behind some scrub trees and the barn. That gives me a better view of the house. My eyes scan the windows, but there's not a single light on.

Abandoned?

Hope creeps up.

But. They. Have. A. Cow.

There's a pasture behind the house and a single cow stands out there, a blot that I can only make out because of my wolf senses.

Someone lives here.

I try to keep the panic off my face as I start searching for shadows instead of lights. Silhouettes. I don't say anything though, because I don't want to freak Elena out any more than she already is. I'm sure her heat is enough to deal with.

I slow the van to a trundle. I reach over with my left hand and lower the driver's side window. "I'm going to partially shift," I warn Elena, so that I don't freak her out. She's never seen me half-shift into a werewolf-like monster. I don't know if she can handle it right now, but to keep her safe, I have to know what we're dealing with. "Don't look, okay?" I instruct, hoping against hope that she'll listen. The surest way to get Elena to defy you is to give her an order.

But the heat must be draining the fight from her. "Okay," she breathes, and I can't believe my ears. But then, I think about her tone. It's disconnected; it doesn't sound like she's paying much attention. In the rear view, she's not looking at me and her hands look busy again.

Good. She's distracted at least. I'll be quick, done before she even looks over.

I let the shift come over me, a tingling sensation rocketing through my upper body, heating my bones and reshaping them like liquid metal poured into an invisible mold. My clothes stretch awkwardly and the side seams on my pant legs burst, but I don't give a shit. My shirt stretches as my pecs grow massive, but it doesn't rip apart, just chokes me uncomfortably. A few seconds later, my wolf head nearly brushes the ceiling of the van and I have to duck to see out the windshield. My monster claws are so huge they have a hard time gripping the steering wheel. But I slowed the van enough that I don't worry about my monster's driving skills right this second. Instead, I tilt my nose to the cracked window and let my wolf take over.

Scents drift in—so many—it's like a patchwork quilt of smells.

Sort through them, I order. He does. There's cat piss and old horse shit coming from the barn but nothing fresh, new. Definitely nothing from the past week. The rose bushes give off a sickly sweet scent he doesn't like. The smell of green hay and cow patties drifts in from out in the pasture.

But the human scents—where are those? I bug him, redirecting our nose towards the house as the van inches slowly closer.

I sniff.

There's a faint scent of detergent. The barest hint of car oil. But no pungent sweat. No body odor. No perfumes or deodorants that leave scent shadows trailing after them. No chemically shampoos. I don't smell any of the things that mark occupied human places.

The cow is probably an escapee. Like us.

I breathe a sigh of relief and let my body shift back to human, my clothes hanging awkwardly now that they've been stretched beyond capacity. I glance up at the moon just as we reach the edge of the cracked-out cement driveway. The moon goddess is bright and soft, her light gently streaking down, landing in a narrow strip on the front door. Almost like she's pointing at it.

No way. Weird. It has to be a coincidence.

But the moonlight on the door grows brighter. I glance up to see if it just popped out from behind a cloud. But there aren't any clouds close to the moon.

Is it possible?

Is she real?

Did she fucking guide us to an abandoned house so that I could keep Elena safe?

Wolves are supposed to be her treasures. Omegas are supposed to be ours.

This seems too damn extreme to be luck. I furrow my brow up at the silvery moon. Maybe … just maybe, we got some divine help.

3

JONAH

My mind is blown. My wolf projects a smug image of a moon goddess inside my head. I'm trying to decide if I had a moment there or just a crisis of atheism.

But that debate cuts off when Elena jerks open the back doors of the van and bolts for the house. Her long, lean runner's legs pelt through the overgrown grass despite the fact that she's in heels.

She vaults over a low bush and scrambles up the wooden steps. She's literally gone before I can snap my jaw shut after it fell open when I stared at the moon.

Fucking track star.

I snap out of my reverie and shove the van into park, yanking out the key and kicking open the door so that I can follow my mate inside. I don't know what the hell a beta can do about a heat, but I'm about to find out.

My fingers are shaking from excitement and intimidation as I pocket the key. My chest and the tips of my ears grow warm. Nervous.

The porch steps creak under my weight, as does the front door, which had a lock at some point. But someone sawed out the deadbolt, leaving a hole into the door so that it swings open easily.

Fucking great. Easy for vagrants and vandals to wander in. As I glance backward at the road, I realize how far we are from the highway. The farm isn't as visible as I'd imagined. Especially at night. In fact, as I peer around, I can only see two distant porch lights from neighboring farms. Both appear to be several miles away. The tension in my shoulders eases and I walk inside. The likelihood of a visit from someone tonight seems rather low. I blow out a relieved breath and step on in.

I glance to the right. The front room is a mess. A formal sitting room with a fireplace has been desecrated by spray-painted orange dicks all over the old flower-print wallpaper. Empty crushed beer cans are stacked inside the fireplace and spill out onto the hearth. There's no furniture in here, but I see a disco ball nailed roughly up in the corner. Teenagers clearly use this place to party. Fucking awesome. Hopefully none come around tonight. Maybe the sight of the van out front will scare them off. If not, the sight of my wolf will.

I debate shoving a chair by the front door, but I don't see one even when I glance over to the formal dining room on the left. Nothing's in that room at all. Improvising, I decide that stacking a couple beer cans in front of the door will be good enough. My wolf will hear that, even if I'm sleeping. Then at least I'll have a warning that someone's around. I grab five and carefully pile them up. Then I trudge across the wooden floor to the adjoining room, calling out, "Elena?"

"Upstairs."

I hear her reply clear as day in this furniture-less place. Her voice echoes off the walls. I walk down a narrow hallway between the living and dining rooms and through an empty kitchen to a set of stairs at the back of the house. I climb slowly. Nerves suddenly hit me. Elena's shifted. What if she's different now?

My stupid mind pictures her pussy changing shape, turning into a square or a triangle. God, I hate my fucking brain sometimes. It's so stupid. But … my hesitation sticks. I've never been around an omega before. They're supposed to be built for alpha cock. What if … oh fuck. What if my dick's too small for her now? What if she thinks it's—like—little? What if she needs something more? What if I can't give it to her?

I pause on the stairs, grabbing the wooden railing. My heart beats really fast—even faster than it did when we rolled through Black's gates tonight on our way out and I waved at his security team, faking like I was the caterer. Heat flushes my neck and I have to remind myself to breathe. I think I might be having a panic attack.

In some room up there, I hear Elena moan. And it's definitely a sex moan, the type she gives when she gets close. My wolf urges me to go up. He can't wait. Her new scent is driving him mad. But what if? What if? What if? I remain a statue.

"Jonah! Now!" she barks, as if she's a fucking psychic. As if she knows I've stopped.

My legs jerk in response. I dart up the stairs and past a moldering bathroom to a bedroom with a slanted roof and dull yellow walls.

I stop in the doorway, shocked to see a queen-sized mattress on the floor of the space complete with fresh sheets and a violet comforter. But I guess, if this really is a teenage party spot, they need someplace to bone.

Elena lays back on top of the comforter, her hair spread on the pillow, her legs splayed wantonly. Her skirt's tossed up around her waist and her tiny thong is just a couple tangled slashes of red beside her. That hand of hers is working in furious circles. Her black polish contrasts the soft pink of her folds.

The moon is peeking inside from the window, watching—just like me—and I swear if that goddess is real, she's fucking touching Elena right now. Moonlight caresses the sharp definition in Elena's calves, the solid muscle of her thighs, over her flat stomach, even squeezing her nipples between light and shadow.

I stare, drinking in the sight until Elena notices me. Her head turns and those glowing golden wolf eyes find me.

But instead of softening into a smile, her face contorts in fury. "Jonah, you better fucking eat me right fucking now." She grits her teeth and I grin.

The order washes away some of my insecurity. Maybe it won't be any different than last week. Not if sex makes Elena hostile and argumentative because she's too wound up to be vulnerable.

I stride into the room and yank off my shirt—which is already sagging and deformed from my shift. I note that we're gonna get hot and sweaty fast since this place has no air conditioning. That won't be great for her heat. Maybe I should make sure she ends up on top.

As I have that thought, I kneel carefully on the wooden planks in front of the mattress, shoving aside her discarded high heels. I plant my hands on the edge of the bed and crawl forward. I don't let myself think about the fact that she might compare me to Black. Well, I think about it. But I dismiss it. She could have stayed with him. She picked running. She could have run alone. She didn't. She's with me.

She chose you. So make sure she knows it's the right choice.

I get close enough to gently push her hand and a bit of her ruby skirt aside so I can get to work. And that's when I realize—holy shit. I was wrong. This isn't going to be the same as last week. *Elena is different.*

Her thighs are already coated in slick. This is not your normal girl's wetness. She's drenched and her pussy is already fluttering. She doesn't just want it. She physically *needs it*.

Goddammit.

That sets off a primal part of me that erases half my brain, just wipes it white. No more thinking. Time for action. I lean forward, my tongue darting out to lick up her inner thigh like I usually do to prep her. White chocolate and anise flavors explode on my taste buds, making me growl.

My growl sets her off and she gives a plaintive whine, a soft submissive sound that she's never made before. It's a sound that goes straight to my dick. My teeth come out and I nip at her, a human nip, but I mark that inner thigh lightly, showing her who she belongs to.

"Yes, make me yours," she breathes.

Those words twist me up like a corkscrew. Fuck. She's never said anything like that before. I lift up slightly, staring through the valley between her chest to meet her eyes.

"Jonah." She's teary and her thick lower lip is nearly trembling, raw and naked, lipstick nearly gone, skin bare. She holds my eyes as she whispers, "You're the best thing that's ever happened to me."

The fabric of the universe rips above us. And night flips to day.

No. It's not day. It just got four times brighter. The fucking moon has just put her hands all over the two of us, trying to turn this moment into a threesome.

I crawl up Elena's body, blocking the light. Because nobody gets to intrude on this moment. Not even a damned goddess.

I stare down at my love, at her soft skin and the eyelashes framing her eyes, reveling in this moment. I let her words soak into my skin for a second before I dip my head and gently brush her lips with mine. The kiss is light, gentle, soft. Everything I'm going to be for her. It's a promise. I'll treasure her forever. She's my everything.

When I lift back up and stare into her eyes, they flicker gray for a moment, and I see my Elena beneath the wildness of the omega heat. Her face is soft and open, vulnerable—just as beautiful as I always imagined it would be when I dreamed about asking her out for real. It only lasts a moment before the golden glow that defines a wolf staring out through human eyes returns.

Her heat comes back with a vengeance and I see sweat bead along her forehead. Her naked pelvis lifts up to grind against my pants. Her breathing grows shallow and a series of semi-frantic "Uh, uh" noises issue from her mouth as need washes over her again.

I reach down to her hips, clamping a hand on them. "I'm going to take care of you. But I want you to repeat that phrase for me, Elena."

"What?"

"The one you just said." I lean down and brush my lips over the column of her neck, feeling the vibrations as she whispers, "You're the best thing that's ever happened to me."

All the hairs on my arms raise up. Even though it's the second time she's said it, it still gives me goosebumps.

She says it again as I shove aside the panels of her dress covering those breasts. I see a red lace bra that hides nothing. Tucked in the middle is that stupid fucking ring Black gave her. That claiming he was arrogant enough to do without even knowing her or how amazing she is. The diamond gleams, huge and gaudy. I yank it out and toss it across the room. It hits the wall with a sharp *thwack* and she instantly tenses underneath me.

"I only kept it on me so we can pawn it—"

I shove aside her bra cup and suck her left nipple into my mouth, cutting off any other explanations she wants to give. I don't care about that shit. Not right now. There's only us. Only her and her need. I don't want him intruding on her thoughts at this moment. I want to be the one intruding on any thought she's ever had about him.

I lap at her little bud, then suck it deep. Her breasts aren't huge but they're perfect. Perky. Delicate like her. And I love getting to touch them. Tongue them. I love how though her skin is so soft, her nipples turn into hard little beads when I get her really riled. Once, she even let me spray my cum on them.

I picture that moment for a second. She'd come to my apartment with sullen eyes and didn't want to talk. She'd wanted to fuck. But after round one, she'd been more gentle and tender with me than ever before. It was the first time she'd given up control. She'd let me take her doggie style and then when I'd pulled out, asking where she wanted my cum, she'd let me choose.

I slide my hand down her front, down past her belly, and let my fingers toy with her sopping pussy. So wet. My fingers slide in easily, and I curl them, gently sliding up and down until I find that spot on her inner wall that makes her squirm. Once she's writhing, I lift my head from her nipple so that I can blow on it.

She whimpers, but it's a whimper of pleasure.

I grin. "I'm gonna stripe your chest with cum again," I promise.

She shakes her head, and I can see her hands fist the blanket. "No. *Please.* I need you. I need your cum inside me, Jonah. Play with me. Then fuck me and fill me up. Make me yours."

God. If only I was recording this. I can't believe those words came out of Elena's mouth. I love how filthy and dirty she's being. She normally is pretty fucking naughty with her words. But that 'please' and 'make me yours' nearly break me. That's not the dominant Elena I know. That's a new, sweeter side of her. That's her omega. That's her vulnerable side. That's her admission that we are *more*.

My chest grows warm and melty.

I like this combination of sweet and fierce. I like how her hand comes to my back and her nails rake harshly down my shoulder blade while her mouth whimpers, "Please," again.

I do what she asks. I play, moving my hand faster, plunging in and out. I use my thumb to gently swipe back and forth in the vicinity of her clit, making it grow stiff. Then I dive back down for that nipple, which is getting unacceptably soft in my absence. I curl my fingers inside her cunt and drag the pads up and down as I pump in and out of her.

Elena's moans grow louder and louder. Eventually, they morph to screams.

That hand on my back comes up to squeeze the junction between my shoulder and my neck, a sensitive spot for a shifter that I've admitted to her makes me see stars.

Her thighs clamp down on my arm, which makes finger fucking her harder, but I don't give up. I embrace the burn in my arm and keep going—just like a good submissive, a good beta—until a shout rips from her lips.

I feel her pussy pulse around me, clenching down on my fingers. A gush of slick follows, glazing my wrist.

The scent wafts up and I feel my own eyes flicker to wolf eyes. Everything sharpens as I stare at her.

She looks so damn hot with her head thrown back, the pulse in her neck pounding, her eyes closed as her hips buck. The urge to rut fills me—but Elena chose me because I can control myself.

I wait, gently dragging my fingers up and down, drawing out her spasms, until her body relaxes, and then gently slip my fingers free. I sit up and yank on my pants, ordering, "Get naked."

Elena hurries to comply, undoing the button that holds up the neck of her dress and then shimmying out of it. I've hardly gotten my pants around my ankles before I feel her breasts press against my back. "More. Jonah. More." Her lips trace down my neck and she playfully bites me.

Mate! My wolf howls in pleasure at that bite as I finish yanking off my pants. He doesn't wait for me to pull off the socks too. He forces me around on my knees so that I can get my hands on that slim waist of Elena's and drag her body to mine. He's so eager for this moment. Every other time I've been with Elena, the worry that her wolf would come in and reject me hovered like a little storm cloud. But now … the sky is clear.

I pull her against me so that she straddles my legs as I sit back on my knees. I make sure she's settled on top of me, dragging my hands up and down her legs for a moment, just reveling in how soft and smooth her skin is. My perfect, precious mate. I tilt my head to gaze up at her and I reach up and fist her black hair with its white streaks. Her cheeks are pink and flushed from her recent orgasm, but her eyes are still full of lust.

She's so incredibly beautiful, so hot that I can't stand it. I lean forward, unable to resist. I kiss her, and she sucks on my tongue violently as she impatiently reaches down and tugs at my cock. Normally, she'd have me tease her with it, but tonight, she just lines us up. She's soaked and ready.

But then she does something unprecedented. She waits. Elena doesn't just take her pleasure from me like usual. She hovers and those eyes, though golden and wild, are weepy again. Tears form in the corners and her voice is husky as she says, "I need you to forgive me."

I drop her hair to cup her cheeks. "You're mine?" I ask. Because even though she's said it, I want to make sure.

"I'm yours." Her tone is strong and sure and absolute. It puts an iron band around my heart and squeezes, just as permanent as any wedding ring.

"You're forgiven." I lift my hips and surge up into her, feeling so much—just so much more than anything I've ever felt. It's perfect. And as I slide into Elena, something happens that hasn't ever happened to me before. Lights pop inside my head. Just burst like there's an electrical surge. I barely stop myself from coming because the moment is just so intense. I've never felt this connected to anyone ever.

My wolf howls and my own eyes flash wild and feral for a moment.

I pull back and lift her slightly so that just the tip remains inside. I take a slow, deep breath to calm myself before I drag her hips in a slow circle, reveling in the moment, edging myself. She's never ever gotten this wet. And the difference it makes on my cock. God. It's perfection.

I tease her, thrusting shallowly, circling, until she growls, takes control, and fucks me roughly. She rides me so hard my bones hurt from how she slams down. But I embrace it, love it, watching her come undone is worth any price. Her dark hair becomes plastered to her face and neck, her breasts bounce temptingly in front of me. I love the way her thighs are splayed open, and I can watch my dick glide in and out of her in this position. It's the perfect view. And that tight, wet heat fits me like a glove.

I reach out around her and let my fingers dig into the soft flesh of her ass as she slides up and down. I hear her breathing grow shallow as she gets closer and I reach between us, my fingers pinching that super slick clit until she's mindless. She doesn't stop, dredging up the heat from my balls. My dick swells as she smashes down onto my lap again and again. I glance down between us, watching my hand on her clit, watching the way my dick fills her up.

Elena's hands come to my shoulders, and she shoves me backward. I don't hesitate. I fall on her command so that my back hits the mattress, bouncing slightly. Elena slams down onto me a couple more times before she lifts up, panting, pulling off of my wet dick, and letting me feel just how cool the night air is as opposed to her hot cunt. Then she flips herself around, that hot pussy gaping, growling, "Knees up."

I maneuver my legs and bend my knees, putting my feet onto the mattress. I watch her squat as she grabs my dick, her ass flexing, showing me the little rosebud of her asshole. I lick my lips. I fucking love how she moans when she slides down onto me, the stretch even more pronounced than before. And in this position, with my cock rigid and hard as a rock, I get deeper into her than I ever have. I don't want to leave.

She gives a little squeal and I watch her pert, muscled ass and the perfect curve of her hips as she starts to bounce. I sear the moment into my mind because she never uses this position and the sight of her ass cheeks spreading as she humps me roughly is too hot to forget. Elena fucks me hard and fast, searching for release. I reach my hands up to help her. With my left hand, I pinch her nipple. My right slides over her slamming hips, down that soft taut skin of her belly, and finds her clit. I leave my palm on her clit so that it rubs against her with every pass she makes but bring my fingers down to her soaked pussy. I spread her lips and slowly slide two fingers in alongside my cock, hoping that the stretch down there will give my little omega what she needs. Her body is looking for a knot. I don't have one. So I try and give her the next best thing. I curl those fingers toward her g-spot.

She starts to shudder, her rhythm breaking. "Jonah. Jonah."

Fuck. When she chants my name like that, I go full savage. I glue my hands in place because she clearly likes them. Then I move my hips to help her, to keep the rhythm going. I thrust upward as hard as I fucking can. My dick is so full and thick; I swear it's never been this swollen before. I feel hard as a rock and I'm on edge, pleasure shooting up my spine in narrow lines just shy of orgasm. But I wait for her.

I force myself to glance at the walls, tracking the water stains, instead of watching the way Elena's writhing from my touch, the way her thighs quiver. Just a few more seconds. I can tell she's close by the soft gasps escaping her lips. They grow faster and shallower as she approaches orgasm.

I allow myself one last look at her hourglass figure, at the smooth curve of her waist before it flares to her hips. God. Fuck. Yes.

Her pussy clamps down on me and the sensation makes me pant. Moan. I can barely hold back as another gush of slick erupts from her tight cunt, soaking my balls in wet heat. Stars flicker at the edges of my vision as Elena's nails dig into my shins.

"Yes. Yes. Yes!" she chants.

"I love you," I whisper.

When she goes over the edge, I let myself follow. And as we come, our wolves' instincts surface. We both howl wildly as the moon bathes us in silver light.

4

ELENA

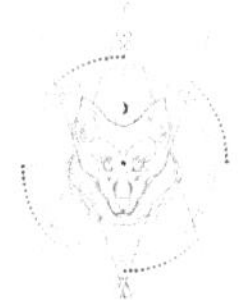

AFTER MY ORGASM SUBSIDES, I collapse back onto Jonah, lying over his body with my arms flopping by my ears, boneless, but also utterly and completely … restored. He sated my heat. My fever has broken, though based on Black's comments that omegas in heat need ten orgasms a day, it's a temporary respite. But Jonah also did something else, something more.

Giving myself to him completely, emotionally—I've never done that before. My heart still aches, like he penetrated that too. Which, I guess, in a way he has. Jonah's burrowed so deep into my soul that he's part of me. And I want him to be. In fact, I can't believe I feared connection like it was a shadow in a dark alley. This feeling … it's reverence. It's prayer made flesh. Every word I've ever uttered to the moon goddess—all the hope and despair and longing I put into my pleas to her—all those feelings are here, encased in this magical, glowing peace.

I finally know what love feels like.

And it's so damn grand that I'm certain this is the very best moment of my life. I don't want it to end.

But eventually, my muscles grow strained, because Jonah's not quite as soft as a mattress. I use my legs to lift my hips and slowly slide off his chest and he grunts, then takes a big breath.

"Excuse me, was I squishing you?" I ask as I turn my face to his, settling my head on his outstretched arm.

"Nope. Not at all." He lies easily, as if me accidentally suffocating him is no big deal so long as I'm comfortable. A beta to the bitter end. That brat.

I poke at his chest playfully. "You were just holding your breath, then? That gasp had nothing to do with my fat ass laying right across your ribs?"

Jonah chuckles as if he knows I'm looking for an excuse to scold him, which, I realize with a start—I am. I am because part of me wants to return to our normal, comfortable interactions. Ones full of dominance and submission instead of this newfound and uncertain space where I see him as precious. Jonah's smarter than me though, at least this one time. He sidesteps my question by brushing my hair back from my forehead.

"You look gorgeous. Are you thirsty? Hungry? Need anything?"

Gah. He's so perfect. And I love him. Saying that phrase in my own head is trippy because it isn't something I ever expected to think—ever. I don't say it aloud yet, I'm not quite ready. But I stare up into his pale blue eyes and let my gaze say it for me.

His expression softens and I know he feels the same way I do. That confident truth flows through me like a low ocean wave caressing the shore—powerfully gentle but impossible to dispute, hold back, or stop. Not that I want to do those things. I want this emotion to lap at my toes forever. I nestle into his shoulder, my cheek settling right on his ridge of muscle, and I just let the feelings wash across me then recede only to douse me all over again. I look at the angle of his nose, the sharp cut of his jaw, my eyes tracing him adoringly.

The brine of our lovemaking and sweat permeate the room and my senses are filled by Jonah. His scent, his touch on my spine as he hugs me to him, the sight of his body so languid and calm. I've never reveled in the aftermath before. Too often, I want sex fast and dangerous, the thrill combining with the orgasm to set me off mentally and physically at the same time. This is wonderfully different. Some feminine part of me purrs and I curl further over Jonah, draping my leg over his thighs, utterly relaxed.

I peer out the window in the middle of the wall just past our feet and spy the moon goddess staring down at us. I swear I feel her smile. It warms up my chest in the most delicious of ways, making me thankful and teary-eyed all at once. I pull my eyes away from her, not wanting to ruin this precious moment together with crying or philosophy. I just want to be with Jonah. Just be. So instead of thanking the goddess, I look back at him. I drag my hand up and trace the planes of his pale chest, which are smooth because I make him shave. I drag my fingers lightly over the closest nipple, not really trying to start anything, just mapping out the planes of his perfect body.

I want to travel over every inch of his skin. I want to repeat what we just did a million times until my mind is full of lovemaking memories and not just hot, filthy sex. I want … I just want everything with him. My heart's already full to bursting and I want my mind to be the same. I don't just want this single year of memories with him. I want them all. So many memories that I could empty out the change jar my mom keeps on her dresser and have more beautiful Jonah memories than cents.

This feeling of falling … I thought I knew what I felt for him when I believed I'd lost him. I didn't. This connection is so much more intense. It makes me giddy and weepy at the same time because it just means *everything.*

Poetry suddenly seems so much less stupid because I would die to keep this feeling. I would kill for it. Luckily, I don't have to do those things. I just have to run. And hide. Forever.

That thought sprouts bitter flavors on my tongue along with images of Black's looming face, spoiling my perfect afterglow. I shove it aside, not wanting to let it intrude, and turn my head so that I can kiss whatever part of Jonah I can reach. I let my lips brush over the top of his pec, over his heart, marveling at how one simple gesture of affection can jolt my chest like a defibrillator.

I give myself three more minutes of solid cuddle time before clean-up necessities take over and I excuse myself to the dilapidated bathroom. I return just a minute later, only to see Jonah hasn't moved. He's still laying there with a grin dragging up the corners of his lips. I easily slide back in beside him, deciding we should take a few more minutes to revel in our little bubble before returning to reality.

When I lay my head back down with a contented sigh, *she* reappears.

My eyes grow wide in shock. What the *motherfuck* is happening right now?

My wolf, with her midnight black hair and white streaked muzzle, paces across my vision like a video game character projected into reality. She just pops out of nowhere and walks across the room, across our legs, and up onto Jonah's chest, as casual as can be. In my eyes, she's only about three inches tall, no bigger than an action figure. I watch, disbelieving, as she sits down on Jonah's left pec, her tail curling around her paws.

I'm stunned—not just speechless but thoughtless. Why here? Why now? Why is she back? I could ask her directly, but I feel so strange and disconnected from her right now that I hesitate. Am I hallucinating?

She seems to understand my confusion, though. Her head turns to gaze at Jonah. And I have my answer.

But my wolf doesn't stare at him with adoring eyes. Her eyes glow unnaturally bright, and she stands up, pacing up and down his abs. Unlike me, I realize that she's not feeling happy and light like she did the first day she appeared. No. That unhinged feeling that came over me during my fever in the van returns with twice as much force and I realize that it's she who's making me feel that way. Because my wolf is operating on instinct right now. Whatever triggered this heat has roused her and she paces toward me with an intent look in her eye.

I want to mark my mate.

Her eyes, normally a silver hue the color of the moon, flash a heat-driven molten gold as they lock onto mine and her words inside my head send a million worries spinning. Love is one thing. But mating? Mate marks. My parents had those, and though I know very little about the shifter world, I know that mate marks are forever. Forget diamonds. Nothing screams devotion like a scar that permanently circles your neck.

What if Jonah's not ready for that? I ask her, trying to deflect from the fact that *I'm* not fucking ready for that.

She gives a dismissive chuff, swishes her tail, prowling closer to my face, willing me to let her take over.

We need this.

No. We don't.

You want the heat to keep driving you mad? An omega without a mate has no center. No one to ground or protect her. Her scent calls out to the wildest alphas. It's dangerous. She rapid-fires images at me in quick succession. None of them have happy endings. All of them are brutal. I don't bother asking how she knows all this shit when I don't, because for all I fucking know about wolves there's another dimension they go to when they aren't inhabiting our bodies and turning our lives to shit.

We're too young.

I gave you two extra years. Her jaw tightens and I see just the tips of her fangs appear. Not enough to threaten, but enough to show me she's frustrated as fuck with me. *I waited until you'd found a good mate, someone who'd actually care for us. I waited! I'm done waiting.*

First of all, that's a fucking revelation to me. I had basically decided I was a glimmer.

She chuffs a laugh, which only ticks me off.

Well, you don't get to waltz in here and just demand things like mate bonds.

My wolf's eyes flash. Her animal instincts lash into me despite my effort to shove them back and for the first time, I recognize the pure brute strength of the shifter inside me. Her need pulses through my veins, the rapid-fire pounding of my heart, and the urgent desire to sink my teeth into Jonah curls my fingers. She proves me wrong. She does get to fucking waltz in because even now, my head turns to gaze up at his neck and I lick my lips as I spy the thrum of his pulse.

Still, I wrestle my wolf for control. She retreats, though whether it's because she's an omega who doesn't fight or because she actually needs me on board for this magical bond to work, I have no clue. But I take a second to shake off the urgent hormones flooding me and think.

I'm torn. I'm not sure what the right thing to do is. Part of me feels like a long, drawn-out conversation with Jonah needs to come first. Actually, getting to New York needs to come first. Then finding a place. Setting up a home. Then the long-drawn-out conversation. My wolf has no patience for my human worries, even though I try to shoot her images of shelter and water, and food. She doesn't even seem to care much about Alpha Black, even when I feed her a picture of his werewolf monster form chasing us. She didn't ever meet him, because she ran at the first sign of trouble, leaving me stranded.

We could have had our mate weeks ago! Why didn't you fucking show up when I was at his house, huh? I accuse. I want to blame her for the fact that I even met Black. Because all my problems started then. If she'd come, even a single day earlier, my life would be A+ perfect. Instead, it's a raging dumpster fire.

I came when you were happy, she retorts.

Well, you ruined that! Anger ripples through me but giving into that emotion apparently weakens my control over my mind. I feel my eyesight flicker and change, just like it did inside the van.

She disappears from sight, and I can feel her merge with me, those wild emotions surfacing again, raging like a forest fire. Goosebumps rise on my arms even though I'm hot as an inferno and I feel a bead of sweat form at my hairline. My hands tremble, as if the magic or this moment is too huge to remain contained within my skin. I'm about to fly to pieces.

I scramble to regain control but this time she doesn't relent. *No. We aren't ready! Fluffy, you wait—*

But then Jonah lets out a contented little hum. And under his breath he whispers, "I love you, my sweet mate."

My human senses probably wouldn't have caught those words because he said them so softly. But my senses are shifting. I'm shifting. And when I hear those words, my wolf explodes with need, her primal instincts eclipsing all my common sense. The urge to bite is so strong, I equate it to the time I accidentally set my palm on my curling iron. I'd ripped it away so quickly it had taken my mind a second to catch up on what had just happened. The wanton flush of omega heat inside of me bursts back to life, burning me from the inside out. Instinctively, I know that biting my mate is the cure. Biting Jonah will end this wild attack on my senses and calm the swirling inferno.

My body melts and morphs and suddenly, I'm a small black wolf nestled in Jonah's arms. I expect him to grow startled, to jerk away in surprise. But he just smiles, eyebrows raising, those light blue eyes of his softening.

"Oh, Elena," he says softly. His hand reaches out to stroke the fur of my back, sensation sizzling down my spine at his touch.

Mate. My wolf and I both say the word together.

I have to put my mouth on him. There is no choice.

We—my wolf and I—reach down and nuzzle him. My tongue comes out and laps at Jonah's skin. It tastes completely different as a wolf—there's an undertone of blackberries to his icy mint scent that I never knew was there before. It's twice as delicious as before and I lick over his collarbone, swallowing down his beads of sweat as if I'm drinking a blackberry mint mojito. Both my wolf and I crave the taste and spend a long minute savoring his flavor. When my muzzle reaches the junction between his neck and shoulder, he tenses.

I yank backward when Jonah stiffens so that I can peer down into his eyes. Is he afraid? Unwilling?

We can't do this yet! I try to tell Fluffy.

She ignores me and lifts my lips from my fangs, the urge to mark as primitively essential as the need to jerk my hips when I'm near orgasm. She's too far gone.

My eyes travel back to Jonah, ready to apologize, to try to scream for him to bat me away so that I don't bite him when he doesn't want it.

"God, I've wanted this forever. *You* want it?" he asks, so gently, always concerned about me. Warmth floods my chest as a tear forms in the corner of his eyes and a tiny smile curves his lips.

Told you. Fluffy's smug, but I'm too relieved and awed and overwhelmed to care about her attitude right now.

Jonah's smile erases my hesitation and I let my wolf take back the reins. I lean back down, my jaw hinges open, and I carefully set my teeth against his frail human flesh.

"Yes," he whispers in excited anticipation.

I snap shut, biting hard, piercing deep.

I feel Jonah's muscles bunch beneath me, and he gasps but I don't let up. To get the mark to stay, it must be deep, it has to shred his skin. Shifters heal too fast for it to be any other way. But as the metallic taste of his blood coats my tongue, I feel a primal satisfaction flare through me. It ignites my mind and sends fire rushing and billowing down my spinal cord, through my tail. I release my teeth, licking my chops and lifting my black nose to give a wild howl. I cry out to the night, the moon, the world, that I'm taken.

The inferno inside of me blazes and my cheeks heat. Scent fills the room. White chocolate and black licorice. Flowers. It's so strong I can taste it.

My heat restarts, my mental faculties burn to a crisp, crumble like ash, blow away.

Sex. Now. My wolf thinks. Actually, what she does is send me a series of images of Jonah rutting me. Human form, wolf form, she doesn't care—just as long as she gets fucked.

Some tiny human part of me is horrified but the hormones racing through my system are as strong as some sort of hallucinogen. The color of the moonlight cast around the room changes from gray to a dull stone-blue shade. Beneath me, Jonah's skin takes on a yellow cast as I feel slick heat up inside of me and start to drip down.

I whine, trying to wrest control from Fluffy, to shift back to human so I can take over. She doesn't relent. Her images of fucking get more intense. She wants a turn. She wants to be held down. She wants to be controlled. She craves an edge of pain and then the sharp bite of his teeth. All the things I don't want. My omega wolf craves submission.

Jonah realizes what's happening when I stay frozen on top of him, slick slowly gliding down my fur onto his belly. He slides me gently off his chest, then kneels beside me on his hands and knees. I watch in wonder as he shifts. It takes less than a second for fur to sprout from his skin as his bones rearrange themselves. By the time I finish blinking, he's done. His beautiful gray wolf sits beside me. Fluffy has never met his wolf before, and I spend a moment just staring at him in awed admiration, the admiration bit no doubt spurred on by my wolf who loves the way he looks.

I paw the mattress with delight.

Our mate is hot, she tells me, which makes me chuckle.

Jonah gives a happy yip.

God. I guess we're doing this. Giving up control is difficult, it's not natural for me. It involves a level of vulnerability I typically shy away from, and I've already given it up once tonight. But this is my wolf. She's part of me—now and forever. I try to relax, then hand the reins over to Fluffy, trusting her.

We're going to have to work on your name for me, she says, before circling Jonah once, checking him out, pleased by things that I'd never notice, like the shape of his ears or the length of his tail.

What do you mean? I ask. But she doesn't reply. She nips at Jonah's face. He nips back.

We playfully wrestle for a moment as wolves, affectionately biting each other. Eventually, I'm able to sink into the playful silliness of the moment, learning his tells, the way his eyes narrow right before he goes for my face so that I can teasingly jerk it away. Then Jonah rises up on his hind paws and puts his forepaws on my shoulders, in what feels like a hug to me, but Fluffy disagrees. To her, that's foreplay.

Suddenly, my tail wags, and I'm hurtling off the bed.

Wait. What? I'm confused as I scamper down the hallway, nails clicking on the scuffed wood floors.

But Fluffy says, *Chase*. She sends me images of running through the woods—and then images of getting caught. My chest trills with excitement as I skitter down the stairs, snorting a wolf-laugh as a naughty thrill spirals through me. Apparently, she loves the chase. Craves it. As we head down the stairs another round of heat hits me, making my neck burn. But despite the fact that need invades my very bones, my wolf takes the heat in stride. The instinct doesn't feel as overwhelming to her because she's used to being driven by instinct. She doesn't fight it the way I tried to in the van.

Jonah's paws thump down the stairs behind us as I dash for the front door. A sort of nervous excitement fills me—like the kind I used to get playing tag on the playground. Only, when Jonah catches me, we're both going to win.

I get to the front hall. Dammit! The door's closed and even though there's a hole where the knob should be, it opens inward. I can't just shove at it with my nose and burst outside.

I glance back. Jonah's getting unacceptably close. I speed up and try to change direction all at once and I slide into a couple of beer cans stacked oddly right next to the door frame. I don't have time to question why the heck they're there because Jonah's blackberry and mint scent wafts over me. Hurry! I want him to catch me, but not easily. I want to draw the anticipation out so that when he wins, he's proud and rough with me. I hustle through the living room and a short hallway at the side of the house, looking for another way out. My nose smells the field, the green hay. I want to run through it, stretch my limbs, lay down, and hide in it. And then fuck roughly while rolling through it.

But how to get out?

I enter a kitchen that's the size of a shoebox. A water heater stands exposed in one corner. There's a stove. A sink with open shelving above it and a speckled white laminate countertop sitting on two cabinets from an era where housewives supposedly had time to clean endless stains off white surfaces as they cooked. An open window just above the counter beckons me. Yes! I can see the moon through the window urging me to come play beneath her watchful eye. I leap up onto the counter, which is small and narrow, forcing my feet close together. I lift onto my back paws so that I can stretch my front paws onto the ledge, bunching my muscles to leap—but I freeze with one paw on the windowsill.

The moon isn't the only thing outside waiting for me.

Clustered in the tall grass are at least a dozen snarling wolves.

Their fur is every color of shadow imaginable, from pale gray to deep black. Their teeth are pulled back and their gazes scan the house, slowly coming to rest on me. My eyes immediately scan for a pure white wolf, a ghost amongst the demons with glowing eyes, but I don't see him.

Either Black's around front or … these aren't Lobos.

Fuck!

Their growls drift in through the window and trail eerily over the fur on my ears, making me shiver. I skitter backward, nearly falling off the counter. I stumble into the sink in my effort to save myself, twisting my paw. Something pinches and pain ricochets up my leg.

Shit. Fuck. Shit.

I'm not the only one trembling. Fluffy's mind has turned into a scattered mix of fearful images, and she wants to hide in one of the cabinets underneath us.

Jonah skids across the floor behind me, smashing into the cabinets beneath me when his paws can't find traction on the old, weathered, grease-splattered linoleum. I'm jolted when he hits. His eyes go wide, and he stares up at me as soon as he catches the scent.

To my utter shock, I hear him speak inside my head. His voice is clear as day and sounds exactly like his human one.

Elena, run. He sends me an image of the front door.

I don't question him. I jump clumsily from the sink, my twisted paw stinging as I hit the ground. He turns, his tail brushing across my muzzle as he bolts out the kitchen down the hall in the middle of the house that leads to the front.

I follow down the narrow hall, favoring my injured paw, not running nearly as fast as I'd like to since the instinct to run and hide is practically shaking me to pieces. My heart screeches a heavy metal song and I curse the wooden planks of the floor, how I can't dig in and push off like I could in dirt. Faster. Faster. Faster.

I hear a noise. A howl. My heat subsides as my panic wallops that need roughly aside.

Who are they? I ask Jonah as we careen toward the front door.

Not Lobos. I can't speak to them. You can only speak to pack.

His response shakes me. Yet another thing I didn't know about the shifter world. Goddammit. Black should have given me a fucking handbook while I was trapped in his basement. I feel like a clueless imbecile. Beyond that, I'm not sure if I'm relieved or scared right now that Black isn't the one after me, because my wolf's stomach is wobbling in ways I can't define.

We reach the front door just in time to see a huge, thick-fingered, hairy monster shifter hand wrapping around the edge of the rough-cut hole where the doorknob once was.

My heart leaps—trying to escape my body and make its way to the moon goddess. My pulse races and all my fur stands on edge.

I think ... I think Jonah and I are about to die.

5

BLACK

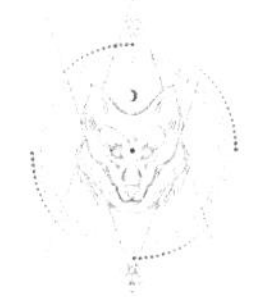

"I'LL FUCKING KILL HIM. And then I'll hang his rotting body in a cage on the grounds—right near the gate to my house—so that everybody sees it," I snarl as we hurtle down the highway in Pluto's Audi like a dart. Anger infects my veins and it's contagious. It spreads through my blood and contaminates every fiber of my being. I am fury.

My mate has been stolen. By a goddamned beta. It's all I can do not to punch out the passenger window.

"Cops might have a problem with that," Pluto quips from beside me, where he drives, shifting gears and lanes like a Nascar racer as we blur around cars, just a smear in the shadows. "They don't tend to like bodies going on display."

"Fine. I'll string up his animal carcass then," I say.

"PETA will have a problem with that."

I barely refrain from decking him. I could too. Easily. I'm nearly seven feet tall and I've got at least fifty pounds on him. I raise my fist and speak through clenched teeth, "Motherfucker, your humor is just as shitty as your Orlando-Bloom-knockoff look," I retort, glaring at my best friend.

"You just hate that all the ladies love me," he jokes, though he speaks the truth. Women flock to him like flies. Clean cut, pretty-boy bastard.

He's the opposite of me. Dark and huge, I intimidate the fuck out of nearly everybody. The women who simper and want to ride my alpha cock get off on the combination of fear and sex. I can smell it on them. But Elena ... my little mate. She'd been full of fire and fury. And delicious lust, the kind that melts your insides until they drip like a popsicle. And, oh, she'd dripped.

"Stop fucking thinking about her. I can smell that shit, you know," Pluto grumbles, reaching for the AC and turning it on to try to erase some of my scent.

"Get used to it. It's gonna happen a lot," I retort.

"We're gonna turn our meetings into video conferences then," he states. As if he makes the fucking rules.

My wolf growls, seeing the words as a challenge, but I shush him since Pluto's just joking. The idiot knows being presumptuous gets under my skin. The very idea of discussing pack business over a video call that could get hacked by humans nearly makes me chuckle. Imagine their reactions. They'd piss themselves. I laugh softly, which makes my neck sting because I haven't shifted to my wolf form to fully heal—because my fiancé's been taken. Tonight should have been my greatest victory, a night I made history. I'm now the fucking king of the shifter world.

But I have an inkling that tonight is going to go down in my memory as one of the worst events of my life, the night the most precious thing in my life was stolen by a rat bastard who's going to lose his fingers one by one. My mind quickly falls back to anger, and I stare out the window, suddenly irritated and unappreciative of my second's attempt to lighten the mood.

My wolf imagines bloodshed. Jonah might fear me. But what my wolf has in store for him … the darker side of me grows exponentially. The lines I won't cross begin to blur. All because of a lithe, gorgeous little spitfire with a submissive streak that she struggles to hide. Her gorgeous, flashing eyes come to mind and the anger coursing through me tangles with guilt. Because I left her unsupervised with that idiot.

Fuck. Elena. I'm sorry. I'm coming.

I barely suppress a shift as my wolf's wild yearning for his mate surges through my body. I clench my hands and breathe deeply until he growls at me and agrees to wait until the car's stopped.

We've been barreling down the highway for half an hour, after debating what the fuck to do once it was determined Elena was gone. Pluto had argued for driving since the catering van at my place had conveniently gone missing, the owners of it shocked and dismayed. I'd agreed, but I'd sent elites and glimmers to the bus and train stations and the airport anyway. Just in case.

I'm not taking a chance with my fiancé's life.

Two glimmers follow along in a car behind us, though I doubt they can keep up with Pluto's pace. We're heading into farm country because Pluto's dead certain they'd head for New York over Los Angeles. He thinks there are too many nature preserves and parks around Cali, too many shifters in the vicinity.

He'd better be right.

I unclench my fist. I bet she's scared out of her mind right now. He better not have hurt her or I'll make his death last a long fucking time.

My wolf appears on the dashboard in front of me, lips curled back, fangs exposed in a growl. I crack the window to let him try to scent her, though the air is rushing by so fast, and the smell of gasoline burns my nostrils. I lean back in my seat, letting him take over my nose while I try not to acknowledge how fucking sore I still am. My neck still feels like someone took a band saw to it. I breathe deeply, letting the smells wash over me as a sign pronounces we're leaving Colorado behind. Pluto must be clocking close to one-fifty for that to be possible.

I don't say a word. Whatever it takes to get Elena back. Whatever it takes.

If he's hurt a hair on her head ... killing an omega is an offense punishable by death. After the last pack wars, the treaties spell that out. Even an idiot knows that law. We go over it enough at howls. So, then why the fuck did he take her? He had to know the consequences.

I picture him—that young, cocky blond fucker with a shaved head. Murky, Pluto had to remind me of his name. Elena's little classmate. He'd reeked of impotence and submission when I'd seen him. I hadn't even thought twice about leaving him alone in the basement with her. But apparently, that was all an act. That beta kidnapped my mate. He stole her right out from under my nose. I didn't suspect a thing. He's got to be a plant.

Is he working for the Dark Nights?

That's the only logical reason I can think of for a beta risking his neck on something so stupid. Maybe Stone was blackmailing him. Threatening his family.

Doesn't fucking matter though. Murky is … no, *was* a Lobo.

My wolf snarls. Exile isn't good enough for him. *He was a wolf.* He shoots me an image of snapping Murky's neck.

I don't bother arguing, because then he'll just try to force a shift on me. I tap my knee while I try to puzzle out his motivation. Murky was supposed to come to me for protection. Wolves are supposed to look to their alphas, it's what we do. We're built to be protectors, dammit. I would have figured out a solution. I would have come up with a plan to counter Stone's. That fucking Dark Night alpha is haunting me from beyond the grave. What was his plan? What was he thinking?

Was Stone planning on stealing her away during the fight? Just spitting on the outcome of the challenge?

Maybe he wanted this beta to pass Elena off to his son, Thomas. Then the Dark Nights win an omega either way. I wouldn't put it past the fucker. He'd stack the deck by stealing her. I'm doubly glad he's gone right now, knowing the underhanded things he's willing to do. I might be a demon, but Stone's the goddamned devil himself.

My thoughts steam and smoke for a second as I reconsider every order I gave about Stone's honorable burial.

But then my mind circles back to Murky.

"What's his real name again? This beta?" I ask.

"Jonah, I think. You can pull him up on my computer if you want." Pluto jerks his head toward his laptop bag, which is laying on the backseat.

I grind my teeth together, not even registering the twinge of pain that runs down my throat—which is still healing because I shifted right from monster to man. I didn't bother turning into a wolf to recover, not when my omega's been taken from me. I reach for the laptop bag, wondering if I'm going to find out anything in there or if it will just leave me more fucking frustrated than before. But it's better than sitting. Alphas don't fucking sit and wait. They act.

I drag the bag onto my lap and unzip it, determined to find out more about this stupid beta. This betrayer. I'm going to rip his throat out. Who the fuck does he think he is? I just killed the most powerful alpha rival I have. Does he really think he can get away with this?

I retrieve the computer and toss the bag in the back. I've just hit the power button to start the thing up when a scent rips across my nose. White chocolate. Flowers. And a new smell mingling with it, one that turns my dick hard as a rock. Anise.

"She's here," I announce, slamming down the window button. I don't give a fuck that we're blasted with air or that our ears pop because we're on the highway and only one window's open. I tilt my head into that breeze, close my eyes, and try to trace the smell.

"Fuck man! I can't fucking see with that wind blasting my eyes," Pluto gripes.

I ignore him, inhaling that scent, drinking it down like wine. It's so pungent. So intense. And then ... mingled with it ... I catch the scent of Elena's arousal.

What the fuck?

I toss the laptop into the backseat and lean my head out the window, causing Pluto to curse and swerve further away from a semi-truck coming up on our right-hand side so that I don't end up beheaded.

I inhale. Searching. Seeking.

We're going too fast. I can't tell where it's coming from.

"Pull over," I yell. "I need to track her scent."

"We're on a goddamned freeway!" he retorts.

"That's an order, Pluto." I pull out my alpha-command, letting it rumble through my tone like a bass drum.

My second snarls, hating when I use my alpha tone to control him, but he darts around between the cars, moving us side to side like a chess piece until he finds a decent gap and can decelerate, pulling off onto the shoulder.

As soon as we're stopped, the car tucked into the middle of a field of high grass and Pluto grumbling about how this is going to ruin the undercarriage of his baby, I toss open the door and step outside. I realize we've fucking pulled over in the middle of 'Little House on the Prairie' land. Flat. Fields. Sky that drapes over the ground like a blanket, only broken by the occasional bank of trees or windmill. But otherwise, we're in the middle of nowhere.

I tilt my nose up and ask the moon goddess for her help. Then I start to unbraid the scents of the plains.

I find Elena's scent immediately. It's so bright that it shines like the north star. It's up ahead. My feet start moving, following her scent, trying to find the scent of that bastard beta too.

I vaguely hear Pluto yelling behind me, but my mind is overtaken by the need to find and protect my little mate. My wolf keeps urging me forward, the drive to protect her so strong that it lashes my stomach. Who knows what could be happening to her right now?

She's an omega, which means she won't be able to protect herself. Her wolf won't fight for her. That's *my job.*

The need to find her is making my wolf anxious to shift. But I won't let him because I need to be cautious about my approach. I need to get a lock on her location first, then make sure I sneak up from downwind, so they can't smell me coming. My pulse thrums in my sore neck, adrenaline pumping as my body prepares for a second fight of the night, something I haven't had to do in years, not since the early days of becoming an alpha wolf.

I've done it before, but I've never had this much motivation to win because my mate's never been on the line before. There's an ache in my chest as her scent comes to me, mingled with tikka masala sauce and something minty. Fuck. My wolf snarls in anxiety, punching at my ribs, trying to make me lose my calm and shift. Now.

He wants to run at her and grab her by the nape of her neck, dragging her away to someplace where he can lick her clean and erase all the shit that probably spilled onto her soft skin when my spunky little mate realized she was stolen. God, I hope she gave them hell —that beta and whatever Dark Night's he's working with.

I'm never letting her out of my sight again.

Pluto tromps after me through hay and wild grass that reaches my waist. He grabs my arm and yanks on it, stopping my dazed walk in Elena's direction, interrupting my wolf's attempt at a mental coup.

"Do you smell them?" he asks.

I scrunch my forehead and stare down at him, nonplussed. "Of course, I smell her. Don't you? Is your nose broken?"

"Not her, fathead. *Them*."

I scent the wind, but don't smell anything other than her for a moment, until the breeze shifts and brings with it smells full of fur and feral markings. A nutty scent ... not too far from Stone's smell reaches my nose.

Shifters.

Dark Nights.

And their scents are far too close to my mate's.

My monster emerges. My wolf wins his battle for control. My heart goes apeshit—smashing my ribs as if it aims to break through them even as they expand and transform. My tendons squeal internally as they stretch for the second time tonight and I push my forty-two-year-old body to do things only meant for twenty-somethings: Fight more than once before dawn.

Pluto transforms beside me. I watch ears sprout from his head and a snout take the place of his nose. His arms elongate into wild clawed hands that stretch beyond any human reach and his shirt rips to pieces as his chest expands. He's finished only seconds behind me, and our golden eyes meet.

A war drum pounds inside my head, urging me forward as my hands erupt into claws and the moonlight makes me glow like a phantom, my pure white fur gleaming.

All ideas about strategy and approaching from downwind flee from my mind as the only thing that's truly important takes precedence: saving Elena.

My wolf and I merge our minds until instinct and the need for bloodshed are the only things driving us. *We will protect our mate or die trying.*

I dart through the field, nothing but my nose guiding me through the tall grass as I peel away from the highway towards the unknown.

In less than ten minutes of full-on sprinting, the smells grow strong enough to be joined by sights. In the distance, a white catering van sticks out like a sore thumb in the driveway of a ramshackle farmhouse. That's where all the smells are concentrated. I stare at the building and curse the fact that fucking werewolves can't see through walls like Superman.

I want to know if she's okay. If anyone's touched a fucking hair on her head … I'm going to shred them into spaghetti.

Pluto nudges me with his shoulder and then jerks his head, indicating with a claw that we should circle before entering. I bare my fangs at him, irritated that he's trying to command me. My wolf nips at his shoulder—he can't stand anyone questioning the hierarchy.

Pluto yields his neck like he's supposed to, which calms my wolf enough to focus. And then, we do exactly as Pluto suggested because he's right. As much as I want to charge straight in there and claw anyone between me and Elena, I need to figure out the best approach. I need to make sure they don't hurt her as a way of controlling me, which means I need the element of surprise on my side.

Pluto and I dart through the weedy hayfield, staying low, ignoring the way the thick stalks irritate my fur and try to scratch the skin beneath. We head for a barn near the house. Grasshoppers chirp around us annoyingly and somewhere an owl hoots. Once, I heard that owls were death omens. That seems appropriate tonight since I'm about to rain pain and death down on the fuckers surrounding my mate. I'm going to water the ground with their blood.

Adrenaline clenches my heart, sharpens my vision, and makes the scents around me double. There aren't any live animal smells drifting from the barn, but Elena's scent ... it's a fucking siren song. I swear, it smells twice as intoxicating as it did earlier, probably because I'm so desperately afraid for her right now, so eager to save her and wrap her up in my arms where she'll be safe.

Pluto's hand grabs my forearm, and his eyes grow wide as he stares up at me, my monster dwarfing his.

I can't go in there, he mind-speaks to me, the way wolves can only with their pack mates.

I need backup, Pluto. What the fuck are you saying? I'm pissed that my second could even consider stepping back on me.

He shakes his head, taking a step back, retreating from our goal. *No. Black. You don't want me. I think ... I think Elena's in heat.*

My knees nearly buckle underneath me. No. Hell fucking no. No way my poor mate went into heat the second they stole her. That would make her so damned vulnerable.

Irresistible.

I bolt away from the barn towards the house, heedless of whatever danger might be coming my way as nightmarish images assault me. Her heat better have just started. God, no one better have touched her. I will not let those fuckers turn my precious mate's first heat into a nightmare. My pulse pounds as I scrape the front steps with my feet and bolt like lightning across the porch.

The front door has been ripped off the hinges and hangs limply like a broken arm. Madness and frenzy drive me across the wooden floor, down a hallway, towards a tiny kitchen where I see a shifter finish his shift into hulking monster form. Two small wolves huddle in the corner of the room behind him, in the space a small kitchen table should sit. I can instantly tell the wolves are shifters by their scent. And small is a relative term. They're small for shifters but large for actual wolves. A quick sniff confirms their identities. That beta and … my mate.

She's shifted into her wolf. Her wolf finally reappeared. And the perfume drifting off her tells me that Pluto was right. Her smell is darker than before, has a black licorice undertone.

Fucker! I curse my second for being right, certain he'll hear me even from a distance, our mental link cultivated over the years so that it's strong as iron.

I told you she's in heat.

I'd be ecstatic on any other occasion that her animal has returned, but this timing fucking sucks because a wolf's rank determines their reactions. She and the beta stand zero chance. In human form, she'd at least fight for herself, but I can see her cowering right now, truly an omega—about to turn and offer her neck.

My blood runs cold as the monster fucker in front of me—whose scent I don't recognize—swipes at them with his claws. The beta takes the hit, giving off a little whimper as he's tossed into the wall.

That's an interesting development. Murky's protecting her instead of handing her off. But I don't take the time to analyze. I don't have a second. I move.

The only sound I make is the inhale I take before I dive headfirst at the creature in front of me. I slam into his back, and he falls to the floor with a surprised *oof*, his kneecaps cracking against the wooden planks, his teeth landing just shy of the beta, Murky's, feet.

This monster's got a walnut smell not too far off from Stone's ungodly horrid scent, which just confirms every theory I had on the drive over. I don't give the bastard a second to push up off the ground. I use my massive claws to rake across his biceps, trying to shred them so he loses the use of his arms.

A satisfying howl erupts from his black muzzle as I dig in deep and twist. Cruelty makes my mouth curve into a smile that showcases my fangs as I slam his arms down against the floor with my claws still embedded in them. Once. Twice. Three times.

But then there's a whimper from Elena. I glance up, wondering if the bloodshed is too much for my sensitive little mate. Her eyes aren't trained on me, however.

Those silver disks set in her midnight fur are looking at a spot directly behind me.

That's all the warning I get before a fist smashes into my back and rakes across it. A trail of blazing heat arises, and I know the asshole has drawn blood.

Instead of making me afraid, I feel like I just drank a triple shot of espresso. I'm energized and full of light and completely ready. My mind maps out a plan and instead of whirling around like this fucker expects, I trust-fall into him. He's not ready for me, or the combined weight of my monster and my bloody friend —who comes along for the fall because my claws are still stuck in his arms, tenderizing his biceps.

Both of us smash down on the new arrival and I yank my claws out of the arms of Thing One in order to reach up to try to find the neck of Thing Two without looking. His claws come down at the same time, skidding over my ribs.

Fuck. I thought that one move through but didn't go beyond it. Now, I've got one fucker under me trying to claw me open and one above me who—though his arms are almost useless—is trying to rise up. I have zero doubt that he's about to kick the living shit out of me.

I'm getting fucking sloppy in my old age.

And maybe senile, Pluto's thoughts break into my head. *If you do go senile, can I have a hall pass for Elena?*

Anger and adrenaline shoot through me, re-energizing me.

Fucker! I yell at Pluto through the link.

You're welcome. Now kick some ass. I'm hunting wolves on the perimeter.

That asshole riled me up on purpose, but it did the trick. Suddenly, I'm not thinking anymore. I'm doing. I reach back with my arms, planting my hands on the floor. I wait until idiot one's weight is off me and then I shove my weight onto my arms, yanking my knees in and quickly kicking them out to smash the back of his knees where he stands. He goes stumbling forward and I whip around to face my second opponent just as that asshole gets a good gut stab in. His claw slices across my belly.

Red lightning flickers in my eyes and pain leapfrogs wildly around my body as I reach down and grab his muzzle. I clamp it shut until I can get my claws in right at the base of his jaw. Then I yank down on either side, popping his lower jaw out.

He gurgles a scream, and his claws retreat from my body, leaving only a nipping sensation in their wake as my shifter magic struggles to knit my body back together. The wound he gave me is rather shallow, so it doesn't take much. I rise to my feet and give the brown-furred shifter with the broken jaw a kick to the 'nads.

I turn to finish off the other monster, but that's when I spot a black wolf on the windowsill. He's not in monster form, he's solely an animal. But those can be just as dangerous. They're smaller and faster. Though they lack massive claws, their teeth are just as deadly. And working together in wolf form is actually the best way to bring down a werewolf.

He leaps just as I spot five other wolves dart in through the kitchen door.

Six on one.

Dammit to fuck.

I twist to avoid the first wolf's leap. Then I grab the shoulders of the asshole behind me. His arms still haven't healed all the way so he can't lash out. I lift him up and hurl his body across the room at the pack of five wolves, who scatter to avoid it. His head hits the countertop at an odd angle with a crack that makes me certain when he collapses in a heap, that he won't be getting back up.

I snarl, taking up a position in front of the beta and Elena.

My thoughts flicker to the beta's for the first time. *You will die to protect her,* I order Murky. He can at least make his last moments useful, even though he's a pack-betraying coward. I pour all my alpha voice into that order, trying to ensure he can't undermine it.

Of course, I will, he says back, simply, as if I'm stating the obvious.

That rankles me and makes me want to turn on him, to verbally eviscerate him before I strip his flesh from his bones inch by inch. But I don't because I have other foes to face first.

Two wolves launch at me, and I bat them back with my arm. But the way their teeth shred my skin, yanking it down like an unruly sleeve sends fire up to my shoulder. I howl in a combination of pain and fury. Then I yank a cabinet door from its hinges and wield it as both a weapon and a shield. I use it to block their leaps at me and slice it in their direction so that the corner smashes into the sides of their furry faces. One after another.

I can't help the wild laugh that escapes my lips when one of the wolves slips in the puddle of piss that's formed around the dead monster's body. Bloodlust has taken me over and the burn in my neck right now isn't just from my injury from Stone. It's from pure violent hunger.

Two of them leap together, coming at me from either side so that I can't fend both off. I throw the cabinet at one like a Frisbee. I reach for the other with both hands, grabbing him by the neck and twisting. His neck breaks as easily as a chicken's. A third wolf, a gray one, runs at my belly and I punt him across the room. But that leaves an opening for the final two.

I feel teeth close around my thigh and I hardly have the chance to think, Femoral artery, before pain erupts like lava and my legs give out.

I blink as stars explode on the edges of my vision. I reach down with my claws and grab one wolf's back. My monster gets a surge of adrenaline and I snap his spine, but his teeth stay embedded in my leg. I don't pull him off me as I grow dizzy. I'm worried that if I do, I'll bleed out sooner.

I stare blankly at the remaining wolves as all the energy I just had dissolves. My leg grows slick and I blink slowly. Did I win earlier just to stumble now? Just to die in front of some anonymous gang of wolves? What will happen to Elena if I die?

That thought sends me stumbling forward, tripping over my useless leg, which now feels more like a hollow log than a limb.

I raise my claws, ready to swipe at them, when a human figure darts forward from behind me. Murky has shifted back to a man. He snatches up the cupboard door I'd thrown and swings it wildly. Fucking fool. They're going to rip him—my thoughts fritz and I feel my body taking over my mind, the magic heating my bones and morphing them, shrinking them. I spiral downward until I'm in wolf form—the form I need to be in to heal.

But there's no time for healing. I need to fucking fight. There is no one else. Murky's about to die and then my Elena will be ripped to shreds. Metallic fear tastes bitter on my tongue as my imagination rapid-fires the things they'll do to her once they get their filthy hands on her.

No. I can't fail my mate. I try to give my wolf more control, to let his feral nature take over more. But he's just as beaten and battered as I am.

I'm here—Pluto's voice cuts through my internal torture just as his monster form steps through the door. I don't have more than a second to stare at him charging towards the other wolves before my vision flickers as everything turns the color of my name.

6

ELENA

I CAN'T BELIEVE how many times in my life I've shallowly said, "This is my worst nightmare." Old me was an idiot, a fool who didn't know what I know now. My worst nightmares were nothing, *nothing* compared to this. If I could time travel, I'd go tell her: there are monsters out there. And all of them want to take everything from you.

The scene in this kitchen is proof. Proof I'm not looking at because I'm curled into the corner in a ball, trembling, eyes tightly shut as a supernatural battle rages two feet in front of me.

A set of wolves from another pack came here and werewolfed out to attack us—and my guess is to drag me off like their own little trophy. An omega.

Black showed up, but he's no better than they are because he wants to throw me back in his own cage. My heart gives a little twinge of protest and even my wolf whines, *Alpha,* as if she's disappointed in me for judging him when he's defending us.

Look. He's not defending us. He's defending his pride.

No. Alphas protect the weak. Treasure. She sends me an image of cuddles with Alpha Black which does all sorts of horrible things to my insides, making them twist and plummet like I'm on a roller coaster. *Stop it.*

She doesn't defy my order. She stops. But she gives an annoyed little chuff inside my head.

I crack my eyes open and realize that Jonah isn't right in front of me. My gaze darts over to him, where he's shifted to human and is hitting a wolf with a board, another werewolf behind that wolf—his opponents stacked up like dominoes. Shit.

Where is Black? Why isn't he taking on that monster? My eyes drift across the narrow kitchen and I realize he's fallen down near the water heater. The huge, massive alpha is down, his white fur slathered in pink, eyes closed. Suddenly, my throat is smushed and clogged.

Black! I yell at him via the mental link instinctively, turning toward him.

He doesn't answer.

Every muscle from the inside of my knees up to my thighs collapses and my wolf legs give out.

One of the attacking wolves dives in my direction.

I shove my wolf roughly away because she rolls onto her back, trying to expose her belly for him. *Fucking no!* I shout at her as I shift into human form, the heat of the change crackling through my bones as if someone just set off an entire case of Black Cats.

I come to on the ground laying down, a naked human, on crusty linoleum that's got a gray film on it, just as the wolf's front paws land on my chest. I latch onto them with my hands, heart thudding wildly as I spin onto my side and try to take the wolf with me.

To my surprise, the wolf doesn't attack. He shifts too, into a muscled brute with shaggy dark gold locks and a pug face. He sneers at me, easily breaking my hold, his hands sliding up to my shoulders because my wrists aren't strong enough to smack them back down. I thought I knew fear before, with Black, but that is nothing compared to now. Black was angry and wanted to punish me. This brute has death in his honey-colored eyes.

He inhales and gives a malevolent smile. "Omega."

I knee him in the balls and that smile distorts into an outraged expression.

My wolf trembles, scared out of her mind. My limbs shake involuntarily, and I realize that this is probably my last moment. I recognize it in a dazed sort of way, not really processing, my body shaking too hard for any of my thoughts to coalesce into anything that makes a scrap of sense.

An explosion of red startles me, makes me instinctively cringe, and toss up my hands as a barrier in front of my face. The man holding me looks startled as his neck bursts apart. Claws rip right through him and I see their gleaming tips amongst the carnage. Blood splatters my face and I have to close my eyes so that it doesn't get into them. When I blink, the brute is gone, tossed aside. In his place is another monster—another werewolf. But a familiar-looking one. My mind is too overwhelmed to place him. I'm having a hard enough time with my racing heart. I just know that somehow—this werewolf doesn't generate a lot of fear in me.

He glares at me for a second, fierce anger making my wolf shove my shoulders into a submissive hunch before I can bat her back and straighten. The werewolf brings his claw up to his wolfish nose, smearing it in the blood of his enemy before he shifts into a human and it dawns on me that I'm staring at Pluto. Black's friend.

"Check on Alpha Maddox." He orders before he turns and bolts from the room, transforming back into a monster as he lurches into the hallway with a ragged howl.

I realize I was holding my breath only when I finally release it. I pant, eyes still panicking, searching the room for more threats. But Pluto eliminated them. I see two dead monsters and six dead wolves. And Black. The huge white wolf hasn't moved from his spot on the floor. That can't be good.

Before I check on Black, my eyes scan for Jonah. My love is curled up in the fetal position in human form near the sink, just outside the light of the moon goddess. I cry out and rush toward him, stumbling around the body at my feet as I try to make my way closer to him.

My fault. This is all my fucking fault. Jonah and Black. Shit. A sob bubbles up in my throat but I shove it back down. I've had plenty of practice doing that over the years. Besides, if I cry, I'll be useless. I need to see how badly Jonah's hurt and if there's anything I can do.

Alpha, my wolf urges me, wanting to follow the damn orders of Black's elite. But I counter with, *Mate,* and shove a mental image of Jonah at her.

She sets the images of the two of them side by side—my image and hers. But I can't be in two places at once so I dismiss her as I step closer to my beta; there are still two wolves blocking my path. That's when Jonah shifts. My hand flies to my mouth as relief gushes down my spine.

Thank the goddess.

If he's shifting then he's healing. He'll survive. I stand a moment, just letting the realization seep into my skin before I let my thoughts turn to our next problem.

Pluto is here. Black's second. The Lobos have found us, which means they mean to take us back.

Or me back.

That thought haunts me.

I glance over at Black, wondering what the fuck that means. He's lying there in wolf form, not moving, his eyes closed and head on his paws. He's covered in blood, though I have no idea how much is his. He's soaked up so damn much of it that he practically looks pink. Why the hell did he fight?

I get why he came after me. He's an alpha. God forbid someone fucking leaves him, not when omegas are property—meant to obey and serve and whatever other bullshit propaganda those alphas feed themselves. But he could have just let those fuckers take me and waited for a strategic moment to steal me from them. He hadn't. He'd John Wayned his way in here.

"Why did you fight?" I whisper, my eyes tracing the lines of his muzzle, the soft black of his eyelashes against that white fur.

He'd fought like a madman, even with the terrible odds.

He'd fought like—like he cared.

Fuck.

A chunk of my soul falls away, like a piece of ice breaking off from a glacier. I feel dizzy and I stumble where I stand, too much blood or too many thoughts rushing through my head. It can't fucking be.

He's an asshole. A total asshole. Entitled. The epitome of an alpha.

But he swept in here with a purpose, like a crusader. I didn't see a moment's hesitation from him. I didn't see fear of death. For that split-second when his eyes had met mine, I'd seen something else—concern. Worry. He looked at me the way my dad had looked at me when he'd dropped me off on the first day of fourth grade when we'd moved houses and I started at a new school. Black's eyes held that same trepidation—like he wanted to protect me from things but knew he wasn't able to.

Oh. My. God.

I gnash my teeth before I spin on my heel, unable to deal with the uncertainty that's planted a seed in my belly.

No. I can't think of Black as a protector. He has to stay a villain. Because even though I know shit-all about wolves, I'm certain I know the consequences for Jonah and me running off. I'll be damned if I feel soft toward Jonah's executioner.

I need to check on Jonah. Then I need to figure out how the two of us are going to get out of here alive. How the fuck are we ever going to escape the Lobos again?

I step carefully over each of the dead wolves, my bare feet unable to avoid all the blood splatter, which clings stickily to my toes, already clotting. I crouch next to Jonah, gently laying my hand on his fur. His chest rises and falls slowly underneath me, almost as if he is peacefully sleeping. I drag my hand along his fur and try to reach out mentally, talk to him the way we did before.

Jonah? I ask.

He doesn't respond.

I try again. *Jonah?*

Still nothing.

Maybe that mental talking only works when we're both shifted. Goddammit, what I wouldn't give for a manual on this shifter crap. I look around for my wolf, eyes scanning for her hiding behind the broken cabinet door or something, like a video game character who's stuck in a corner, handled by some inexperienced newb—which is basically what I am.

She's not there. And when I close my eyes and reach out to her inside my head, she's gone. She's left. She stayed long enough to panic. To show our fucking belly to an ass that was going to kill us. But she's gone now? Why?

Fucking hell. I'm furious at her for disappearing again, especially when my current best plan is for Jonah and me to shift to wolf form and run away.

Does she not give a single shit that she's leaving me unprotected and vulnerable? Selfish bitch! And that heat? Why the hell did she have to bring on that heat? We'd still be on the road. We'd still be safe. Jonah wouldn't be hurt if my stupid wolf hormones hadn't turned traitor and made me into a mindless lunatic.

As if that thought triggers my body, I feel the flush of the heat's fever start back up in the base of my spine. Hell no. I'm not going to do this. I reach for Jonah and shake him roughly. I know he needs to heal, but he can do it in the van while I drive. I don't know where Black's little lackey went, but I'll run him over if I have to. I'm not doing this. I'm not staying here and letting my stupid shifter instincts shackle me any longer. I'm going to fight this heat and find a way to get rid of it —permanently.

Slick dribbles down my thigh and I shake Jonah harder, very conscious of the fact that I'm completely naked.

His wolf whines, but when I lean down and whisper, "I need you to shift so we can find the van keys," he gives a quick, wolfish nod—eyes still closed—before transforming into my precious Jonah. I try not to focus on the bite marks that cover my mate, or the blood still trickling from one of the wounds near his abdomen. I don't allow my gaze to look any lower than his mate mark, where the skin is scarring in a beautiful circle. I resist the urge to trace the mark because now isn't the time for tenderness. We need to stay on high alert. "Jonah, we have to leave," I gently say, wrapping an arm around his trim waist so that I can help him to his feet.

Jonah moans as he stands and it takes a second before he blinks and really seems to come to. That's when his eyes gaze around the room and widen in horror. "Elena!"

"Shh. It's okay. Just stay quiet. We need to find the keys and sneak out of here before anyone else comes." I decide not to mention Black's friend. No need for Jonah to worry more than necessary. Maybe that guy ran off for reinforcements. And maybe they're far away. Hopefully.

I help Jonah navigate around the bodies and out of the kitchen, into the dark hallway. But once we're away from all the death, Jonah stops. He leans back against the wall across from me, groaning. I reach for him, concerned, worried that his internal injuries are worse than I thought and I should have left him as a wolf.

"Are you okay?"

"No," he replies through clenched teeth, his eyes closing as his head bows down.

Fuck. I can see pain's shadow flit over his face.

"Okay. Stay here then. I'm going to run upstairs and find the keys. They were in your pocket, right? So hopefully they're on the floor?"

He shakes his head, sending panic slicing through me. "They're not? Where are they?" I ask frantically, hoping like hell he didn't leave the keys in the van. Otherwise, I'm certain one of these attacker fuckers snatched them. Who wouldn't?

"Elena," Jonah's pale blue eyes fly open and he stares at me. "We can't keep running."

"What?" I pull away from him, stunned and infuriated. We've hardly been on the run for two hours. "What the fuck?"

"You're in the middle of a heat." Jonah keeps his tone soft as his hand lifts and he gestures down the hall, toward the kitchen carnage just out of sight. "You're in a heat that apparently will call to wolves from miles around and I can't protect you."

"What the fuck? I just saw you fight off those wolves."

He snorts. "Yeah. Right. You saw me smack a couple around. Some who were already weakened by Black."

"Well, next time, we'll stay out in the open where we can run away easier."

"Elena, what kind of guy would I be if I let there be a next time?" He shakes his head, hand coming up to shove through the short bristles of his blond hair. "This can't happen again."

My stomach implodes—shock and hurt concuss my system as Jonah's eyes drift away from mine, back down to the ground. Submissive but not submitting. He doesn't want to be with me. "It's too much for you," I whisper. "Too dangerous."

"I don't give a shit about me," he retorts roughly, angrily. "But knowing I was in there, not really able to protect you? Knowing that my wolf would fucking roll the hell over and my human form was just going to be kibble for them? Easy pickings? And realizing that as soon as they were done with me, they'd take you and do unspeakable things ... yeah, it's too much for me. You're right." He shoves roughly off the wall and turns away from me. His voice is thick as he limps toward the front door. "You need an alpha to protect you, Elena. I thought … I thought—I was an idiot."

The front door is broken, and Jonah walks out of it, down the porch steps into the moonlight. The goddess watches as my mate breaks my heart.

7

BLACK

My wolf magic zings through me, stitching me up like some internal, sparkly Cinderella bullshit as I fight tooth and nail to wake back up. I don't give a shit if I heal or not. There's only one thing I need right now, and it's not to be stitched back together.

Where's my mate?

I bat and paw at the supernatural swirls that try to keep me down. Finally, I break through and blink awake. It takes a second to get my bearings. I realize I'm laying on a hard floor, my elbows sore and stiff beneath me, my wounds—most of them healed—my neck still stinging. I wonder if Stone dipped his fingernails in silver dust or something. Wouldn't fucking surprise me. The bastard would be sadistic enough to do something like that.

I shake out my fur, which is stiff with dried blood as I glance around for Elena. I carefully eye every dead wolf on the floor, heart pounding, but she's not one of them. She's gone.

Shit. Those assholes must have gotten her.

My wolf lets out a bereaved howl inside my head before turning wild, untamed. He's bristling and ready to fight again.

Even though I'm pushing it, I shift back into monster form, because I don't know what's waiting around the corner. I have no idea how long I was out or where they're hiding. My muscles scream at me because they're starving, depleted, and don't want to hold this form another second. I ignore them as I step over a couple bodies carefully, about to call out to Pluto mentally and find out what the fuck is going on.

But that's when I spot her.

Elena stands naked and alone in the hallway, her hair disheveled as she faces away from me.

I'm stunned, stupefied, frozen in utter disbelief. How? My eyes scan her figure, searching for wounds. I don't see any as I try to process what is going on right now. How did my mate—an omega—survive? Who saved her? And where are they?

I come up to Elena slowly, letting my feet make a sound so that she's not startled. It doesn't work, since she gasps and whirls toward me anyway, tears gleaming in her eyes and—

Is that *blood* on her face?

I rush to her and gather her up in my arms, ignoring the way she stiffens and pushes away, probably so frightened that she doesn't recognize me in monster form.

But I can't let go. My instincts are too intense—I have to check on her, see if she's hurt, and what I can do about it.

I purr, trying to calm her, to let that rumble in my chest tell her that I'm not a threat as I lean down and sniff the droplets splattered across her face as my eyes roam across her features. I don't see any rips or nicks in her skin. I tuck her in tighter, hugging her hard as my shoulders sag in relief.

My sweet little mate is okay.

She must be fucking moon-blessed because I have no clue how my girl was able to walk out of a massacre like that kitchen scene and not have a scratch on her.

Thank you, I tell the goddess, hit by a solid right hook of gratitude so strong it makes my head spin.

Thank you.

"Let me go!" Elena finally finds her voice, though it's lower and scruffy from her crying, and probably from all the screaming she did when they took her.

I don't let her go, because I know that's just the stubborn side of her, the same stubborn side she's shown so far. I purr louder.

"You giant bastard, let me fucking go!" She tries to kick out even as her cheek slides down on my furry chest so she can better hear my purr. They've clearly traumatized her. I realize that her mouthiness is her defense mechanism. It's the only one my omega has.

Who knows what they did to her. I'm not going to ask. But someday, someday I'll fucking rip out the teeth of every damned elite Stone has in retribution for hurting my sweet mate. Right now though, my wolf just wants to hold her, hug her tighter until she relents and stops fighting and realizes she's protected, adored, cherished.

I hug harder, nuzzling the top of her head.

But Elena doesn't react the way I want. She doesn't calm down. She keeps kicking and screaming at me and I realize she's been traumatized by these fuckers grabbing her. I don't want her mentally mixing me in with them. My poor, sweet mate. So ... slowly, I set her on her feet.

That's when the beta fucker bursts in through the open front door, armed with a stick, screaming nonsense as he charges.

Elena stiffens at the sight of him, obviously scared witless.

I push her back against the wall behind me so that she's protected. Then I issue a growl to Murky—one that every beta in the pack knows, one filled with alpha command. It means *Stop!*

He freezes.

I point at the floor.

He kneels.

And as the moon goddess peeks in through the window, curious about what's going on, I spot a mark on his shoulder. A bite mark. A fresh one, still pink, the skin not fully scarred over.

His nonsense words suddenly make sense. He'd screeched, "Don't you fucking touch my mate!"

Cotton fills my ears. Then a waterfall. I'm hollow. No. I'm falling through the sky, a jagged mountain rushing up at me.

My wolf yanks away control from me and sniffs. I smell her on him. Despite all the gore in the house, her scent is so strong that I can smell her on him. I turn so

I can see her, backing up a few steps. I smell him on her too.

I roar.

Elena and her beta quake, as they should.

She marked him.

I'm livid. Burning.

But I spot a shadow darting outside, a hundred yards past the front door, and I realize … this fight's not over.

There are probably other Dark Nights roaming outside, more driving in, more shifting to attack. I wouldn't be surprised if Thomas Stone tried to pull all of the alphas in the Dark Nights here tonight to try to circumvent this territory change.

In fact, if I was him, it's exactly what I'd do. Steal the other alpha's mate, get him to chase after her, let him think he's won, then slaughter him.

I make eye contact with both of them, then point upstairs with a single claw. Murky nods, immediately understanding.

I fucking hate that he's compliant right now because I want to rip his throat out. But he's a fight I'm going to save for later. After we survive.

I don't wait to ensure he follows my orders. I don't want to see if he touches Elena.

Mate, my wolf growls, wanting to spin around and gut him and then take Elena and rut her in monster form to show her who she belongs to.

NO! I shove him back.

Survival. Always survival first.

He snarls but then we catch a scent. Not the beta's or Elena's. Red colors the edges of my vision as I wear my anger like a cloak.

I move faster, stomping and smelling, putting all my focus into the solitary quest for more Dark Nights. They'd better be out there, skulking in the trees, because someone needs to taste my wrath, have it bubble up red in their throat. Someone needs to drown in it.

I hurtle out the front door of the farmhouse, the steps creaking and moaning as I launch myself off the tiny porch and into the field. It's not nearly dark enough out here for my mood. The goddess is flooding the damned plains with her light. I want to flip her off—her and her divine plans. Her destiny. It's bullshit.

I scent blood and pump my legs fast to go around the corner, to the back of the house, the windows that face the now-gory kitchen.

I gnash my teeth as I find four shifted Dark Night wolves in the grass. Their throats are missing and eyes glazed.

Pluto clearly found a way to make himself useful even though he didn't come inside. Somehow, the fact that he had my back doesn't make me feel better—because my mate didn't have my back. My own mate betrayed me. She took my ring then disappeared.

Even worse, she mate-marked the beta who ran with her like this is some goddamned teenage love story.

An invisible eagle screeches, digs his claws into my chest, and then flies off, leaving me flayed—peeled open—still alive because he was startled and couldn't bother to finish the job. Everything throbs. My half-healed wounds. My head. My chest.

I have to force myself to keep moving, sniffing, searching along the back of the house, but it gives me purpose, something to focus on other than the shifters indoors. The smells out here are a thick batter full of wolf scents. Some of them I recognize from indoors. Some of them I don't. So there *are* more to hunt.

The hair prickles on the back of my monster neck, my ruff stiffening as I peer out into the darkness.

My heightened senses catch movement in the tall grass a hundred feet away. I'm off. I sprint, my claws scythes that slash the hay, beheading entire swathes of it with each swing. I don't try for subtlety. I want whoever's fucking out there to hear me. I want them to be scared —their heart in their throat. I want them to run, to flee. I want their fear choking them just before *I* do.

A flash of fur catches my eye and then a scent. It's got a metallic edge and woodsy flavor, like a hot saw whirling in a lumber mill.

It's not Pluto. I grin, pouring on speed, and my wolf howls inside my head, eager for this chase, this release, this speck of justice.

Bunching my muscles, I push myself to go faster, stooping to use my front claws for extra traction. I speed up until I feel my lungs burn and the wound on my neck, still raw around the edges, aches from the biting snap of the hay as I rush through it.

I get closer and adrenaline merges with giddiness. I see the paw pads of the wolf in front of me just before they disappear in the grass.

I'm close.

I let out a growl, not enough to steal my breath, just enough to shoot shivers down the spine of the bastard in front of me. Then a strange, warped smile crosses my wolfish face. Nearly there.

I hear a yip and a second later I barrel into the fucker, who's slowed at the edge of a murky brown pond, having to change direction to run around the edge. He glances back and I can smell the urine dribble down his leg when he spies my monster form. He knows he's dead.

I grow even more excited.

He doesn't have room to turn to fight, so he tries to pour on speed. But I'm bigger, faster, and full of righteous anger. There's no way he's getting away. I force my exhausted limbs faster until I'm looming over him, my massive arms near his midsection. I lean forward and clamp my teeth down on the back of his neck and then I stand with him dangling from my mouth. The snap of his spine is as satisfying as the crack of asparagus stalks. I shake him once, twice, then I fling him from my jaw.

I watch as his limp wolf form soars up underneath the stars and then crashes down into the pond with a splash. His eyes go dull before he sinks beneath the surface. I lick my bloody chops, satisfaction rumbling through me. One threat gone.

But a sound interrupts my gloating.

Pluto's voice appears inside my head. *Maddox, by the highway! There are more!*

I'm off like a shot, skirting the pond and heading for my second.

Where?

North of the house. Quarter mile.

I push my legs faster and harder, though the farther I get from the house the rockier the ground—it hasn't been worked over in years and so my easy run gets more complicated. Just like my life.

Nope. No thinking about that fucking bullshit storm.

You okay? I ask, trying not to let the tension I feel slide into my thought-projected words. But Pluto and Matthew are fucking family to me. Hopefully, there's just a stray or two. Those wouldn't be any problem for Pluto. But if there were ...

Ooof—

I don't think he meant to send me that, but the pack link can fritz when you're injured. *Dammit.* I don't like the fact that Pluto's probably hurt and I'm not there to back him up. Nothing else can go wrong tonight. It just —it can't.

I try to speed up but lactic acid has already built up inside my limbs. My muscles have gone from hot to cold so many times tonight that they simply won't push any harder.

Pluto! I call out his name, but nothing else, not wanting to distract him from a fight.

You fucking fucker—

His thoughts project into my head and randomly break off again. But at least he sounds pissed. Pissed is good for an alpha. It feeds the darkness, allows us to sink more fully into our animals, and lets the feral side of ourselves take control.

I break through the stupid grass and can finally see what Pluto's facing. In a gravel turnoff for truckers to snooze away, he's monstered out and fighting three others who are also in werewolf form. I don't smell anyone I recognize, but I'd bet my last dollar that one of them is Thomas Stone.

I'm breathing hard, grateful they haven't spotted me yet. At least three-on-one, soon to be three-on-two, isn't bad odds.

I take a second to glance towards the road, though it's dark out tonight, so I doubt humans could see us from the highway, with its little streetlights blinding them. Most cars zip past, but my eyes widen as a silver one pulls off the road, heading straight for us. Dammit to fuck.

I don't give two shits about some human girl running home to daddy saying she saw monsters on the road and getting labeled delusional. I'm concerned that a car means backup is here for the Dark Nights. Cars can mean guns. Silver bullets.

I jet left toward Pluto, my right arm scything at the Dark Nights as I try to put distance between them and my second. Heart stampeding, and huge claws dragging, I know I'm wearing out. I'm reaching the end of my capacity. Even my wolf's panting inside my head. The aches in my chest aren't as easy to ignore and that damn wound in my neck, which still hasn't healed, feels like someone's holding a pan fresh from the stovetop up against me, searing the skin. My monster form won't hold much longer and either my shift or silver bullets—because I'm damn sure that car is driven by a Dark Night based on the scent—will be the end of us.

The car screeches to a halt, tires squealing as it fishtails in the gravel. I reach Pluto at that exact moment.

Into the grass, I snarl an alpha command as the other monsters all hightail it towards the vehicle. We both dive for the grass, letting our wolves take over and shift us into pure animals, muscles eclipsing thought as we dash madly as far as we can get. We have more instinctual survival skills in our pure wolf forms, we're a shit ton smaller, and it's not nearly as exhausting. But I push. I strain. I hurry because I'm sure I know what's coming.

We dart toward some scrub bushes.

The crack of a gunshot sounds behind us, just as I expected. Pluto and I stop running and crouch as the gun spits death in our direction.

If we just wait, backup is on the way, Pluto tells me. *I called Warcraft right after I dealt with the four outside.*

Good. If they come into the grass, split up, I order, though the alpha tone slips from my voice. I'm fucking exhausted. I'm panting and my eyes are hooded. If they just wait out there with their guns for ten minutes, I'll probably be easy pickings because I'm fighting a second round of magical sleep with every fiber of my being. My body wants to heal itself completely and rest after all these battles. But I can't. Not yet.

My wolf's ears perk when the car starts to roll along the gravel. Are they going to drive into the field after us? Or are they leaving? Are they going to head back for the farm to grab Elena? Fuck. Concern jumps into my throat even though it shouldn't—because I'm too fucking weak and worn out right now to convert it back into anger. I should have made those two hide somewhere else. The barn. Something.

I have to know where the car is headed. Even though it's stupid as fuck, even though they're traitors, that beta and Elena are still under my protection. I'm the one who gets to make the ruling on their punishment. Me. Not a Dark Night.

I try to peer through the grass, but as a wolf, I'm too short. I pad forward when it sounds like the car is moving away from us, the little *click-clack* of the gravel knocking together underneath the tires growing softer.

What are you doing? Pluto demands.

Checking on things.

Don't be stupid.

Don't call me stupid, stupid. I retort, a little dazed and light-headed from exhaustion.

I hear the undercarriage of the car scrape against the highway as it tries to climb the ridge between the dirt and the gravel, which must have washed out due to rain. When I break through the grass, I see the driver tensed on the wheel, flooring it so that a semi barreling down the road doesn't turn him into a silver pancake. But he's the only one who's tense. The other guys in the car have shifted back to humans, and none of them see the threat. One pulls himself up through an open sunroof, gun in hand, looking in my direction.

I don't move, despite the fact that my pure white wolf is visible in the moonlight. I won't give him the satisfaction. Not at this shooting distance, with him in a moving vehicle. He'd have to be an expert shot to hit me.

I stare up at the man, knowing instinctively that this is Thomas Stone. He's got the same jaw as his father, though his golden-brown curls scream Matthew McConaughey. He tilts the barrel of the gun in my direction.

Pluto barrels into me from behind, knocking me sideways as the shot rings out. I fall to the ground, unable to catch my balance, my snout smashing into the dirt before I can get my paws underneath me.

MOTHERFUCK! Pluto screeches behind me.

I whirl around, fear leaping up my throat, eyes scanning him. The bastard better not have gotten himself killed saving me. Idiot. I look him over as best I can in his prone position—he's gone fetal on his side, curled up in a ball. I can't fucking see in wolf form where he's hit, his fur is too thick. But I can smell the blood. I lean forward over him and sniff. I find the sizzled flesh and fresh wound on his left shoulder. But I don't scent the silver, which means the silver bullet isn't lodged inside of him. It passed straight through. Relief washes over me so intensely that my knees nearly give out.

Stop whining like a bitch. That's just a little love bite, I tell him, teasing so that I don't start verbally lashing him for being so stupid. He could have fucking died.

No, 'Thanks Pluto, you took a bullet for me?' His wolf eyes pop open, annoyance a greater emotion than pain.

Well, I mean, it's not still in there. So does that really count as taking one?

I'll remember that next time.

Good. I'm the alpha. I take the bullets.

He growls, but not bitterly, as he pushes up to his paws.

Oh. Already healed? See, told you it was just a nip.

I'll give you a nip.

You can try.

We walk back toward the house, both of us limping—me, from a combination of my neck wound and pure exhaustion, and Pluto from the scar that was certainly forming on his shoulder, because silver always leaves scars.

You did it for the scar, didn't you? I ask.

Well, it will make a good story. I saved Alpha Maddox in his weakest hour...

If that's the story, then I'll start telling the one about how you 'mixed up' headache meds and little blue pills and ended up with—

Pluto cuts off my threat with a nod in the direction of the farmhouse. *What are you going to do about them?*

He redirects my thoughts exactly where I do not want them to go, to what I've deliberately been trying to avoid—to the fact that Elena marked someone else.

My mood plummets, like the temperature just before a storm rolls in. I stare at the house, the utter wreck of a place that's as good a metaphor for my life right now as I've ever heard. The only thing that would make it more accurate is tossing a tornado on top.

I'll figure it out, I tell Pluto.

I'll be out here.

As I make my way up the creaking steps, the smell of curdling blood hits my nose. So much death tonight. I killed another alpha. Then Pluto and I just killed a dozen or so more Dark Nights here. But what the hell did I just fight for?

Nothing.

I fought and killed for her.

But it amounts to nothing.

I shove aside whatever trembly note runs through my stomach because fuck regret.

I could kill her beta right now and blame it on his collusion with the Dark Nights. I could kill *her* and tell everyone she got caught in the crossfire.

I could do a lot of things. But I won't.

I won't become one of those alphas who kills just for convenience. Crossing that line wipes out a whole lot of others, and while I live in the shadows and do things most betas would piss their pants to know, I have my own set of rules. One that has nothing to do with the goddess and everything to do with that face in the mirror that gazes back at me every morning.

I won't kill them.

But I *am* an alpha. And I will punish them. Question is … what kind of punishment fits their crime?

8

ELENA

I'm back in my tattered dress, a layer of dust graciously added by the bedroom floor to make this thing look as trashy as it truly is. I clench the keys to the van in my hand, but Jonah won't budge from the bedroom. He won't leave with me. He won't even go downstairs, the stubborn fuck.

"You need Black."

"Bullshit!" I counter, furious, squeezing the keys until they dig into my palms, not even a quarter as painful as his rejection. "I need *you*. And we need to keep moving. They're gone. This is a second chance. I don't understand why you're being this way. The van is right there. *Right. Down. There!*" I jerk my arm at the bedroom door, indicating the stairs.

Jonah just shakes his head, a hand at his waist where he's holding up his stretched-out, sagging pants. His light blue eyes are tired, and though his words resist me, his shoulders slump. He hates arguments and confrontations. He's so damn go-with-the flow normally that I know this isn't really him speaking. It's trauma. It's got to be.

I can convince him. I can. I just have to calm the fuck down first. That's easier said than done when my pulse is racing and my fingers are trembling from horror, anxiety, fear—essentially every negative emotion is pummeling me right now because we only have this narrow window, this tiny slice of possibility.

I'm desperate, so desperate to be with him. Doesn't he want that too?

I drag a hand through my hair, grinding my teeth in frustration. My first instinct is to yell at Jonah, shake him, boss him around because when I get upset, that's what I revert to. Fury to cover up fear and sadness. Yelling to keep the tears at bay. But I tried that a few minutes ago and it didn't sway him. Besides ... I don't want to go too far with that. Memories of my parents and their "whispered" fights behind closed doors pop up in my head. The last thing I want to do is repeat history. I refuse to become my mother.

I blow out a breath, trying to talk myself down without letting the sobs that threaten to close my throat break free. If I cry, then I'm done for—and I can't be done yet. Someone has to keep fighting for us—for that perfect moment Jonah and I just experienced.

The attack was too much and he's freaking out, that's why he walked off earlier and it's why he's frozen now. I get that. I can respect it. It's definitely too fucking much for me, I'm grappling to suppress my own shock and trying to help him find a way to motivate so we can get the lead out and get a move on. But obviously, I'm screwing up.

Maybe I just need to be bluntly vulnerable. Maybe I need to share what I actually fear. God, I don't know if I can say it aloud without bursting into tears. But I try.

"Jonah, honey. He'll hurt you," I whisper the last bit brokenly. It's an understatement. A euphemism. It's the best I can do, because even that word has me grimacing in pain and placing a hand over my heart—like it's already happened. As if my soul's already torn by it.

"I know." He sags back against the wall and shakes his head. "But I can't protect you. More wolves will show up like that."

"Not if we're running fast enough."

His eyes water. "It won't be that bad."

I start to hyperventilate. How can he say that? How can Jonah stand there calmly talking about his own death? No. No. I refuse to listen.

I reach for his hand and yank on it, trying to drag his ass from the room. Even though I work out for the track team, I can barely get him to budge an inch, much less the five feet I need to get him through the door. "I will never be with an alpha. You know that." I don't talk about my parent's relationship. But it's not like my dad's bruises were a secret to those in the pack. Unlike a woman who'd hide them with makeup, his were visible all the fucking time. But maybe Jonah was too young to hear about all of the DeMarkus drama. Maybe I have to tell him … "My mom used to beat the shit out of my dad." I lay it out there, even though saying it aloud feels like lighting a blow torch inside my own stomach. The words burn.

Jonah's eyes turn soft and his hand comes to my face. "I didn't know that." He pulls me into a hug, leaning down and kissing the top of my head. That simple gesture makes the omega heat between my legs flare back to life but I ignore it, clamping my thighs shut. No more of that bullshit.

I will fight it off this time. I will, I tell myself, as the fire creeps up my spine.

"But Black won't do that to you," he tries to reassure me.

“Bullshit! He’s a fucking bastard.”

“Elena, you didn’t see him in the hall. The way he held you … I thought you said he just claimed you because you’re an omega.”

“He did!” I retort, pulling away from Jonah, starting to pace.

I hate the direction this conversation is taking. I don’t want to talk about Black. Or that hug, which made me feel safe and warm and cherished. That hug was a millisecond and it was nothing compared to how Black treated me before that.

He’s so damned arrogant and cocky and demanding. I’ve no doubt he’s going to be furious and just as deadly as those Dark Nights. He won’t be able to stand that I defied him. Alphas will not be undermined. I know this for a fact.

Dammit. Fuck this calming down and sweet-talking Jonah into running bullshit, I reach for him again and uselessly yank. He won’t budge.

I eye him, wondering if I could toss him on my shoulders and fireman-carry him down the stairs while I explain the whole messed up Black scenario.

“He chased me through the forest and then locked me in his basement. He spanked me!” My cheeks flare at the memory, humiliation and arousal both flooding my system as I scoff, "Who the fuck does that?"

Jonah tilts his head as he studies me. But then his expression collapses into pain as he grits his teeth and mutters, "Aw shit."

"What?" I lean toward him, ready to swoop my shoulder under his armpit and prop him up, worried he's got some kind of internal injury he's been hiding. But he shakes his head.

"You feel something for him, don't you?"

His lower teeth scrape across his upper lip and his eyes drop to the ground, but not submissively. He looks down like he can't bear the sight of me.

"Don't be stupid. I don't feel anything," —My chest tightens but I continue anyway—"Nothing but loathing."

"Elena, you're a wolf now. I can fricking smell it."

"That's the heat. The heat *you* started," I counter, well aware that the space between my thighs is flaring back to life now that death isn't imminent.

Slick trickles down my inner thigh and I get the urge to straddle Jonah's thigh and ride it until I make myself fall apart.

But I ignore the stupid, ridiculous hormones magic shoved into my system. And I'm going to keep ignoring them. I'm going to treat this whole heat thing like period cramps—an unwelcome fucking annoyance attached to being female.

Jonah's tone breaks when he says, "He held you like you were the most precious thing in the world down there."

"Precious to his ego maybe—"

"There was no one around, Elena!" Jonah shouts, pushing off the wall and then tilting his chin, his expression something I've only ever seen in the movies before, in one of those tragic scenes where someone just found out they're about to die. He looms down over me, vibrating with pain and fury so strong that I can feel them on my skin like a shock of static electricity. "There was no one there to see Alpha Maddox play the big, bad alpha. He wasn't playing. And don't pretend you believe your own bullshit."

I take a step back, toward the hall, shaking my head at his ridiculous accusation. "Black doesn't even know me." The arrogant prick doesn't know what I like for breakfast, much less what I value. So who gives a shit about attraction in light of that?

Why is Jonah treating it like it's so important?

"I didn't say he did. He doesn't know you. But what he feels for you …" Jonah makes a fist and it comes up to his forehead. "God, I'm an idiot. I'm an idiot for thinking your wolf didn't change you. She connected you to him, didn't she?"

Jonah's going insane. He's running off onto a tangent that's so far afield of what we need to discuss that I find it hard to believe we're in the same room, much less the same galaxy. "No! She didn't. I marked you, remember? She hasn't even fucking met Black because she keeps disappearing. I chose *you*—but I only get to be with you if we fucking run!"

A soft desperation blows across the back of my neck as I stare at him, begging, pleading for him not to do this. I can't watch him die. I can't.

There's a noise downstairs. And just like that, our time's up.

I gasp and run to Jonah, the fight in my veins abandoning me immediately. I wrap my arms around his shoulders and squeeze him, pressing my cheek to his chest as my heart pounds. I can feel the frantic drumming underneath his skin. Though he sounds calm when he speaks, there's no denying it ... Jonah's terrified.

"The window. We can still make it," I whisper against his skin as I clutch him.

He pulls me close and folds me in tight. Why does it feel like he's hugging me goodbye?

He kisses my hair, my ear, my cheek. Then he pulls away, his eyes glossy. "I can't protect you, Elena. He can."

I yank out of his grasp and punch his pec as hard as I can as sobs rack me. "No. No. You hear me! No." I have to swipe at my eyes because they're blurring so much that Jonah's face has turned into smears of color. I won't let this happen. It can't happen. How the fuck can he just give up?

I turn and run from the room, out into the hall, desperate to stop this.

But how can I fix something so shattered?

I toss down the keys, my only hope, as I pace the upstairs hallway and struggle to get myself under control before Black appears. It's him downstairs. I can tell by the woodsmoke and caramel scent already drifting up the stairwell. My fists clench and unclench as I breathe deeply, trying to calm my spasming diaphragm and end the sobs.

I'm not just heartbroken— I'm also fucking furious. My hackles are up because I'm backed into a corner all over again. Before, it was marrying Black. Now, it's losing Jonah.

I swipe at my nose and try to rub the moisture from my cheeks. I wish my stupid wolf would reappear because I want to yell at her some more, get angry at her for the mate mark. Without it, I could have lied. I could have told Black that Jonah was helping me while I puked and we were taken together. I could have made Jonah look like a victim too.

I knew we should've waited. We weren't ready.

But now … now the truth is branded right into Jonah's skin. And Black saw it.

There is no lying.

My throat clenches and releases like I'm crying, though I refuse to let any more tears fall.

They won't get me any pity from that brute.

Maybe I can take the blame. Say I forced the bite onto Jonah, say I had a knife. I made him get me out of there at knife-point. I got the knife from … from … fuck! He knows I didn't have access to that shit.

With every creak of the stairs Black ascends, my heart threatens to burst free of my chest. It wants to fly out of my body, crash through the glass window behind me in a wild bid for freedom. I don't know anything about alpha males, and what I know about Black would fit on the head of the pin. The only thing I know he wants in life … The only thing I have any power to give … is me.

I'm out of time to think, or debate whether that would even work because a moment later, Black's face appears in the stairwell. He's dragging like he's exhausted. He's completely naked after his shift and covered in a combination of blood and small cuts. A scar on his neck still oozes a thin line of blood and his long hair is wild and free, a leaf stuck in it.

I swallow hard because my mind instantly compares Black to Henry Cavill. They both look amazing roughed up. Hotter than when they're clean-cut and ready for society.

The heat flares between my legs and I clamp them shut, reminding them who the hell is in charge of this body.

I know Black can smell it by the way his nostrils flare, but his lips clamp shut as he continues to slowly ascend the stairs. But his eyes … those dark eyes. I can see buzzards circling in his gaze already—in his mind, he's looking at a dead woman.

"It's my fault," I declare, though I'm utterly disgusted by how thin and reedy my voice sounds right now.

Black doesn't respond. He doesn't acknowledge that I spoke. He simply stops and stands at the edge of the hall, those eyes charring me where I stand.

Desperation festers inside my stomach, tasting foul and rotten as I step closer, doing one of the few things I know alphas like: keeping my eyes downcast and showing my neck. "Don't kill him," I breathe, pleading even though I promised myself I wouldn't. But the thought of a world without Jonah is terrifying.

"And why shouldn't I?" Black growls, his voice so low it's hardly human.

Hairs rise up on the back of my arms at his tone and I have to fight the physical instinct to back away slowly from him. Instead, I force my trembling body to take a step forward. "I'll do anything." I don't even negotiate, the plea just escapes from my lips immediately.

The truth is out there between us, waving itself like a white flag—surrendering everything.

"Get on your knees," he says, taking a single step forward.

I hurry to comply, to show him that I mean what I say. I slide down to my knees, ignoring the discomfort of the wooden floor. He takes a step toward me, letting his right arm monster out, his forearm growing massive, four-inch claws descending from his furred fingers.

I have to clamp my mouth shut so that I don't squeal in terror as he steps closer, that claw clenching and flexing in a way that tells me he's considering snapping my neck.

"Don't move," he tells me as he grows close.

I squeeze my eyes shut and try to stay in place, though I'm trembling from head to toe and panting in panic, every nerve ending tensed—just waiting for him to deal that final blow. It'll be quick. His footsteps grow louder and closer until I can tell he's right next to me.

He takes a step past me and I envision him coming up behind me so he can hold my hair while he slices my neck. It would be cleaner for him that way. Less messy if he's behind me. Oh fuck.

But he takes another step away. And another.

My eyes fly open as I realize he's not about to touch me —he's headed for Jonah. I turn on my knees, reaching for him. "Don't!"

Black whirls around, eyes glinting gold. "I told you not to move." He marches back over to me and grabs my shoulder, roughly turning me back to face the stairwell. "If you want that beta bitch to live … you'll do exactly as I say from now on. Forever."

I might puke. I'm shaking so hard that I can barely nod.

But then I inhale and get a whiff of his scent. And fuck my stupid body. I wish he had just swiped a claw across my carotid—because that scent relaxes me. The shaking slows and stops as he holds me roughly where he wants me. And instead of puking, my body betrays me. I grow sweltering hot. His hand squeezes my shoulder and my brain flickers.

This can't be happening.

I try to breathe through my mouth.

"Raise your right hand," Black orders.

I slowly bring it up to my shoulder.

"Faster," he snarls.

I shoot my fingers up to the sky.

"Good. Now, take off that dress."

I gulp and struggle to hurry, pushing the straps down my shoulders as I shove down a million shitty, snarky things I want to say. "Bastard," slips out under my breath and suddenly, Black's fingers are instantly on my chin, squeezing hard.

"What was that?"

"Nothing, Alpha."

"Lying won't be allowed either … if you want that prick to live. Do you understand?"

I give another nod. He roughly pushes my chin away. "Continue."

Humiliation and rage slap at me while I slide the dress to my knees, then carefully down my legs before I resume the kneeling position he assigned me—terrified. I can only think of one reason why Black wants me naked. He's going to do terrible things to me. He's going to order me to let him. And I'll have to do it. If I want Jonah to live, I'll have to do it. Even if it's mortifying, sick, twisted. I anticipate Black's hand coming down and squeezing my breasts.

But he doesn't touch me.

I hear a sound from the bedroom behind me and I know it's Jonah, making me stiffen. Black notices and chuckles as I hear Jonah's feet pad out into the hall. He inhales sharply in shock.

"Don't move." Black murmurs next to my ear. "If you do, then I refuse your offer. And he dies."

I try to stay perfectly still. But then Black lets go and walks down the hall toward Jonah. And it's a fight to keep my limbs still. An impossibility. It goes against every instinct. My body cries out that I should get up and turn and run—shove myself between Jonah and Black. But if I do … it's over.

I'm Orpheus, kneeling in Death's kingdom, bargaining for my love's life. And I can't look back.

Not when I hear Black's claw scrape along the wall, shredding the old wallpaper deliberately. Not when I hear Jonah gasp. Not even when I hear them both walk into the bedroom and the door closes, trapping Jonah inside with a monster.

9

BLACK

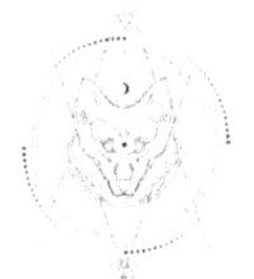

I DON'T LOOK at the beta. I don't dare. Inside, my wolf is snarling. Right now, he wants blood. He wants justice—his wild, untamed version of justice, which is really just revenge by another name. An alpha wolf can't stand to be undermined. Pack hierarchy is absolute, stratification is essential to our lives. Order is paramount. A place for everyone and everyone in their place.

Elena doesn't understand that.

She's been human too long. Her wolf came too late and isn't an alpha, won't instantly overpower her rash human decisions—her wolf is probably scared of her sometimes.

The beta, on the other hand, knows the score. I glance back and see him laying on his back on the bedroom floor, a hand clasping his pants, exposing his human neck—a neck I could snap like a twig right now with my claw if I wanted to. He knows it too. And he's laying there, accepting it. Waiting for it.

He knows he deserves it.

The thought does cross my mind, the image of breaking him is mentally satisfying—especially given the fact that this room is corrupted with the scent of Elena's heat, and the smell of his cum defiling her.

That fucking bastard.

I have to look away from him when I scent that. I have to close my eyes and bunch my fists because if I keep looking at him, or at those mussed sheets, I *will* kill him.

It's a struggle to calm my buzzing pulse and throbbing temple, but I do it, talking my body down from lashing out and destroying every single stick in this house. I could huff and puff and easily blow it all down.

But death is the sort of punishment that's one and done. Killing makes me into the asshole, instead of them, because no one likes to think ill of the dead. Their crimes would be erased by their ends. They don't deserve to have their crimes erased. Murky and Elena have earned punishment for every single waking moment remaining to them for the fact that they are cowards and *cheaters*.

Goddess, that riles me up. I haven't been cheated on in years—I've made certain of it. Planned for it. And the second I let down my guard …

Elena deserves everything I'm about to do to her.

My wolf howls in agreement, pacing, his ears low, eyes glowing. I open my eyes and stare at his tiny figure walking in front of me in midair. He's itching to transform, wanting to fuck her human body in his wolf form so that she's terrified. He wants to sink his teeth into her neck as he ruts her from behind. He wants to feel her pulse fluttering inside his jaw so that she knows her life belongs to him. He wants her to wet herself every time she sees us walk into a room.

I breathe slowly and deeply, trying to keep my body calm so he doesn't wrest control away from me and do just that.

Don't worry, I reassure him. *We'll make her realize her mistake.*

We'd better, he snarls in reply. But he doesn't fight me for control, so he must trust that my plan is working so far.

Behind me, Murky coughs from the dust in this place. I don't turn and acknowledge him because I'm too fucking riled up not to hurt him. And if I hurt him, I might not be able to stop myself. If I kill him, there's zero doubt in my mind that Elena will go feral and simply run again—getting herself killed.

For some reason, that image isn't nearly as satisfying as picturing Murky with a snapped neck. My stomach twists uncomfortably, probably because I don't hurt women as a rule. But this will be dominance—not violence.

I lean against the door and I can practically feel her hatred blazing through the hallway like a fire, heating up the very air around me. I'm waiting, letting her burn herself out before I go back out there and initiate the next part of the punishment I decided upon the second I saw her crying at the top of the stairs.

If Elena's worst nightmare is to be with me ... well then, that's exactly what she deserves.

A cruel smile crosses my face as I think of Murky's worst nightmare. I have a pretty good idea what it is, even though I know practically nothing about the blond-haired beta. And I'm going to take a lot of pleasure in making sure their nightmares recur again and again.

My wolf's eyes flash as he sees my plan flicker across my mind. He likes it. He likes it so much that it makes him wildly happy. He howls inside my head and I have to clench my teeth hard so that the howl doesn't erupt from my lips. If I give him an inch right now, he'll take a mile and I'll end up shifting. If that happens, he'll destroy both of these wolves—both of these stupid, arrogant, selfish children who think that they can run off together and find their happily-ever-after. Who think they can shun the pack and me.

Now … their only purpose in life is to serve me.

I inhale, bracing myself to have to argue with Elena the second I step outside the door. I have zero doubt she's left her spot to check—she's so entitled and has zero patience. I yank the door open, expecting to find her on the other side. But she's not there. I turn and look down the hall, only to see her sliding right back into her spot.

Caught her. She did get up.

"I told you to stay put!" I bark, enjoying the way she jumps at the sound of my voice.

Yes, the fear's there. I'm sure the hatred is too. I wait, giving her the chance to mouth off like she has in the past.

Her shoulders hunch, but she doesn't retort like I expect. She must be holding it in. So at least there's a tiny centimeter of progress. I'm not actually sure I'm ready for progress just yet. I want every opportunity to punish her. But … of course, Murky's impending death is top of mind right now. If I wait, she'll slip up. In a haze of anger, she'll forget—and that's when I'll pounce.

I walk down the hall and step around her to revel in the way she's grinding her teeth, clenching her fists. Oh, yes, the fury's there, just below the surface. She can hardly contain it. Good. If I feel that way then she fucking should too, I think as I gaze down at her. I can't help the fact that my eyes also drift across her small, shapely breasts.

Her nipples are stiff. I remember the feel of them in my mouth for a moment and have to shove that sensation aside.

Part of me wonders how close she is to the next cycle of her heat. I hope it's close. Because I can't wait to watch her beg me for my cock and then hate herself for doing so. And she will, I'm sure of it.

Elena licks her lips, her eyes still downcast in the fakest show of subservience I've ever seen. "Is …is …" she trails off. She can't ask it.

But guess what, little wolf? I'm going to make you ask.

I wait, shifting my feet into a comfortable, relaxed stance. I've never broken a strong-willed omega before, but I imagine this punishment is going to be an exercise in patience for both of us. The minutes drag on. She doesn't say anything. And Murky doesn't emerge from that bedroom, because my last order was for him to go in there and stay. He won't leave until I tell him to.

Finally, Elena's breathing grows ragged and uneven, as if she can't take one more second alone with her imagination. Little does she know, I'm going to turn that little mind of hers against her. I'm going to tangle up her thoughts until she has to beg me to undo the knot.

"Is Jonah … dead?" her voice breaks.

There we are. I have to resist a smile of satisfaction. "If he is, it would be your fault for moving from your spot, wouldn't it?"

Her eyes fly up and spit fire at my face. "I didn't."

"That's a lie. I told you there would be no lying. Turn around, and plant your hands on the floor." I wait until she's kneeling on her hands and knees in doggy position, just the edge of her pussy lips visible in that narrow gap between her thighs. It's sinful how delicious she looks like this. Absolutely wrong how tempting it still is despite everything.

But fool me once … I won't let that ass tempt me twice. I crouch behind her and swing my shifted hand down hard, smacking her ass so well that her knees skid across the floor toward her palms.

"Get back in position!" I yell, as if moving was her fault.

She hurries to slide her knees backward and I hear a mumbled, "bastard" from her lips. I don't bother to deal with that. Actions first. Words later. One day, she'll submit completely. Until then …

I spank her a second time, heat traveling up my arm from the blow. Her ass is a gorgeous cherry color on the right-hand side and I stare at it, admiring how good her skin looks with my mark. It's the wrong kind of mark, though, and my eyes drift up to her neck before I yank them away.

"Go get your ring," I tell her, though I honestly have no clue where it is. She could have pitched it out of the window onto the side of the highway for all I know. But I'm hedging a bet on the fact that Elena's not utterly stupid and knows what a pawn shop is.

Elena climbs to her feet and reaches for her dress.

"Uh-uh," I tell her, stepping on the hem of the dress so she can't retrieve it. "Go get it naked. In silence."

She walks down the hall nude, her steps shuffling, and I decide I don't like the look of that. "Actually. Crawl to get it."

Oh. That gets her. Her head whips around and her gray eyes turn thunderous.

I smile at her.

She turns her back to me and sinks to her knees. And then I watch as she crawls across the wooden planks of the hallway, boards creaking under her weight, those breasts hanging deliciously as she turns to enter the bedroom.

I can tell the second she spots Murky, because her spine stiffens, then relaxes. I slide forward a step, wanting to ensure she sticks to the order of silence I gave her. Or maybe, I'm hoping she doesn't and I can paint that other ass cheek red. My paw tingles and my claws scrape against one another in anticipation—it's definitely the latter.

When Elena emerges, the ring clutched inside one of her hands instead of on her finger, my eyes narrow. "Put it on," I snap. "You'll never take it off again."

Oh, the face she makes is so full of fire that I wish I could photograph it. In fact ... that gives me an idea for later. But for right now, I'm just going to make both her and Murky as uncomfortable as possible. I watch her slide the ring onto her middle finger with a glint of satisfaction in her eyes. She's following orders, but not quite.

Perfect.

I stomp over and grab her by the hair as I march around behind her and yank her head back. I smack the left side of her ass repeatedly as I say, "Put it on your engagement finger, Elena. You knew what I meant. I'm not going to spell things out for you."

She isn't able to swallow a whimper after one of my spankings, and even though she hurries to switch the ring, I can smell her slick starting back up. The scent almost makes me lose focus—it definitely makes me hard. An omega in heat is everything I've ever wished for. But the circumstances are everything I haven't.

I drop her hair and stand.

"Crawl to the van," I order as I turn and stride into the bedroom. I stare down at Murky, who's still lying on his back, though he's trembling now. He thinks his time has come—that I'm taking Elena out of here and am going to end him. "Find the keys. You're driving us back."

His blue eyes grow wide but he scrambles to comply, rolling onto his knees and heading out into the hallway. I leave him to scramble around, because of the two of them, he's the more compliant. Every order sets Elena's teeth on edge, and I don't want to miss an opportunity to punish her.

The view from the top of the stairs as she crawls down is magnificent. Her ass is round as a peach and still glowing with my fingerprints. The scent of her slick is the most delicious perfume.

By the time she reaches the front door, I've grown impatient because she's so slow to crawl, so I throw her over my shoulder and carry her myself. The scent of her slick so close to my face is tempting whenever I inhale, so I hold my breath until I can toss her onto the front seat of their little escape vehicle.

I plaster a twisted smile onto my face through the entire ride back, even though I'm uncomfortably cramped in the middle seat between them in the catering van. The seat is vinyl that grows sticky beneath my naked ass as we drive.

But despite the fact that my knees keep knocking into Murky's and this van has absolutely no shocks to absorb the bumps of the road, I hold onto that grin because halfway through the drive back, Elena's cheeks flush and her arm grows burning hot against mine.

I smell slick collecting between her thighs, though she keeps them clamped firmly together. She leans her forehead against the passenger side window in an attempt to cool herself down. But it's a warm night, and I'm glad she can't.

I watch her as her fingers end up clamping down on the door handle and her breathing grows shallow.

Her need grows more and more intense, but she fights it. She tries not to say anything as her heat overcomes her again.

Perfect.

Both I and my wolf prance in cruel delight. This is going to be grand. I'm going to wait until she begs for it, because she will. And then she'll take me, gladly, and revel in it. Until the heat wears off and she hates herself for asking. Not just asking but pleading.

I press my lips together to control my smirk, though I can't extinguish it completely.

Murky shoots concerned looks at her and then up at me. But he doesn't speak—he knows better.

Eventually, she can't help it. Her hips start to lift up off the seat, the motion inevitable, driven by instinct.

"Stay still," I order.

I wonder if the sight of her anger is ever going to grow old. I doubt it. My dick hardens—either from the way her eyes flash gold as she glares or the way the scent of her slick completely overwhelms the smells of the Indian food drifting in from the back.

She rips her gaze away from mine but I'm delighted to see it doesn't help—because when she lowers her eyes, she notices my cock growing in length, reacting to her heat.

She licks her lips before she realizes what she's doing.

Yes.

I let out a full-on chuckle as she turns back to the window and pretends that I don't exist.

I congratulate myself on picking the perfect punishment for her. My wolf chuffs his agreement.

Two puppets at my beck and call.

I can't wait to get them home and pull even more strings.

10

ELENA

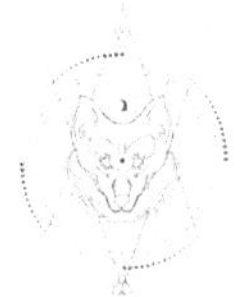

I HATE him with the passion of a thousand suns—or whatever the fuck that saying is. Though right now, I'm not sure if I hate him or my wolf more. My body is betraying me. Minute by minute, I can feel the heat swell inside my low belly, need growing more and more pronounced. I fight it with everything that I have but it doesn't let up.

He knows it too. That just makes it worse.

His arrogant little smirk gets under my skin like a splinter, a painful little irritation that I can't seem to dig out. Black knows I'm lusting after him and that I hate it but can't help it. He knows my shifter senses are slowly taking over my rational mind—and he finds it amusing, the fucker.

Another round of heat cripples my anger. Time loses all meaning as sweat skates down the back of my neck and plasters my hair into strips. My nipples pucker and ache for lips to touch them. My thighs rub together but it's not enough—my body screams for more friction. Even closing my eyes ceases to bring relief because when they're closed all I picture is Black. I imagine his big throbbing cock sliding into me and soothing this all-consuming need. His knot. Goddess, I think all kinds of dirty things about that knot—how it will stretch me and rub against my g-spot, how it will spread me open and make me ache and drive me higher all at the same time.

His arm brushes against mine and even that incidental touch nearly drives me to madness. I want to latch onto Black's hand, to shove his fingers where I need them, and use his entire arm as my own personal sex toy.

Black Maddox—dildo extraordinaire.

I chuckle at that thought because the fucker really is a dildo, but that only earns me a dark look. Apparently, somehow, Black knows I'm laughing at him. Too bad in my current state, his hostile glares aren't nearly as intimidating as he intends them to be. Instead of looking angry, he looks intense—the same kind of intense fire flared in his eyes when he fucked me hard.

And I've done it again. Full circle. My thoughts are back to lusting over Black. It doesn't seem to matter that Jonah is in the car too, or the fact that he just sated my need a few hours ago. The fact that he's my fucking mate doesn't even dampen my lust the slightest bit. My body is entirely attuned to the pack alpha because I'm fucked in the head and something's wrong with my shifter instincts.

Mates are supposed to be for life. Forever. They're supposed to be loyal. At least, that's what I thought from the snippets I've gathered over the years. But my shifter senses make me feel like a harlot. Maybe omegas are different. Maybe their heat tempts all the alphas because they're supposed to fuck all the alphas—well, I won't let my pussy be a pincushion for all those pricks, thank you.

It's Jonah or nothing.

And since Black caught us … it's going to be nothing. Unless … Black said I had to follow his orders from now on. Is he going to make me … fuck him? Is he going to force me to be a sex slave?

My mind rebels but my body sings at the thought of Black tying me up and having his way with me. I've never wanted that before, to give up control to someone, but right now it sounds perfect. Deliciously wanton and mindless—which is exactly what the heat is driving me to be. I think back to the way Black's experienced touch worked my body before and I know he'd drive me wild.

I imagine him calling me downstairs at his huge mansion, into his office, and then grumbling, "Shut the door," as he closes his laptop and puts it into his briefcase. In my mind, the hulking brute shoves his shoulder-length black hair behind his shoulders and leans back in his leather executive chair as I approach.

"Come here." Another order, which for some reason, makes me grow even wetter.

"Drop the panties, climb on the desk, and spread your legs."

Mmm. The idea of being fully clothed in a dress sans panties, with my pussy exposed for him to see, riles me up and a little shiver of pleasure drifts over me.

I imagine Black staring down between my legs, tracing my opening, then dropping his pants and boxers and taking me roughly, without warning—holding me down and fucking me hard. He makes me slide across the desk, my hands reaching to hold onto the back lip until he comes. Then I imagine him standing back up and playing with my clit so he can watch my pussy spasm while his cum drizzles out.

Oh my god.

Imaginary Black then slides my panties back on, and whispers, "I have to get back to work. I want you to walk around the rest of the afternoon thinking about my cum inside you."

My hand drifts to my clit. So fucking hot.

No.

I clench my teeth so hard that my jaw hurts and shove my wandering hand back to the car door, taking the handle in a death grip. I *will not* touch myself thinking about that asshole giving me dirty orders.

I bemoan the fact that my wolf has disappeared, because I'm furious that my body is feeding me these sorts of lurid images. I feel her lingering presence somewhere behind the haze of the heat, but I can't find her with my mind's eye. I can't find her to yell at her and scream and rant and tell her to take all of this shit away and shove it where the sun doesn't shine. I just have to suffer through it.

By the time we pulled through Black's gate, tears are running down my cheeks because my thighs are soaked —literally soaked in slick. I've resisted touching myself, but just barely. Every jostle in the road for the last mile has been pure torment because my thighs constantly brushed together and I've had to grind my teeth to bite down on a moan. I haven't sobbed out loud like I did when the first wave hit, but it's a near thing.

And the images have gotten worse. I've imagined Black at least five more times and a combination of Black and Jonah together nearly made me come.

I'm desperate. And I'm sore. Between my clenched jaw, tense muscles, and this fever racing through me, I'm in physical pain. My nerves are on fire and my body is demanding satisfaction. I don't know how much longer I'll be able to stand it.

Jonah slows the vehicle as we near the house and I glance at the clock. It's nearly four in the morning. I should be tired. I should be falling asleep where I sit. But the heat won't let me.

I'm startled when Black speaks. "Stop at the front door."

It's the first thing anyone has said in over an hour, ever since Black hung up the phone with his butler, Matthew—after telling the older man to clear the place of anyone and everyone but himself.

At least my defilement will be a private affair, I snark internally, still certain Black is going to humiliate me even further.

Only after I climb out of the van do I realize exactly how much slick I've made. My seat is wet, the leather soaked. Both Jonah and Black issue low growls when I step out of the van and they see it in the dull gray pre-dawn light.

"Wait!" Black orders.

I freeze where I stand, though part of me wants to flip him the finger as I fight not to shiver. There's a breeze back in Colorado that wasn't there on the farm—a bite to the air that makes goosebumps pebble on my arms. It should dampen the heat. But for some damn reason, it only enhances it.

He climbs out, deliberately sliding over my puddle of slick and coating his ass in my scent. Then he stands behind me, silently looming until Jonah comes around the back of the van. All three of us are naked. To an outsider, this might look like either the start or the end of a great orgy. Three naked people at four in the morning.

"When you get inside, you'll both crawl. Up the stairs, all the way to the attic."

I'm surprised by the order but I shrug it off. *At least he's going to lock us up together.* I take solace in that fact. Maybe I'm tainted now that Jonah's touched me. Maybe Black won't want to lay a finger on me. I ignore the aching pulse that runs through my cunt at that thought, which very much wants to feel Black's fingers—all of them, at the same time stuffing me full and fucking me ... maybe even fisting me for my first time.

I shove a hand to my forehead as I follow Black into his house, trying to remind my body that I'm doing this to save Jonah, and not because Black is a freaking greek statue come to life. My eyes glance over at Jonah, but his blue gaze is glued to the floor.

My heart twinges for a second, but my fevered brain quickly snaps away rational thought and it's all I can do to put one knee in front of the other.

The three flights of stairs we climb are torture. By the time we're done, all of us are breathing hard. And it's not because we suck at cardio. My scent perfumes the house. My need has triggered both of theirs.

I don't know what's about to happen. But *something* needs to happen. Soon. Or I might just die.

Black turns the knob to a door at the very end of the hallway and holds it open, silently gesturing for us to crawl inside. Jonah enters first and I follow, surprised to see a small staircase just inside the door. When I crawl off the landing into the attic, I gasp. The space is magnificent. The ceiling slopes down on either side, like most attic spaces, but there's still plenty of room in the long space and a beautiful plate glass window at the far end where the moon goddess peeks in. The walls are cream and the wooden beams have been painted a soothing pale green. There is a huge, fluffy mattress on the floor that must be custom-made because it spans from wall to wall, a huge, orgy-sized mattress. Pink, flowered sheets adorn it with enough pillows to make a pillow fort—something I haven't done since I was a child but suddenly seems like the absolute best thing in the world, after orgasms.

I need an orgasm so badly that I'm about to run to that bed and give myself one while they both watch.

"Stand up." Black orders, his voice sends the hairs on my back rising.

When I climb to my feet I realize that dressers and tables line the sides of the room. Each table has a variety of boxes on top of it. Dildos, vibrators, whips, and things I've never even seen before like octopus tentacles. That should freak me out. As should the sex swing I spot hanging from the ceiling. But they don't. They entice the fuck out of me and make me dazed as I realize something.

Black had this room put together for me before I left.

A combination of guilt and fury rattle my mind. First of all, the gesture is arrogant. How dare he operate under the presumption that I'd turn into some kind of sex fiend at the snap of his fingers! But then I feel guilty because I realize Black obviously planned for my heat. He knew that I'd need something like this, a cozy little sex dungeon that's cute instead of scary.

Fuck him for knowing that. Goddammit. It only makes me want him more. And then, I'm furious with myself for wanting more so I stare off at the sex toys and find something to resent. Black obviously assumed I'd be some kind of kinky sex fiend based on all the weird shit he bought. Why? He's so damn cocky to be sure of that.

We only ever had vanilla sex.

Vanilla with whipped cream on top, sure.

And nuts. Don't forget about his nuts, my horny-delusional mind thinks.

My eyes wander to said cock. Yeah. Black's cocky. At least nine inches of cocky. Fuck. And that knot at his base is swelling. I have to grab onto the nearest support beam, a tall, square wooden post with a couple of metal eyelets in it to keep from swooning as the heat rolls deliciously down my spine, clouding my thoughts and filling my head with dirty pictures. I imagine Black chaining me to the pole and spanking me again.

Slick floods the room with scent and we all growl at the same time. My eyes flit unintentionally to Black's. But he doesn't move a step closer. My eyes flicker to Jonah's and his gaze burns.

What's Black going to do to us? How's he going to destroy us? I'd have thought that—with my scent—the huge alpha would have jumped me by now, pulled my hair, and fucked me in front of Jonah to proclaim his dominance. He hasn't. And I don't understand.

I let Jonah read the confused expression on my face. He just gives me a sympathetic "I don't know" shrug in response as his eyes travel down to my beaded nipples.

Black interrupts our nonverbal exchange when he commands, "Grab a pillow."

There it is. I knew it was coming. I knew he was going to turn this sexual to punish us. But I swore to follow orders and when I see Black step closer to Jonah, I hurry to comply.

Don't think. Don't question. Just do. And then it'll be over. I give myself the shittiest pep talk in the history of the universe.

I march stiffly over to the mattress and grab a furry pink pillow, hoping that my choice will somehow annoy Black. Maybe if he fucks me on it, the furry texture will tickle his knees. That's the sort of retaliation I'm left with now. Tickled knees. I can't do anything real, say anything real, because if I do—Jonah's life is put on the line.

I carry the pillow over to Black and stand expectantly in front of him before I realize he might have asked me to get the pillow for myself, so I could kneel on the wooden floor and give him a blowjob. My core throbs at that thought but I'm furious at myself because I might have just picked my own torture device.

Stupid, Elena. Fucking stupid.

"Follow me. Crawl." Black turns and leads the way out of the sex room.

I'm shell-shocked for a second. I'm concussed by those words … and his actions. My cheeks flare red and I want to cry.

Isn't he going to fuck me?

He dragged me up here, with Jonah … torturing us both with all the mental images of what's going to happen. I half expected him to shove his knot into my ass.

But he waits in the hall as Jonah and I slowly and silently follow him, the furry pillow clutched awkwardly against my chest and rubbing against my nipples as I crawl on three limbs. I'm feeling desperate enough that I might just hump it if Black doesn't touch me soon. I'm right about the stupid texture. It becomes a form of torture, nearly chafing my sensitized skin. The tears threaten but I manage to rein them in … until we reach the basement.

That beautiful room, that perfect nest upstairs … is just going to waste? He's not even going to use it? Some little omega part of me cringes and moans in despair because suddenly the idea of sex in a regular bed, or on the floor, or anywhere that isn't that small cozy room, sounds fucking horrible.

Necessary, my body insists. But my mind turns wistfully to that little room.

I watch Black walk calmly across the main room of the basement—noting that the ping pong table and broken television are gone, replaced already with brand new ones. He doesn't turn to go to the table on the right, nor does he turn left and head to the little bar area. He walks straight to his storage room and pulls the door open. "Elena, go inside. Jonah, wait there."

I start to cry. My hormones sweep over me and this need becomes more powerful than my dignity. He's not going to fuck me in the nest. But … he's going to lock me up and not even fuck me at all?

I thought alphas couldn't control themselves around omegas. So … what the hell is this?

All my anger and outrage at the idea of him taking me morphs into an inferno of fury at the idea that he won't.

He's going to leave me screaming and crying in that storage room, humping a pink pillow in the dark.

Another round of slick glazes my core and primal need washes over me. My knees grow weak at the thought of marching into that tiny, dark room and trying to finger myself like I did during the first wave. I won't be able to get there. Nothing I did last time got me there. He's going to torture me using my own omega heat. A tear rolls down my cheek.

"Please," I beg.

"Please what?" Black asks calmly, a smile tugging at his lips. But his cock knows exactly what I'm asking for. It bobs against his toned stomach.

"Please, fuck—don't do this." I twist my words at the last second. But we both know what I'm asking for.

Black struggles with himself for a moment. I can see him fighting. He wants me just as desperately as I want him. But he reins it in. How the fuck is he doing that? How the hell is he controlling his instincts? His wolf? I want to fucking do that.

Instead, I rear up on my knees and clasp my hands in a prayer position, all shame evaporating.

Black shakes his head and gives me a regretful look. "I can't trust you. Just like I'd originally thought. This is where people I can't trust sleep." He gestures again at the storage room, which gapes open with all the appeal of the gates of Hell.

It's a low blow, but well-deserved. He's right. But my brain hardly processes what he's saying because a bit of precum has appeared at the top of his cock. My eyes shift to wolf eyes. I feel them heat and morph. All of my surroundings slightly change color. And then I can smell that caramel and woodsmoke scent mixing with the salt of his precum—making me feral.

I don't ask. Don't look at Jonah. I'm operating on pure instinct and desperation as I crawl towards him. The scent of his precum, of that bead dangling on the tip of his swollen red cock dazzles me like it's a fucking treasure.

I reach for it. But Black's arms are longer and he grips my shoulders, stopping me.

"What are you doing?" he growls.

"Please," I respond. "I need it."

"What?"

"I want your cock!" I snarl.

Black relents, letting go of my shoulders.

I dive forward and take him into my mouth.

11

ELENA

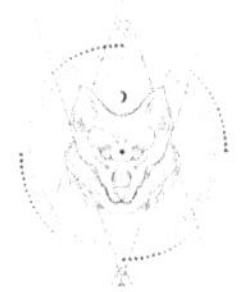

God, the taste of him. My eyelashes flutter and the heat that's been burning up my spine blazes like I've been tied to a stake and set aflame. I've never hated or wanted anyone more.

Instinct steamrolls everything else, flattening my thoughts. My hands drop the stupid fuzzy pink pillow I've been clutching and finally reach for the cock that's made me ache with longing for hours. I slide my fingers slowly up and down his shaft, enjoying the feel of him, that bulge at his base where he's going to lock us together and breed me.

Fuck.

What?

My mouth drops open and I lean back, shocked for a second. But I've already gone too far. Black doesn't let me go. His huge hand reaches for me and he fists my hair, not too roughly, just enough. His eyes devour me as he says, "Oh no, you don't. Keep going. Jonah, get the fuck over here and put your mouth on her clit. You're going to make her wet. And then you're gonna watch me fuck the girl you love."

Black shoves me back down onto his cock before I can screech out a protest. But I can't deny the power of the mental image Black painted. The idea of the three of us linked together makes my thighs feel weak. And the taste of him inside my mouth is so obscenely good that I forget to hate him for a second.

A hand gently traces up my ass and I smile around the girth of Black's cock as I feel Jonah's bashful touch.

"Deeper," Black growls down at me, one hand still tangled in my long hair and the other cupping my cheek so he can guide me.

I struggle to swallow him down, but the knot near the base of his shaft makes it hard. It's swollen to the size of a baseball. I bob on his cock trying to get a rhythm and gradually go deeper as I feel Jonah gently push my thighs apart so he can lay down on the floor in between them. I can feel Jonah's skin brush mine as he leans up. His warm breath fans across me until I feel his tongue dance across my thighs.

Mate.

His touch makes my heart thrash wildly.

I'm so desperate for release that I lean into his face before he's ready, my hips already gyrating. He has to grab onto me and settle me onto his mouth. But when he latches on ... his tongue spades against my clit. I gasp, which lets Black thrust deeper into my mouth.

My eyes flutter closed as I work the alpha's dick while the beta at my feet works me. My caustic hatred for Black burns away in the light of the fact that this is probably the hottest thing I've ever done.

Jonah hits just the right spot as Black's hand leaves my cheek and he leans down to pinch a nipple. He pinches hard and tight and then tugs.

That's all it takes for me to swoon and nearly fall over as an orgasm steals across my flesh. Pleasure rattles me from head to toe and just stokes my heat. Because it's not enough. I'm hungry, starving, dying. I have to have more orgasms. More of this.

I slide my lips gently off Black's mushroom tip and blink up at him. He stands over me, panting, those giant pecs harshly defined by the angled light streaming in from the tall and narrow basement windows and the one light on over the ping pong table. His sleek six-pack causes my fingers to rise so that I can trace them and that rare, amazing Adonis belt.

"Please," I beg again because the word worked so well for me before. Maybe he'll listen again.

His dark brown eyes glitter as he asks, "Please what, Elena?" like I'm a child.

I should be offended. I should rail at him for making me beg like a whiny bitch instead of commanding him to fuck me like I know he's dying to.

A tiny part of me knows this but my wolf instincts love the way his fist tightens in my hair and he wrenches my neck back, taking complete control of my body.

I'm a marionette and when he tugs at my hair I move exactly where he wants me, tilting my head back and exposing my neck, my torso stretched as far as it can go because I don't want to leave Jonah's amazing mouth.

Jonah swipes over my slit again, causing pleasurable trembles to rocket through me.

"Please, I need it," I repeat, hardly able to form words. I feel drunk and delirious with want. My wolf senses ravage my mind and a howl erupts from my lips, filling the basement and making Black smile.

But the bastard doesn't relent. He doesn't give me what I'm asking for. Instead, he orders, "Be specific."

Asshole. I can't think with the river of pleasure that's rushing through me, churning into rapids, dunking me under while whitewater swirls around me. My head can hardly surface long enough to gasp, much less form words. The sight of his cock is making me delirious. I reach up and cup my breasts then pinch my own nipples in frustration, needing more stimulation and about to do desperate things to get it.

"Your cock. I need your cock," I wail, my hands reaching for it again.

I yank away from Jonah, because his mouth is wonderful, but I need the feel of a thick, hard dick pounding into me right now. I need someone to hold me down and maul my breasts while they ruin my pussy. I want an orgasm that hurts, that I can feel days later, that punches straight through me.

Black's eyes narrow and he gives me a crocodile smile. Then he pulls on my hair, dragging me up so that I stand over Jonah, who waits patiently and silently, lying on the carpet below.

The intensity grows in the air around us and I watch Black's eyes go from human to bestial—as he joins me on the plane of existence where nothing matters but this.

Our human anger and distrust are wiped away as our wolves acknowledge something more primal than rage: Lust.

With a growl, Black spins me around so that I'm facing Jonah and can see just how turned on my beta is, his cock swollen. Jonah licks his lips, which are still wet from my slick as Black plants a hand on my back and pushes me down.

"Hands on the carpet. Do *not* touch the beta." Black orders, sending me into a position reminiscent of downward dog in yoga. I plant my hands on the plush carpet on either side of Jonah's head so my breasts dangle deliciously over his face.

Black addresses Jonah. "And you. Don't even think about touching yourself. You watch while I fuck your little mate until she can't even remember your name."

I bend my neck to look back at him. Jonah grits his teeth and nods as his eyes drift to my hanging breasts and then up to meet my gaze. Instead of wearing the betrayed expression I expect, I've never seen him so turned on. He clenches his teeth and I can see that his canines have shifted. He's feral too.

He mouths one word at me. "Hot."

And then Black pulls on my hair and instead of bending to stare at Jonah's face, I'm faced with the beta's cock. A bead of precum oozes from the tip of Jonah's dick and I can't help but lick my lips because I want to taste him. I want to feel him.

But I have to follow orders. There's something deliciously sick and twisted about being denied. I've never craved it before, never had it turn me on so much. But it does. I become hyper-aware of that tiny bead on Jonah's cock as it slides down, and the fact that I'm forbidden from touching it makes it all the more enticing.

That is, until I feel Black lift his cock and drag it along my slit, coating himself in slick. Then my focus shifts. Just knowing that an alpha cock is touching me floods me even more, I gasp in pleasure as my body produces more slick. He slides back and forth, teasing me, letting me feel how thick his knot is. It's so damn big that I have to widen my legs so he can fit between them.

I bite my lip in anticipation. God, that's gonna hurt so good.

He lines us up and teases me with the tip, pushing in and then backing out twice. I growl, because I'm done waiting. I shove back against his cock, forcing him in. But I underestimate the knot, which stretches me too far, too quickly. But as soon as I pause, Black snarls, "No you don't." He pushes hard, his knot stretching me so much that I inhale and hold my breath so that I don't cry out. I don't want to give him the satisfaction. So instead, I bend my head and look again at Jonah.

A concerned look crosses my mate's face but I just focus on staring at him, tracing the contours of his brow and nose until my body has adjusted to the intrusion. It takes a good long minute, one in which I curse myself, but then … Black swivels his hips.

I nearly pass out.

It's. That. Fucking. Good.

That knot drags up and down my g-spot with his every movement. Each motion makes me want to roll my eyes back into my head but I resist because I want to draw this out just a little bit longer.

But Black doesn't. He's through playing, teasing, torturing, forcing me to beg. Now that he's inside of me, he's ready to rut hard and fast.

He grabs my hips from behind, and to my surprise, swings my legs up on either side of him, yanking me into an unwilling push up. "Hold yourself up with those hands and *do not* fall." Then he slams into me with the force of a wrecking ball.

Every part of my body jolts forward and flies back deliciously as his cock bludgeons me over and over. I've never had this much g-spot stimulation in my life.

And … there's another factor. He has me spread so wide with that knot that the lips of my pussy stretch and even the hood of my clit pulls thin and taut, rubbing against my sensitive nub with each stroke. It's gentler than a finger but at the same time, the tease of that stimulation combines with the internal rub of his thickness and it's so amazing that I see golden specks flicker across my vision.

"Yes!" I scream without meaning to. "More!"

But when Black gives me more—his hip bones slamming into my ass and making it turn to jello—my arms can't take it. I end up sliding across the carpet my torso falling down, my nipples scraping across Jonah's pecs. Fuck. Yes.

"Murky, move! Grab her shoulders and hold her still!" Black shouts as he continues to ram me relentlessly.

Jonah slides out from underneath me and then he crouches in front of me, helping me straighten my arms back into a push-up position. His eyes are gold as he stares at me. Deliciously, wildly gold.

His cool fingers press down on my shoulders and hold me in place so I can take Black's brutishly fulfilling fuck. Every smash of his hips into mine feels like the culmination of an argument. He presses into me and I flex my ass and shove back. We're yelling at each other without words. I'm screaming at him for his presumption and he's snarling at me for leaving. Our mutual anger makes us both ruthless. With Jonah holding me, I find myself wrapping my legs around the back of

Black's waist, heels digging into him as he ruts, trying to get him to change his pace to what I want.

"No you fucking don't," he growls, fully aware of what I'm doing. "You're going to come when I want you to come."

"Not if I make you come first," I retort, finally able to find my voice through the haze of the heat—possibly because I'm not fighting it anymore, but embracing it.

His chuckle irritates me and I decide to make him eat his words. I flex, using Kegels to grip him again and again. *Godfuckingdammittohell.* That feels too good. When I squeeze down, the stretch of his dick becomes even more intense and I have to stop or I'll make myself come.

"I hate you," I snap.

"If you weren't an omega you'd be dead right now," Black snarls as he drills my pussy, changing angles and going slightly left until he finds a spot that makes us both moan.

My eyelashes flutter as an orgasm washes over me. At the same time, I hear Black give a huge groan and he stills. I feel his cock pulse as he fills me up with his cum and for some reason the knowledge that the alpha just bred me, without protection, makes me clench all over again.

But when I come down from that high, I realize the truth of Black's words. If I wasn't an omega, I'd be dead. Of course, if I wasn't an omega then I wouldn't be here in the first place. Black wouldn't have dragged me here. He also might not have saved me in the forest. We'd never know.

Undone by his own orgasm, Black slides down to the carpet, still tethered to me by that swollen knot so that I end up sitting in his lap until he lays down on his side and I have no choice but to follow.

I'm filled with a yearning to cuddle close to him. I want to feel his stomach press against my spine and his arms enfold me so that I feel safe and comforted. And I want Jonah to snuggle close to my front, making me feel adored and cherished.

But as the high of orgasm and the intensity of my heat fades, I resist those stupid longings—knowing that they just spring from another instinct created by my omega wolf, another idiotic magical attempt to enslave me and chain me to an alpha. So when I settle on the carpet on my side, I deliberately scoot away from Black, as much as I can considering his dick's still lodged inside me. And the thing hasn't seemed to shrink an inch. It's still pressing me open, tapping against my cervix when I move.

Bastard.

He doesn't deserve to have a cock this good. He deserves one as shriveled and twisted and tiny as his heart.

I wrap my arms around myself as I feel my vision change, shifting from wolf-eyes back to human. With the shift, all my human emotions come rushing back. Guilt coats my mouth and it feels like I'm sucking on a penny, a disgusting, metallic taste manifesting how I feel about myself right now. How could I do that? How could my wolf do that? She marked Jonah. She chose Jonah.

I blink as I stare dully over at my mate, who stares back at me with a look as dazed as my own. Sleep looms on the edges of my thoughts like a dark cloud.

I bargained to save us ... but for what? This? Amazing angry sex with no afterglow? Now that I've had the afterglow, anything less is devastating. To know Black used my body against me and then fucked me without feeling a damned thing ... he might as well have bashed my chest in with a wrench. He truly proves my theory that alphas are heartless, cruel masters. Nothing more.

He proves that I was right to carefully avoid alphas all those years. But now, I'm just as trapped as my father once was. And suddenly, I see why Dad thought he only had one way out.

Maybe I should have just let Black end us both. Then, instead of here in the dark—defiled by a monster—Jonah and I would be up with the moon goddess, dancing together among the stars.

That's my final wretched thought before exhaustion finally claims me and I drift off to sleep.

12

BLACK

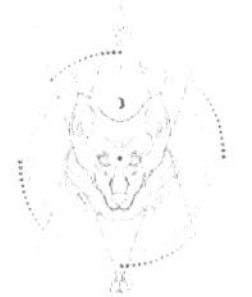

I DON'T MEAN TO, but I fall asleep. One moment, I'm staring at Elena's back as she tries to get as far from me as possible. The next, it's mid-afternoon and I'm working in my office. The front door opens and I look up to see a beam of sunshine burst through my front door. Elena walks in wearing a summer dress and sandals, a shopping bag draped over her arm. I can see her from my desk because I left my office door open, like I was waiting for her.

She turns to look at me and smiles. It's the biggest, most beautiful smile I've ever seen and just the sight of it makes me feel slightly dizzy as she walks toward me, and the click of her heels echo throughout the front hall. When she reaches my office, she stops and leans casually against the door frame, studying me.

"Still working?"

"Always."

With her bag still on her arm, she saunters forward and rounds my desk. I take a moment to inhale her gorgeous scent and appreciate the way her skirt hugs the curves of her hips. I push my chair back from the desk and swivel it when she gets near so that I'm facing her. I part my legs and she walks straight in between them and sits down on my right thigh, her legs trapped between mine, her bag dangling on her outer arm as she leans in and nuzzles my neck.

A sense of contentment I've never had before rises up inside my chest and I purr.

"Mmm," Elena murmurs into my neck, before pulling back and standing. Her gray eyes gleam with mischief as she says, "You get one more hour in this office, so work fast. Then I'll meet you up in the nest." She taps the bag as she backs away, winking.

"I can quit now."

"No way. I want you desperate."

Lust roars through my veins, but with it—right alongside it—is tenderness. The combination nearly melts me and I fight to keep a straight face as I raise a brow at her. "No topping from the bottom."

She laughs as she re-enters the hallway. "We'll see about that."

My insides turn into a goddamned Lucky Charms commercial: hearts and stars and rainbows. She's so fucking sweet I can't stand it. I turn back to my work with a smile tugging at my lips but then my back twinges painfully.

I wake up and find myself on the floor of the basement, the moonlight dimming as dawn takes over. I must not have slept long, though my aching back feels every inch of the cement underneath this carpet. Elena's still sleeping right in front of me, my knot still locked inside of her. My hand drifted to her hip as I slept and her skin burns warm under my palm. I quickly draw it away and blink, disoriented by reality.

What was that dream?

I've never dreamed about a girl who's lying right next to me, much less had a dream like *that.*

Sex dreams I get. I've had those since I was in fifth grade. No big deal, even when they're about a teacher. But dreaming about holding a girl on my lap? About watching the door for her to come home? That's weird fucking shit. Especially when my stupid brain should know that bullshit's never going to happen. Not with Elena.

The moonlight in the room wavers and retreats as bitterness overtakes my thoughts and they grow so dark even the moon goddess can't stand them.

The reality is that Elena's agreed to be my slave. She's agreed to do anything I fucking ask, even if I ask for fucking.

That sex tonight … was incredible. It was ten times beyond the best I've ever had. But that was probably only because it was hate sex fueled by her heat and our wolves' needs. There was none of the idiotic tenderness my obviously delirious sleeping mind imagined. Nope, not a drop of kindness in what we did. It was resentful, angry fucking. Getting to press my knot into Elena—and fucking her without any sort of restraint, not holding back or giving a shit about how delicate she is—created the perfect storm. The sex was Level Five catastrophic, wrecking my mind.

I want to do it again. Ten more times. My cock swells where it's still lodged inside of her and I stare down at her slight form with its perfect curves, those long legs, and that lush ass tempting me.

It isn't fair. It shouldn't fucking be this way.

I realize—with a start—that I wanted the dream with her.

I ask the moon goddess why the best sex of my life has to be with Elena … the girl who left me. Who didn't even bother to reject me to my face, just stole my ring and ran.

Even worse, why do I have to dream sweet things about her? Things that only make me wish it all had turned out differently and leave regret weighing me down like a heavy brick.

A fissure forms inside my chest when I think about what could have been. We could have been fucking right now up in that nest. We could have snuggled into eighty pillows after while I stroked her hair and imagined the babies she'd give me one day, dark little spitfires just like her. We could have spent her entire heat perfuming the nest with her scent, lighting it with her smiles.

Elena had captivated me, and then …

I grow angry all over again, and for whatever reason, the anger perks my dick up even more—perhaps because it wants more hate sex with the woman who despises me. The only damn woman in the pack now who'd dare do something like this.

I shove up onto my elbow and peer at Elena's naked back, tracing her spine with my eyes as I debate whether I should try and calm my dick down or go for round two. The moon's leaving and the sun's peeking through the high basement windows, announcing the start of the day and I have a million other things I should be doing.

I should be solidifying my newly acquired territory. I should be calling Pluto and putting together a meeting with my elites. I need to hunt down Thomas Stone and punish that fucker for trying to steal my—

I cut off my thought when I realize I was about to call Elena my mate. Fuck no.

My wolf, who's been dozing, wakes at my vitriol and realizes who I'm directing it at. He quickly stretches his back and shakes out his legs. Then his avatar form paces in front of my eyes, right along the ridge of Elena's back. His white fur is gleaming and he tips his ears forward as he stares pointedly at me before licking his black nose. Then he says, very deliberately, *Mate.* He glances over at the soft swell of Elena's cheek.

That ratchets my anger up another notch.

She's not anymore.

He pointedly turns his nose down to where I'm still locked inside of her because my knot refuses to go down. It doesn't matter that I napped before I woke up and started thinking all these bullshit thoughts. I'm still stuck to her—without protection.

Fuck you, I tell him.

Fuck her, he responds, sending me a barrage of images. He still wants to rut Elena as a wolf. In fact, the fact that she's asleep right now and would wake up terrified makes him grin. He's not done punishing her even though he thinks she's his mate. He wants to make sure she knows her place.

No. Asshole, I cut him off at the pass, but I can't help the fact that my body responds to his demented thoughts and grows hard again inside of her. I gaze down at Elena again. She's curled up into a fetal position, no doubt overwhelmed by the hormones from both her heat and all the fight-or-flight responses she's been through.

I shouldn't give a damn, since they're all self-inflicted gunshot wounds. She ran and got caught by Dark Nights—it's her own stupid fault. But for a second, I hesitate to wake her.

That's when I spot the beta. He's lying on the carpet near a leather recliner. And the asshole is young and fit and doesn't have a single damned gray hair.

His bones probably don't ache from stupid shit like falling asleep on the floor. Worst of all—he hasn't put a toe out of line yet and given me a valid excuse to punch his face in.

His back is on the floor but his head is turned toward us and his blue eyes are open, watching and judging me.

I can see him frown as he stares at me and Elena.

How dare he, the little shit!

He's the one who's done wrong here. I fucking saved his ass even after he broke his pack vows. Murky has no goddamn room to judge me.

He deserves this. So does she.

To spite him, I shove my hips closer to her and start rocking them, my hand traveling to Elena's waist and tugging her back against me in a show of possession. Her soft skin makes my senses burn and moving her lets her mouthwatering scent drift through the space.

I might fucking hate her but the omega's mine to punish and mine to fuck—in whatever order or combination I please. I slide a hand up to grip her tit and she gasps, waking.

She doesn't even hesitate, her hips immediately start gyrating in response to my slow thrusts.

Her walls clench down on my dick and everything inside me tingles. Everything from my toes to my ears is drained of blood as my cock swells inside her again, in that silky heat.

Physically, we're perfect together, her slender form just tall enough that I can bend and still kiss her if I wanted to—which I don't. Sex with her is just that—sex, I remind myself.

I want to use her right now to show Murky his place. I want to use her right now to prove my own place to myself. I'm the goddamned wolf king.

I'm going to rut this omega to show my wolf that all the awe I felt just a few minutes ago was a fluke. And that dreams mean nothing. Elena *is not* and never will be my mate. I don't do second chances because I'm a firm believer in burn me once shame on you, but burn me twice ...

Her pussy clamps down deliciously on me and her tiny hand comes up over mine on her breast, directing me to her nipple. Instead of giving her what she wants, I yank my hand away. I roll onto my back, pulling her with me so that she's laying on top of me, both of us facing the ceiling. I thrust like that for a moment, but it's not as deep as I want to get. I want to tap her cervix so she screams. I push her shoulders up so that she's sitting on my waist, facing away from me.

"Swivel around—carefully," I order. "You're going to ride me." I prop myself up on one elbow to watch, letting Elena navigate the gymnastics of changing from the reverse-cowgirl position and slowly turning so she faces me. As she does, my knot must hit a sensitive spot because suddenly her slick gushes down onto my pelvis. The room fills with her scent and my hands morph into monster claws of their own volition.

Goddess, yes.

When she sees my claws and gasps, I decide not to change them back. Partially because my wolf is howling in delight at her combination of arousal and fear and partially because her smell has my brain buzzing like I just took a hit of ecstasy.

Elena rises up and then grinds down, rubbing her clit against my skin. Her little clit is so swollen I can feel it when she grinds and I reach down between us, pinching it carefully with the pads of my fingers, my claws right near her most sensitive bits.

She inhales sharply, those moon-colored eyes of hers widening with anxiety.

"Nice and slow," I tell her.

She lifts her hips carefully, leaning forward and planting her hands on my pecs. Her long mane of hair drapes down over my chest and tickles my skin. Her eyes find mine and she holds my gaze as she swivels her hips. I clamp down on her clit and bring my other claw up to her neck, carefully placing the sharp tips of each fingernail on the side of her neck and gently tracing down, not scratching, just drawing sensation out of her nerve endings. I reach her chest and drag my claws across her left breast where the pounding of her heart is so intense that it radiates up and I can feel it in my fingertips.

This is just as intense for her as it is for me. That knowledge makes me swell and my dick expands inside of her, so much that I think I can see her pelvis bulge a little. I take my claw off her clit, fascinated and eager to see if I'm right. I place my palm on her stomach to see if I can feel my dick through her body as she impales herself.

"Harder," I grit out. She uses those delicious thigh muscles to lift herself up as far as she can. I press into the soft skin of her low belly and I think I can feel it, the way I rearrange her insides. Damn straight. She's going to be broken after my cock. No stupid beta dick can compare.

She starts to give off tiny, breathy little moans.

That drives me wild and both my claws fall to her hips, holding her in place so I can fuck up into that tight pussy. I nearly forget that I'm fucking to punish her and Jonah because, for a minute, I'm just fucking. I'm just chasing that wild high like it's a rabbit through the forest, trying to snatch it up in my teeth.

I'm lost in the way her cunt grips my cock, squeezing it in a tight, slick, velvet hold. It's dazzling.

I get caught up in the moment, almost thinking my dream is a reality, almost able to delude myself into thinking that I found my omega and we got our happy ending.

For a moment, I don't see her betrayal. I just see her and how breathtaking she is.

But when Elena throws back her head and I see a soft smile cross her lips as she pants, close to her own release—I remember that I don't fucking want her enjoying this.

That snaps me right out of my own lusty-haze.

I especially don't want her closing her eyes and pretending I'm someone else, which is what I'm pretty sure she's doing right now.

She's imagining that I'm *him*.

The words my father said to me a long time ago come back to haunt me. "Women will want your protection. They'll want your money. Good luck finding one who just wants you."

My throat burns as his truth—which I'd scoffed at when I was younger—rings true.

Elena let me fight for her.

But at the end of the day, she didn't want me. I wasn't enough for her. She wasn't willing to get to know me, not even willing to give me a chance. She'd rather humiliate me and run off with a nobody. She'd let me take hits for her, stand in front of her like a shield and not say a word. Not even a thank you. Well, fuck that.

My rage is back.

"Murky! Get up," I bark.

Elena's eyes pop open at that, her lips dropping into a frown that suits her cheating soul so much better.

"Jerk off in front of her and spray her face with your cum," I order him.

That should do it. Women hate facials.

Elena's face turns to stone and I know I've hit the mark. Now, even if she orgasms, she'll stay mad at me —which she should. This is not some kind of orgasm swap like I've done in the past. This isn't tit-for-tat. Elena's here because she made a bargain to do anything to save her precious beta. That bargain means she has to follow orders. She has to give herself to me and hate it.

My wolf growls as Murky steps closer, dick in hand. He can't stand the minty scent of the beta who stole our mate.

Not our mate, I tell him.

Just a stupid girl.

A cheating girl who'll use me every chance she gets. Just like the last one.

I rut her hard and fast, ignoring her yelps as I drive deep. Gradually her yelps morph into screams, and when they do, I'm shocked.

Because she screams my name.

"Yes, Black! Yes, more!" Elena chants.

Goddammit—even though I should hate it, hearing my name spill from her lips gets me so fucking hot.

My knot swells and the edges of my vision flicker and all I can focus on is her as my balls tingle and pressure shoots up my spine. The next time Elena murmurs, "Black," I vanish. My mind is wiped away as I explode with enough force to topple a Vegas casino.

I come down to see Elena's face panting down at me, open-mouthed, as if she's fully aware these orgasms we're having are *not* normal.

Her eyes flash gold for a second and my own wolf shoves into my skin and transforms my eyes so they flash gold back at her.

As soon as my knot has gone down enough to pull out, I do. This sizzling connection between us has me feeling things I don't like.

But as soon as I pull free, something happens—something I've feared over the years, something that's happened before, but not in a very long time. My wolf shoves me aside and rears up. He seizes control of my body and shifts me into my monster, into a werewolf. Elena shrieks, but she can't get away when my werewolf reaches out and grabs her shoulders with his claws. He leans forward and—before I can stop him—he sinks his wolf teeth into her skin, right at the junction of her neck and shoulder.

He marks her as his.

I wrench away in horror, but the damage is already done. The teeth marks are bloody and fresh, gleaming, far too deep to just heal over without the resulting scars.

Idiot, I shove at my wolf, taking my body back and shifting to human. *What the fuck have you done? She already picked her mate!*My wolf doesn't answer, just prances in front of my vision, floating in midair in front of Elena's breasts, cocky and proud of himself. He runs up and perches on Elena's shoulder as she reaches up to delicately touch her small round wounds in disbelief.

That's when—with perfect timing—Murky erupts and comes all over her face.

I'd thought I'd found the best metaphor for my life before, but I was wrong, I realize, as I watch Elena break out into sobs. My life isn't a disaster. It's worse. It's a fucking unwanted facial. The universe has just splattered cum in my eye in a big, gigantic 'fuck you.'

I'm mated to a woman who hates me.

13

JONAH

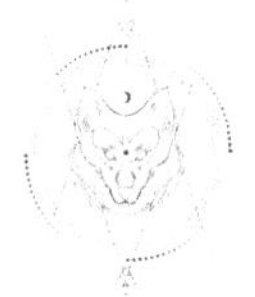

Black's avoided us for two days straight. As soon as his knot went down after his second round with Elena, he left the basement. I haven't seen him since.

Of course, the alphahole didn't leave me alone with her. He sent down his butler to separate us like children.

That's literally what the dude said. "Apparently, my job description now includes timeout supervision. If you make this bad for me, I *will* put live cockroaches in your food. I did it to Alpha Maddox when he continued to throw his used towels on the bathroom floor. So please don't take it personally, but do take it seriously. He did not enjoy the wiggle and crunch combination. I suspect you won't either." Matthew had crossed his arms behind his back and narrowed his eyes at us. I had no idea how old the guy was, he could have been anywhere from fifty to eighty, but his "try me" stare was stone cold.

Then he'd left Elena in the basement, telling her to shower.

I'd followed the gray-haired man up the stairs all the way back to the attic. He'd grumbled several times about having to cancel an appointment with Matilda the flexible wonder. I'd wanted to ask, but decided keeping my mouth shut was better until I knew exactly what I was in for.

Turns out, it was hell.

I've been forced to sleep in Elena's nest, looking every damned night at all the shit Black can give her that I can't. Wealth, protection, fancy lingerie. I found some lacy sets in a dresser up here and I've definitely come in a few pairs of panties imagining my mate, hoping one day Black will force her to wear them and she'll smell me, even if I'm gone. That minor rebellion has kept me sane through the past few nights, when I've spent hours staring at the door, expecting him to burst through and finally give me what's coming.

Death.

His wolf has clearly claimed Elena despite the fact that she marked me. What other outcome could there be but death? Alpha assholes can't deal with the slightest challenge. Each night I trace those marks on my neck, my fingers dragging over the soft, fresh scars. I'm still amazed by them. But I also think that they mean I'm not just marked for Elena. I'm marked for death.

Despite the deal he made with her, I'm certain Black wants to wreck me.

The only way to erase these marks is to wipe me out completely.

Maybe he wants to break my mind first.

I don't know.

Whatever his "master" plan is, I can't figure it out because Black's become a ghost.

I don't get it.

It would be easy for him. Even if I wanted to fight him, my wolf won't. And the thing is, I don't really want to fight him. I look around and I'm sick to my stomach knowing Black can give Elena a life a million times better than I could. I feel like an idiot for ever thinking I'd play the hero and help her get away.

I should have known.

Elena's always been a runner. She runs from her feelings the way she bolts around the track.

The fact that she insisted on leaving him should have tipped me off.

She's caught feelings for him.

Even if she doesn't want to admit it, I can tell.

The harder she resists the more she feels. I remember how she laid down the law between the two of us at the start. How she'd avoid me the next day and be cold as ice.

With Black, she's practically arctic.

That means she feels a whole hell of a lot of shit she doesn't want to admit to—especially since she's always been anti-alpha.

But it's there, under the surface.

I know, because I know her.

Black will kill me.

And one day, she'll thaw out. She'll be just fine with him. One day, she'll realize her feelings aren't full of hate, they're full of fear.

It's a strange place to be—death row.

Sometimes I remember it's coming and sometimes I don't. It's easier to distract myself now that Black's set up other punishments for me.

One of my new punishments is bizarre. I don't even see how it qualifies as a payback for running, unless Black thinks I hate working for free. Or hated my job.

I don't say a word—but the joke's on him because I don't give a shit.

This morning, Matthew showed up at the attic door with clothes that fit. "Put these on. You are apparently going to get to work instead of laze about today." His tone was wry, but the second that I saw real clothes and mechanic's coveralls, I jumped at them.

After I've changed, I head out of the attic to find him in the hallway holding a bagel stuffed with egg and a travel coffee mug. He hands them over and then jerks his head toward the stairs.

I eat because I've learned Matthew's food is pretty damn good the last few days. I'm especially happy to find some bacon slices hidden inside as we go down the steps. But I'm really curious about what the hell is going on. Is Black actually sending me back to work? I'm pretty sure they fired me after I no-showed several days in a row. Of course, he could smooth that over in a heartbeat. But why would he? It doesn't make sense.

Why let me show my face in the pack only to kill me later?

Unless … "Is this some kind of tar and feather thing?" I wonder aloud.

"What?" Matthew crooks a brow.

"Is there a crowd outside with pitchforks?" If so, they're like, really quiet for a mob. I finger the collar of my coveralls, the rough threads thick between my fingers. "Why hasn't Black killed me yet?"

"You're asking why the man *hasn't* committed a crime like he's insane?"

"Well, he kinda is, isn't he?"

"Alpha Maddox,"—Matthew emphasizes Black's official title as if reminding me to address my soon-to-be-killer with respect— "is *not* a murderer."

I think of about a thousand retorts but nothing I can say out loud. He's an alpha. They all fight to the death at some point. Some at many points. Over stupid shit too. But then the memory of Black bursting into that kitchen with a vengeance to save us comes to mind and I clamp my lips shut.

As we cross through the main hallway, I scent Elena and can't help a glance toward the basement door. But it's closed.

She's still in heat. I can tell by the anise scent mixed in with the lighter notes that normally define her.

I hear her moan.

The sound perks up my wolf and drives me wild. Why is she moaning? Is she touching herself? Is she in pain?

Or is Black down there with her right now? Is that why she's moaning?

Maybe that's why Black had me come downstairs, to rub it in my face like he's done before.

The times before … though I hate to admit it, were secretly hot. I never thought I'd get off on that shit, but watching him fuck Elena was … well, I've thought about it while I've jerked off in her panties far more than I should have.

I sniff, trying to see where Black is at, but his scent is all over every part of the house, so I can't really tell. I don't get to investigate because Matthew's already at the front door, holding it open. "Sometime this year, please," he says dryly.

I wrench my gaze away from the basement door and follow him outside as I polish off the last of the bagel, blinking in the cheery yellow morning light. It's going to be a hot one today, I can already tell.

"You're now the official Lobo mechanic. Enjoy that."

The old dude points a gnarled finger toward the gate at the end of the long, tree-lined driveway. Several cars are parked just inside the dark wrought iron. I can tell just by the look of them that everyone has brought in their junkers. The cars that sat in their driveways and wouldn't start or have no brakes for mysterious reasons that are too expensive to investigate but make the car impossible to sell. Problem cars. My favorite kind. My hands itch to touch them.

I love cars. I love the way they're predictable. And they don't fight back. And there's always a solution to a problem with them. They're easy.

Easier than everything else anyway.

I try to control my eagerness in front of Matthew, though, because I'm not sure if he has to report back to Black. I don't want him telling his boss that this punishment is actually a total win for me. Because Black wants this to suck for me, right?

He does, doesn't he?

For a second I confuse myself because it almost seems like Black's actually being nice to me.

But that's just got to be a head game.

He's lulling me into thinking he isn't mad when he is. Then he'll strike. That's what this is.

Having figured out that mental-gymnastics bullcrap, I feel better. Because I'd feel really fucking shitty if Black was actually being nice to me.

"Why did people leave the cars out there?" I ask Matthew as I take a sip of my coffee.

"Partially because Elena's still in heat," the butler tells me honestly. "Partially to piss you off, I'd guess."

"Piss me off?"

"Your tools are all in the fifth garage. Good luck," Matthew walks back into the house without looking back.

"Fucking cryptic much?" I mutter as I walk down the long-ass driveway to get the first car. Maybe this won't be as fun as I think. Well, good. Because I wouldn't want to think Black was a nice guy. That would just fuck my head up even more before he killed me. But even this punishment—working on cars for free out in the heat—is better than sitting up in that attic room reading instruction pamphlets for every dildo known to man because I have nothing better to do than imagine Black using it on Elena.

I'm determined not to let the alpha get under my skin, though I wonder again if he's down in that basement, touching Elena right now.

It makes me jealous as fuck, but my wolf just sits in front of my gaze and curls his tail around his paws like it's no big deal that the alpha is taking our mate.

That's what I fucking hate about the hierarchy. You just have to fucking sit there and take it when someone higher up than you wants something. If it weren't for this stupid hierarchy, if Elena and I were both glimmers, we could choose each other. And we'd be just fucking fine. Hierarchy ruins everything. My dad always chuckles and pats my shoulder when I complain about that shit. "Son, humans don't have it any better. They have their own hierarchy. It's called cash." I can hear his voice in my ears.

I wonder if my family knows what happened. I wonder if Black's spread the word. Does Elena's mom know?

I probably ought to ask Matthew, just to see what he says. I don't know if he'll tell me the truth or not, but it's worth asking.

A couple of blue jays dive bomb each other on my right side as I reach the first car, a dull green Honda Civic with a rusty slash on the hood. I ignore the birds bickering as I pull open the door and look for a key. There isn't one. Odd.

I get out of that car and try the next. But there aren't any keys there either.

Fucker.

Now I get what Matthew meant. I heave a sigh. I'm going to have to push each car toward the garage or haul tools out here. But if I do that … I'm limited to hand tools. No air compressors or other electric tools. Black's a clever bastard, I'll give him that. He probably wouldn't survive as alpha of the pack too long if he wasn't.

I glare up at the house, hoping he can see, then I go back to the green Civic, open it up so I can shove the car into neutral, and brace myself against the front door. I take a deep breath and push, slowly rolling that beast forward. When we hit the first curve, I panic because there is a damn tree looming.

Fuck. I have to lean down to reach inside the car, latch onto the wheel, and jerk it to the side. The car rolls slightly off the drive, into the grass, a couple bushes scraping the window on the other side. Shit!

The car is about to lose a side mirror when something smashes into it and shoves it towards me, changing the car's path at the last second.

"This is my grandma's car," Pluto, the asshole who worked the desk at the last howl, appears above the hood of the car, pushing it from the opposite side. He glares at me.

"Sorry." I shrug. "That tree came out of nowhere."

"I don't understand why you aren't dead."

"That makes two of us," I respond candidly.

"If he's getting soft … that's fucking dangerous." Pluto's eyes narrow as he evaluates me.

The gleam in his eyes makes me panic. I can't have anyone thinking Black's getting soft. If they do, then all kinds of alphas will challenge him. And if that happens,

Elena's in danger. "He's not soft. You should see the whip marks on my back. I think he's just drawing out the torture."

Pluto sniffs. "I don't smell blood."

Fuck. I think quickly. "He does it at night. So I can heal up enough for this shit," I jerk my chin toward the car.

Pluto narrows his eyes but doesn't say anything else. He just turns and walks back to the guard shack at the gate, which I didn't even notice until now. Shack is an understatement since it really looks like a fancy pool house on one of those remodeling shows. I watch him walk inside without a backward glance.

I turn back to the Civic and throw my shoulder into getting it moving again, slowly straining as I push it over to the garage.

I work until late into the night, after the sun has set. It's easier to keep working than letting Matthew lock me into the nest all night so I can stare at sex toys and wonder what other kind of head games Black might play.

The moon has reached the tip-top of the sky when I finish up with a particularly nasty brake job. I swipe my greasy hands with a rag and stretch, rolling my head on my neck to stretch it out.

I hate to admit it, but working did me good. It got my mind off anticipating Black's every move.

But that little run-in with Pluto made me think: I need to warn Black.

Nobody can think he's weak. His second can't challenge him. Otherwise, Elena's in danger.

"My life fucking sucks," I grumble to no one as I toss the rag into a work sink in the garage. I glare up at the moon and point at the goddess, talking to the invisible woman supposedly up there for once. "Why the fuck would you make me have to go warn the dickhead who hates me? Huh? If you exist, you're a bitch."

A cloud slides across the moon, which I'm sure is a coincidence because it looks like a summer storm is rolling in but I still get a line of shivers down my spine.

Fuck that shit. That's what's wrong with belief. All of a sudden, every shadow means something, and if you just had the secret key to translate it—stupid. I flip off my own brain as I walk inside through the side entrance.

I shuck off my mechanic's coveralls, boots, and sweaty socks in a mudroom before walking barefoot into a laundry room only to see clean shorts, underwear, and a t-shirt, along with a note to toss my coveralls and day clothes in the wash provided by the utterly efficient butler. I've never met a glimmer who takes his job so seriously. And he's so damned good at it that he might as well be magical. He can predict what I want before I even say I want it. Craziness.

Case in point, he appears with a plate as soon as I hit the foyer. The plate has a slab of steak, some green beans, and a mountain of mashed potatoes on it.

Apparently, thankfully, Black's punishments don't extend to food.

I don't know why. Maybe he knows wolf shifters get more than just "hangry." But I'm not asking in case it's a mistake.

"How's Elena?" I ask Matthew, same as I have the past two nights.

"Physically, maybe a little exhausted. He had her make fifteen cakes for a charity cakewalk today."

I wrinkle my nose. "He's making her cook?"

Matthew gives me a sardonic look.

"Not to question his judgment, but … I think that might be punishing someone else. Some innocent person is going to eat that."

"You speak as though you have experience."

"Yeah, cooking is not one of the reasons I lo—it's not one of Elena's strengths," I amend.

Matthew bites down on a smile. “Based on the fact that she forgot to put eggs in once and baking powder twice, I’m inclined to agree with you.”

I grimace as I use my fork to stuff a bite of mashed potatoes into my mouth and swallow. Fucking heaven.

“Am I supposed to eat this upstairs?”

“He wants to see you,” Matthew replies calmly, gesturing to the left of the stairs, at a closed door.

I raise my plate slightly. “Last meal?” I ask.

“I wouldn’t know.”

“Great. Thanks.”

“Happy to help.” Matthew gestures toward the door again, as if I’ve forgotten where I need to go.

I sigh and force myself to walk forward, though I can’t control how my feet drag. My wolf paces in front of my vision, worried and anxious about how the alpha’s going to receive us.

Shut up, Mouse, I tell him.

He whines and sits, like a fucking dog instead of a wolf. No matter how I curse him, he won’t stand up and face the music like a fucking man.

The air seems to grow thinner the closer I get to that door. My pulse speeds up until it feels like a shiver inside me.

I reach the handle and turn it, shoving the door open, only to drop my jaw in surprise.

I stare into Black's office, a fancy room with a desk bigger than three people would reasonably need. There's a huge bookshelf off to one side filled with predictably gold-trimmed hardbacks.

I don't see a vicious Alpha standing in front of his desk, monstered out in werewolf form, ready to kill me.

Instead, I see a drunk dude with his collared shirt half unbuttoned, sitting at a meeting table. He reeks of scotch, and the half-empty bottle beside him explains why. He doesn't even turn to look at me as he reaches his hand into a crystal bowl of trail mix beside him. He takes out a raisin and then he flicks it.

It flies two feet forward before it smacks into the chair across from his table.

Fuck.

Fuck.

Fuck.

The asshole's depressed.

"You know, if I believed in the Moon Goddess, I'd call her a fucking bitch right now," I say as I walk inside and close the door.

"Get out."

Hmm. So Black didn't summon me. Matthew set this up. He must be worried about the alpha, which means Black's feelings for Elena run deeper than I thought. Motherfucking hell. And penguin-suited dude wants me to what? Make it all better? Since when do captives have to console their captors?

Matthew's suddenly on my shit list despite the fact that it smells like he can cook a steak to perfection.

"I said *leave*," Black repeats, louder this time, though he doesn't bother to look over.

"Can't. Your butler bribed me with steak to come cheer you up. And he's already threatened to put cockroaches in my food."

Black snorts. "He should. You deserve it."

"Not arguing that." I walk through the room and take a seat at the table he's at, moving my chair so I'm not close enough for him to reach and I'm out of his direct line of sight. I don't want to poke the beast too much.

We sit in silence for a second before I decide not to let my dinner get cold. I cut into my steak and take a bite.

It's perfect and tender and almost worth the bullshit I'm about to put myself through.

Black takes another swig from his scotch bottle. Then he sets it down with a thump and grabs a blue M&M. He clutches between his thumb and forefinger, just staring at it.

I nod my head toward his hand, indicating the candy he's holding. "She taught you the flick?"

He tucks the candy down, clenching his fist. I'm not sure if he's irritated that Elena showed me how to do it too or if it's because I caught him practicing. Maybe both.

"She doesn't teach just anyone that, you know. If she talked about her dad to you, that's huge."

"What the fuck are you doing?" he asks, tossing the M&M back in the bowl.

"Something so stupid and beta that I'm probably going to hate myself later for it."

That makes his brows rise. "I'm listening."

"Look. Elena runs from her feelings."

That does it. He growls and glares at me before shoving the candy dish off the table. I snatch my plate back, just to ensure it's not next, and take a quick bite of mashed potatoes in case this is about to get violent. "I didn't know she actually liked you. When she asked to run, she made it sound like you just shoved a ring on her finger like some barbarian …"

His brow furrows and he leans back in his chair, snatching the bottle for another drink. It's a long one.

That raises a red flag. "You did ask her, right? Like down on one knee and stuff?"

He doesn't answer. Doesn't look at me. I sigh and set my plate back on the table. "Okay, well. I don't know how the fuck to fix that. But you need to fix that. Because in case you haven't noticed, Elena fucking hates taking orders."

He holds up a hand. "If you're trying to excuse her—"

"I'm not. What we did … I know there's no excuse for that. But I'm trying to explain. There's a reason for things. And if you want to keep her, you need to fucking figure her out."

"If! She's *mine*."

His dark brown eyes flash gold and he sends a death glare my way. His wolf is edging closer to the surface.

I decide to give him some time. There's no moment like the present to finish my last meal. And I really don't want to go without finishing it. My thoughts get a little punch drunk as I contemplate the fact that I'm probably spending my last living moments with the alpha of my pack.

I don't say anything else for a few minutes, just cut my steak and enjoy the perfect seasoning, stabbing some green beans to go with it. I watch Black out of the corner of my eye. He sits tense, gripping the armrests of his chair for a few minutes. But eventually, his shoulders roll back and down. In my family, that's always a tell from an alpha dude. When he relaxes his shoulders, he's ready to talk again.

"Pluto, your second, thinks you should kill me. He thinks you're getting soft." I say, before scooting my chair back and ducking as Black stands, tosses the table aside, and launches the liquor bottle at my head. My empty dinner plate goes flying, smashing into a wall and shattering.

At least it was empty, my idiotic giddy mind tells me.

"What the fuck?" he growls. "When did you see Pluto?"

"I worked on his grandmother's car," I respond, casting my eyes down and right, exposing my neck, and speaking quickly. There are things I need to say before he does it, so I can't challenge him head-on. Just a few minutes. I just need a few minutes. Inside my head, my wolf's already rolled onto his back and exposed his belly. "Look. If you need to kill me to keep order, fine. Do it. Don't really get why you haven't already. But, you need to know a couple things about Elena first."

I try not to flinch as Black yanks on my shirt and pulls me up to his chest. He yanks so hard that I'm on my tiptoes. My calves start to burn as he pulls me higher.

"Look. She thought she was gonna be an alpha but she hates alphas because I think her mom beat her dad and he killed himself," I say, all in one breath, trying to smash out the essentials before he wolfs out and does it.

But Black drops my shirt instantly, stepping back and bumping into the overturned table leg. He drags a hand down his face. "She hates alphas?"

I nod, trying not to reach for my neck, where he grabbed the shirt so tightly I thought I might choke. "She hates orders. She wants to feel like she's in charge. It's how she feels secure."

"So you're basically telling me that my fucking wolf picked a mate who's going to hate me forever?"

I shrug. "Welcome to the club. My wolf picked a mate that we can never hope to protect."

As Black and I stare at each other, the storm that's been rolling in finally breaks.

Lightning scars the sky, searing and marking it, the same way Elena's somehow marked both of us.

14

BLACK

THUNDER RUMBLES through the sky and I want to roar like it is. I want the ground to shake underneath my feet, tremble with my rage. I'm fucking furious right now and I'd like nothing more than to claw Murky's neck to ribbons just to appease the beast inside.

But I don't.

Even though my heart's beating like a gorilla pounding its chest, I hold myself back because Murky knows Elena inside and out. And he walked into my office tonight, cool as a cucumber, to tell me the bullshit crap Pluto said questioning my choices.

Murky even offered to let me off him. That's either unhinged or really damned noble. I'm not sure which yet, but it has me intrigued.

So instead of killing him, I stare daggers at him.

He gives a long, drawn-out sigh and points to the pair of chairs that are still whole, not broken by the table I overturned during my outburst. “Can we sit?”

I nod and move to a leather seat and sink into it. All the messed-up emotions I’ve been carrying for the past few days as I’ve tried to sort out pack shit weigh down my shoulders. Thomas Stone and his little band of fuck-ups are trying to make things hard for me. They burned down their pack house and have tied up all their pack finances. My lawyers are having a heyday arguing with theirs over releasing this shit because humans control most banking institutions and really don’t know a damned thing about shifter law. I really need to fly down to Alabama and take care of this. Nothing solves a shifter uprising like snapping some necks … but Elena’s still in heat. I can’t leave her.

I tried yesterday. I made it all the way to the end of the driveway before my wolf shifted and took over, clawing up the town car. Fucking bastard. I had to have Matthew call my pilot and tell him he’d prepped the jet for nothing.

I can’t leave her alone even though the pack needs me to. My wolf won’t allow me to leave his mate while she’s in heat and bringing her anywhere is far too dangerous, especially since I know Thomas tried to steal her.

It feels like my hands and shoelaces are both tied and I'm tripping over myself for a woman who doesn't even want me.

I hate that Pluto's skepticism isn't misplaced. Even I'm second-guessing myself. I'm going to fall on my face and fail as pack alpha if I don't get shit with Elena sorted out soon.

I've never been this guy. I fucking hate *this guy*.

Why am I this guy? I ask internally as I side-eye my wolf, who's too busy baring his teeth at Murky to notice me and how I'm blaming him for turning me into this fucking wreck.

I've always been about the pack. Always.

Taking up the reins as head alpha means focusing on the pack at all times, monitoring threats, ensuring order. I've dedicated the last fucking decade to that.

But it's all going to be wiped out if I can't get my shit together.

If only we hadn't fucking mate-marked a bitch who hates us and left us, I lash out at my animal.

My wolf turns then, his eyes fierce. His pale fur rises, and he lowers his head as he growls at me for calling his mate a name. He even takes a threatening step in my direction, though what the fuck he plans to do to me, I don't know. Shift and piss on my leg?

Try it, I tell him, narrowing my eyes back at him. We're at odds with each other, which hasn't happened before. Our choices have always synced.

One measly little omega waltzed in and now … life's fucked.

You wanted her too, he growls.

And he's right. I did. I still fucking do even though I hate that I do.

We stare each other down for a moment before my wolf switches gears, deciding to redirect his ire.

He shoots me several images of Elena and then of various alphas. He's offended that Elena hates alphas and groups us all together. No matter what her mother did, we aren't all the same. He thinks he's different, even though that thought makes me laugh.

We're not fucking different. We are *the damn stereotype,* I snarl back at him. Though I do wonder what Elena's mother did to ruin the family. Did she really beat her husband? And if so, why didn't Prime, the Lobos' alpha at the time, take care of that shit?

My wolf doesn't want to dig up history. He wants to go downstairs and paddle the little wolf's ass again.

That's not going to help, I tell him. *Especially if she wants control.*

Pack hierarchy, my wolf responds, not understanding that human needs are far more complex than his.

Elena's wolf might be an omega. But she's not.

And I treated her like she was.

I didn't get down on one knee.

There was no romance.

We didn't even go on a fucking date.

I just claimed her. And now I've marked her without asking.

Fuck. My. Life.

No wonder she ran off.

Every woman fucking wants the alpha. That's all I've ever known. I never fathomed Elena was so different or that everything I'd do would trigger her worst fears.

I want to throw something else—smash it—but the alcohol is hitting me hard and my head jitters a little when I lean to put my chin on my hand. Goddammit, I'm too drunk to argue with my wolf right now.

My self-control is shot to shit along with every other piece of this life I've built—which is about to come tumbling down like a house of cards unless I find a way to stop it.

I call out, "Hey Siri, make an announcement: Matthew, can we get some water?"

The little black puck on the corner of my desk sends out the message to my butler.

The beta waits quietly, sitting in his chair and interlacing his fingers, the epitome of patience and submission with his downcast eyes.

"There are alphas in your family, aren't there?" I ask, hating that the little punk seems to know how to act to appease my wolf. I want him to be a bigger asshole so I have an excuse to be one back. I could justify being an asshole still based on the fact that he took Elena, but it's pretty damned clear that she chose to run with him and to mark him. Hell, she probably fucking forced him to take her, he's so damned compliant and unassuming.

"What the fuck does she see in you?" I ask, gripping the chair arms so hard that I'm liable to break it.

I realize, with a start, that I'm jealous.

I've never been fucking jealous of a beta in my life but as I stare at Murky, bile creeps up my throat.

He gives an innocent little shrug. "I do what she wants. I don't push. But it's not like I've got a lock down on anything. You know—she's never let me visit her house. Isn't that weird?"

For some reason, that fact instantly soothes me. If I can be the first to visit her house, then it will feel like a fucking win.

God. This isn't a competition.

I don't know why I'm treating it like one.

She doesn't even want me.

Why do I give a shit if I get to see her childhood home?

I still want her to want me, I realize with a start. Despite everything I've done, I *still* hope I have a fucking shot with her because my wolf marked her, and we have the world's hottest sex, and the best fucking chase, and she's not afraid of me, and her little smirk when she feels superior is so fucking cute... the list of reasons piles up in my head.

Motherfucking hell.

I glare outside as the raindrops pound against the glass and my chest aches. Pressure builds up inside of me just like the atmosphere during a storm, making it hard to breathe.

I realize that I don't even know if Elena's spoken to her parents since she got home. No, not parents. Mother. Murky said her dad killed himself.

No wonder she wears sarcasm like a cloak.

I grimace at everything I've done that's probably just strengthened her hatred of alphas.

Matthew walks in just then with my dinner, which I'd refused earlier, and a huge bottle of water. He stops short at the sight of the overturned table before turning to me. "I think we might need to rename your office the forbidden West Wing."

I reach for the water, hardly seeing him now that relief is in sight. I take the bottle and unscrew the cap so I can chug. "What?" I ask when I've finished.

Matthew sets my plate on my desk and points at it sternly. "If you continue breaking things like a child, then I think it's only fair your office gets named after a children's movie."

Murky snorts and I frown as I turn to look at him. He instantly wipes his expression, but I ask, "What the hell is he saying?" as I jerk a thumb at Matthew's retreating back.

"Pretty sure he just compared you to *Beauty and the Beast*," Murky replies.

I whip my head in the direction of my butler, ready to put him in his place. But he's gone, wisely disappearing.

Murky bears the brunt of my annoyance instead as I stare at him and his grease-streaked arms. "Of course, you *would* know kid's movies. You even old enough to drive those cars you work on?"

"I'm older than your mate, cradle robber," he punts it back but with a light, teasing expression on his face.

"Careful, pipsqueak."

"I'm about to die, no need to be careful, geezer."

I shake my head and take another sip of water. "You know, you make it so fucking hard to hate you. I hate that about you."

He grins. "Well, that's unexpected and ironic."

"Kind of like this damn whole mess," I tell him.

I stare down at the broken table for a second, before I heave myself to my feet and go to my desk. I don't feel like eating, but I know I need to soak up the alcohol churning through my system. So I drag the plate over to me, unroll my utensils from inside the cloth napkin Matthew brought, and force myself to take a bite of mashed potatoes. Then I point my fork at Murky. "Explain more Elena shit. Now."

He clears his throat and sits up a little straighter, like he's in class or something. I fight the urge to roll my eyes.

"Well. She's in school to be a nurse."

That's news to me. It kind of takes me off guard—caretaker isn't exactly the role I'd have pinned for Elena. But then, she's been full of surprises since the moment I found her in the woods.

Suddenly, the way she treated my wounds after the fight in the basement takes on new meaning. I'd thought it had been tender. Was it really more clinical? Was everything I'd thought happened between us one-sided? "What kind of nurse?"

"She hasn't done rotations yet, so I don't think she knows. I think those are next semester, maybe?"

I circle my fork, signaling for him to continue as I dig into my meal.

"She likes writing dirty notes. Coffee, spaghetti, grapefruit in those little snack containers with the juice. Those are her favorite foods as far as I can tell."

I tilt my head and stare at him, soaking in this information but at the same time wondering why he's giving it to me when it's clearly been hard-earned on his part. The idiot really does think I'm going to kill him. I could try to rid him of that illusion, but it's making him spill his guts, so for the moment I embrace my inner asshole and use Murky's misconceptions to my advantage. "Go back to the hating alphas. Tell me what you know about that."

He shrugs. "It's not like she sat down and explained it to me. She didn't even tell me about her dad. I asked around."

"Ok. What do you know about her mom?" I ask, taking another bite.

"Don't you have spy cams or some shit?"

I shrug. "We have a database, but the pack is huge. Too many shifters. And now that we've added Dark Night territory ..." I trail off and wait for him to continue.

"I know her mom has a long-standing rivalry with this other female alpha. They fight a lot." He tosses his shoulders up. "Other than that, I've never met her."

I nod, absorbing that and deciding Elena's parents' situation must have made her jaded. She's fucking young to be that disillusioned, but then again—I probably hit that same wall around her age. Which leads me to ask, "Wait. When's her birthday?"

"You proposed marriage without knowing her birthday?" His disapproval reeks, smelling up the room.

I shoot the fork at him like a dart, and he ducks—his reflexes are impressively good.

"Thought you came here to let me kill you."

"You're planning on doing it with a fork?"

"Maybe."

"Not to critique your murder weapon of choice, but there are a lot better choices out there."

Fuck, this little punk is funny. I glare but my drunken self can't hold back the grin fighting to get free. It breaks loose and completely ruins what I say next. "Get the hell out of here before I decide that *is* how I'm going to kill you. You fucking deserve to be stabbed like a potato."

He stands up but asks, "You're going to, right? Your elites *can't* question you. If they lead a coup, what happens to Elena?"

He's so goddamned selfless I can't stand it. If we were human, the fuckers would paint a halo over his head. It makes me sick. I grab my plate and lob it at him. "Get out."

I expect him to comply, being a beta, part of my pack, and a prisoner. But the little fucker surprises me for a second time tonight. He straightens his spine and pretends he's got a backbone. "No. I want to challenge you." The little fool raises his fists.

My gut immediately tightens, and I'm torn between anger that he dare challenge me and amusement that he thinks he's got a shot.

Murky continues his little proposal like it's not the most preposterous thing I've ever heard.

But when he names his terms, he's dead serious, and his terms make me rise to my feet in fury, because the punk kid says, "Man to man. No wolves. I want to fight you for the rights to Elena tonight."

He's challenging me over my mate.

15

JONAH

I NARROW my eyes and widen my stance, trying to make my posture look confident when I'm totally freaking out inside. I know I'm being stupid as hell right now, challenging the alpha of the entire frickin' Lobos, but Black isn't taking my warning about Pluto, seriously enough. He also didn't know a damned thing about his mate, and I'm offended on her behalf that he claimed her. Finally, I'm brutally, viscerally jealous of the fact that I fucking love her to the moon and back but this dick—he's the only one who can protect her.

He doesn't deserve her but he's the one who gets to keep her.

I know he thinks I stole her from him. But I've taken a couple days of punishment for that, and honestly—finding out how little he knows about the most amazing woman on the planet erases a shit-ton of my guilt.

Just because he threw a ring at her doesn't mean she owed him a yes.

Black pushes up out of his seat and towers over me even though he's five feet away.

Oversized alpha asshole.

I try to calm but when he growls, my throat and my asshole both clench. I'm about to lose, badly, and my body is already prepping for the pain.

Maybe this move will be the end of me, but I don't even regret it. Black's drunker than a skunk in a funk—to quote my grandfather. I'll at least have a shot. Maybe. If he sticks to the rules. But alphas often care more about winning than rules. It's how they stay on top.

I watch Black's eyes stay nailed to me as he rounds his desk, and his office shrinks around him as he fills up my vision. His lips curve up in amusement but his eyes—they don't look like they're laughing.

He glances down at the broken table and the shattered plates on the floor. "Not here. Wouldn't want you to stumble into the table and cry foul like a little bitch."

He's accepting my challenge.

I don't know if that makes me happy or if I'm about to piss myself.

My throat dries out and I can't even nod or say anything. I just swallow like an idiot and wait for him to tell me where and when.

We're doing this. We're dueling over Elena.

This desperate hope scratches and claws at my chest because right now I want to win more than anything in the fucking universe. I want to hold her one last time. I have to blink hard because my eyes threaten to tear up and there's no chance in hell I'm going to let Black see that.

I'm not sure he misses it though because his expression grows closed-off and hard as he steps closer to me. I half expect him to grab me by the throat and squeeze. Instead, he just knocks me sideways as he stalks past, and yanks open his office door.

I follow in a cloud of light-headed disbelief that this is actually happening.

As we move through the front hall, I try not to slide on my socked feet as his shoes make a scuffing sound against the floor. I'm cursing at myself because even though he's only wearing dress shoes right now, those are a major advantage. My ribs are anticipating those shoes smashing into them several times.

I blow out a breath and shake out my hands trying to calm my nerves, but my wolf isn't helping anything.

He's whining in my ear. Mouse really fucking hates this idea, but I shove him into a cage in the corner of my mind and lock him up like a dog in a kennel. *Stay,* I order him. *You'll only make this worse.*

It's already pretty bad. I don't need worse.

Oh, I'm hating myself right now as I stare up at Black's broad back and feel like a coward. I walked into that office and pushed for this. And it's the right thing, I can feel that in my bones. But at the same time, those bones are also urging me to hightail it to the front door and just run.

Fuck. I wish shifters had Avada Kedavra. A flash of green light, then it's all over, Harry Potter style—that sounds way better than shifter claws or teeth. Better than getting punched until I'm knocked out, or kneed in the groin. My balls shrivel at the very thought.

Elena always says I have an MMA build and I fucking love that. I love the way her eyes light up when she looks at my body. But at the end of the day, I'm just a gym rat, not a fighter.

I crack my knuckles as Black leads me past a fancy-ass dining room with at least ten chairs.

Did he turn off the air conditioner or am I nervous-sweating? I can't tell.

I reach up and wipe a tiny line of sweat from my hair-line and blink as the hall seems to grow narrower and darker.

Finally, we reach a room with double doors and some fancy-ass handles.

Black shoves them open and strides inside but my adrenaline-charged brain takes a little bit to catch up. It takes me a minute to register what I'm seeing.

A polished wooden floor gleams along the length of a huge room lined with columns. Windows line the back of the room. A couple rows of padded convention chairs are stacked near the left end, but it's otherwise completely vacant.

I stare around and it takes me a second to recognize that this is a ballroom. I go to howls but never to other fucking pack shit because they don't involve running and *do* involve mingling with the alphas.

I didn't know he had a fucking ballroom inside his house. Or should I just call it a damned castle? When do you get that upgrade? Does it have to be made of stone to be called a castle?

I have the sudden urge to Google shit, which probably comes from the fact that part of me is still rebelling against being here. I try and lock that part away because it will undermine me in the fight.

Instead, I try to focus on the cool factor of fighting in a ballroom.

Black flicks the lights on and I glance up to see chandeliers taller than me dripping from the ceiling. My grandma Tillie always called chandeliers tears of the poor. She hated them and thought that pricks who had them probably cheated someone else to get them. I wonder if she's been here to this ballroom. This is the alpha mansion, so probably. I briefly wonder if this exact room sparked her hatred and why. But she's not around to ask anymore.

"Backing out already, Murkaaay?" Black's tongue stumbles over my name a little but his posture doesn't look drunk. He looks furious.

I step inside, my ears buzzing at the echo his footsteps make as he goes to the middle of the floor and waits for me. I peel off my socks, knowing that they'll be a slip hazard. Then I toss aside my shirt.

Black wolf-whistles, trying to goad me. He doesn't bother to undress, to remove the shirt I could grab and yank. Fucker's annoyingly confident.

"Come on, beta. Let's dance."

I try to keep my stride confident as I cross the distance between us, but a throat clears behind me and echoes around the empty room. I'm so amped up that I immediately spin to face the threat, thinking Black's going to double-team me.

I see Matthew in the doorway, still in his penguin suit, arms crossed in disapproval, and my shoulders relax.

The butler pipes up. "I'd like to ask you to refrain from destroying this room, Alpha Maddox, as it happens to be the most expensive to repair."

"No can do. Murkay here wants to fight."

"Human style," I remind the big alpha, turning back to him with a warning wag of my finger.

"Again, I'll repeat my request," Matthew states.

"Denied. Come on, beta. Let's do this."

Matthew gives a long-suffering sigh and I hear his jacket rustle. Suddenly, a romantic waltz blasts through the speakers, filling the room with sound. "Fine. Be that way. Here's some mood music."

"Turn that shit off!" Black commands, but when I turn around, the butler's already disappeared.

"I like him," I say.

"Shut the fuck up and fight," Black retorts, bending his knees and raising his hands to get into grappling position. I walk toward him and find my steps annoyingly matching the beat of the music.

"What the hell is this shit?" I ask, as I raise my fists, thrown off by the music, which makes me think of shows that Elena's forced me to watch like Dancing with the Stars. How the hell am I supposed to fight with this crap messing up my mojo?

"Heathen. It's Dark Eyes. Only one of the best waltzes ever written." Black scowls at me, where he sways slightly.

I take another step toward him, encouraged by the fact that he looks like he might fucking faceplant on his own. Maybe I can just tap him a little. "How the hell do you—" My question is cut off as he throws a hook at my head that comes during a swell in the music. I duck and he misses. I step back as the strings take over and the absurdity of this moment truly hits me.

His explanation is just as unexpected as his swing. "High school orchestra."

I press my lips together and move in for an uppercut. "Play the harp?" I get in a glancing blow but nothing good enough to make my knuckles ring in pain, so probably nothing that will truly mess him up.

"Piccolo."

"You're fucking with me."

Black lands a gut punch that makes my lungs stutter. I wheeze as I stumble back, away from his second swing. "Really?" I ask—about the piccolo, not the hit.

He follows my train of thought exactly. "The name of the waltz is right. I fucked a girl in the orchestra once in high school." He grins. "You're pretty fucking dumb for believing that, Murky."

"Excuse me for hoping you had some layers."

"Nope. Just asshole through and through," he grins as we circle, the chandeliers twinkling above us and the moon peeking inside through the windows.

I glare at him.

From behind me, Matthew's voice echoes off the walls like he's the damned Wizard of Oz, "You did so play piccolo. It's up in the attic closet, along with your trumpet."

Black glares over at him distracted. "What the fuck—"

"I thought I'd make a TikTok," Matthew's voice trails through the room as I take my shot, going low and swiping at Black's knees. I yank one up into my arms and he goes flying backward, crashing into the floor.

"Erase that shit!" he barks at Matthew, not even concerned about me as I dive on top of him and start pummeling his face. I try to focus on my breathing, matching it to each of my hits as I thrash his cheeks and bruise my knuckles. I ignore the protests that shoot up my arms because his head is as thick as a fucking troll's. Hitting him while he's down is far more important than any pain I feel. "I. Can't. Believe. You. Were. A. Band. Geek."

He roars in my face and shoves me backward so that I smack against the polished wood floor. I quickly do a reverse somersault to back away from him as he rises. The violins start shrieking in the background, in perfect concert with my nerves.

"Band and orchestra aren't the same, you stupid fucker!" he yells. He dives at me and my heart thunders because I can see his eyes flash gold.

Shit.

He's seconds from shifting.

My blood gushes through me like river rapids as adrenaline sharpens my vision and thoughts.

On pure instinct, I jump as high as I can, tucking my knees in. When his head is just in front of me, I kick out and strike him in the chin. His head snaps back and he's fucking pissed. He's falling, but with his massive reach, his arm swipes up and latches onto my shorts. I smack down next to him with a loud thwack.

He pushes up, but I'm not drunk. My reflexes are faster than his right now. I scramble up to my knees and climb on top of him, my hands reaching for his neck. I get an arm hooked nice and tight before he can get a hand in between to shove me away and I squeeze hard as he bucks up, trying to stand and throw me off.

From the sidelines, Matthew dryly says, "Ride 'em, cowboy."

I burst into laughter and shout, "Yee-haw!" If that doesn't get Black to kill me quickly later, I don't know what will. I flex, letting my bicep push against the side of his face as he wheezes. "Tap out," I whisper quietly in his ear. "You know it's just for tonight, anyway. We both know as much as she wants me right now, what she really needs is you."

I expect him to reach back and try to grab me and throw me off because I know he's nowhere near to passing out yet. He's the fucking pack alpha, he's got fight left in him. But instead, he leans forward slowly and taps the floor.

Black Maddox admits defeat.

I let go and stagger away from him, disbelieving. There's no way I should have won. My ribs aren't even broken yet. I fully expected to stumble down the steps and die in Elena's arms.

But here I am with a couple of bruises, nothing else.

"You get her tonight. But you let me go down and tell her first." Black says as he rises to his feet.

I blink, nonplussed, turning to Matthew to confirm that this is reality and I'm still alive—and Avada Kedavra doesn't exist somehow and I missed the moment of my death because it was as fast as a flash of green light.

The butler nods as Black Maddox strides from the room and I stare at his wide back, then down at my hands, where my knuckles throb, then back to Matthew.

"Take the gift, son. Don't question it."

Matthew disappears from the doorway, but I'm stuck still standing there.

Did the pack alpha just throw this fight so I can say goodbye?

16

ELENA

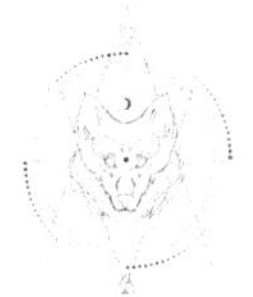

Four hours. It's been four hours since Black's shadow darkened the doorway of the basement. Every time he does, I swear I fucking hate him. But the second he leaves, my eyes dart back up the stairs to that door and I end up fantasizing about him and the way he can just throw my body around, pin me down, and take me.

There's a wild push and pull to our connection and I keep swinging from one extreme to the other when I think about Black. He's furious and unforgiving and so brutish when he fucks. He's spanked me and yelled at me more than once for running from him like a coward— which infuriates me to no end. As if he would have let me leave. That arrogant prick would never have accepted rejection. Those comments of his burn me up. But then his fingers and dick and his mouth have worshiped me, transforming my fury into fire and then guilt. We have a cycle going: Hate. Fuck. Cry. Repeat.

I've been hating him for hours now and I desperately need the next part of that cycle.

I'm panting, aching, lying on the carpet in the middle of the room surrounded by every pillow I could find. Couch pillows, bed pillows, and the comforter stolen from the bedroom down here, and that stupid fuzzy pink pillow that I've come to hate.

I've made myself a temporary nest. It sucks; it's little more than a messy blob on the floor—it isn't pretty or soft or the other million descriptors that my buzzing hormones tell me it needs to be. But it's better than nothing—and I have next to nothing down here.

It would be better if I could have made the nest on the mattress in the bedroom. That was softer than this floor. But Black never seems to make it to the bed with me.

He hasn't set foot in that bedroom since he left me down here to punish me two days ago.

As I touch myself in slow circles, I come to the conclusion I should have had hours ago—he doesn't want to be in that bed with me.

Beds mean intimacy or something to him. And this is all just a punishment fuck. He's pissed that I ran.

Ticked his wolf marked me. Well, so am I, because that mark took away any hope I ever had of leaving.

A small, tiny sliver of me had hoped when I'd pled with him that he'd have mercy and banish Jonah and I at some point and we could run away to New York as we'd planned. But his bite makes that impossible.

He's tied to me, and I'm tied to Jonah and we're a fucking three-ring circus full of sad clowns.

I'm trapped here, fucking on the floor instead of a mattress because neither Black nor I have control of our wolves.

Tears come to my eyes, and I turn and stare up at the moon goddess, pleading for the millionth time tonight that she take all our wolves away.

My wolf appears in my line of sight, tilting her head at me as if in sarcastic disbelief that I could think such negative things about her or Black's wolf. She's downright annoyed that I wish she'd never come, though she's an omega, so she doesn't say it outright.

Instead, she does passive-aggressive shit. She flashes a picture of the huge engagement ring through my head. She thinks Black associates that room with the ring and with our moments before I left and that's why he's avoiding it. She sends me a picture she's fabricated of him covering his eyes like he's hurt.

I want to roll my eyes because that's bullshit. Black isn't sentimental about anything. Least of all me. The only part of him that's attached to me is his pride. Unfortunately, I know all too much about alphas and their pride. It's an addiction for them. Look at my own mother and her obsession with rank. Always wanting to be tougher. Always wanting those bragging rights. Stupid.

Fluffy lays down, not wanting to argue, which only pisses me off more because I've been waiting for her to show up for days so that I can rail at her.

Why the hell do you keep disappearing? I ask. *You put all this shit in motion—you derail my entire life, and then don't even stick around.*

Her nose drops, and she doesn't answer. I clench my fists in frustration and close my eyes, but when I open them back up—she's gone.

Typical.

My heat picks up speed then, the symptoms of desperation intensifying. Sweat rolls down my spine and my pussy gives a greedy pulse, looking for something to hold onto—it has been like that for nearly the past hour. And I don't know why Black hasn't shown.

Normally, I think he can scent me—my flare-ups make me produce another round of slick, which normally draws him like a bee to a flower.

Why isn't he here already?

I whine as my hand circles my clit, bringing me close yet again, but unable to push myself over the edge. My fingers aren't big enough or rough enough for what I need. Black has broken me because all I crave when I'm like this is his cock. Well, in my secret fantasies, it's his cock and Jonah's mouth. Or Jonah's cock stuffing my mouth full as Black rails my pussy so that I can't scream. Both of them holding me down together and riding me—one from below and one from above.

Need builds inside of me and I rub faster, my fingers bringing out pleasurable sparks.

I lick my lips, determined to come this time without him.

But then I hear the doorknob turn.

Like a flash, my hand retreats from my clit, and I scramble to my knees. Last time I wasn't on them when he came down and he threatened to fuck my ass with a dildo while he railed me up against a wall.

That image does dirty things to me, sending a pleasurable shiver down my spine as the door swings open. I can just imagine him shoving me face-first up against the wall and lubing that dildo in my slick—there's more than enough. Then I imagine him sliding the toy in my ass and his dick into my cunt at the same time, stretching me impossibly and filling me up.

Maybe I should get off my knees.

But he swore he wouldn't let me come for hours if I wasn't in position. And besides, it's too late. He's already coming down the stairs, those deep brown eyes scanning my naked form where I kneel, arms at my sides, facing him instead of head down like he ordered—because I just can't help myself. I study his expression, unsure if he looks pleased or not, but then he lets out a soft purr.

My body instantly responds to that noise. My back straightens and my nipples tighten and a warm, cinnamon-roll-like feeling cloaks me. It's soft and deliciously sweet as his purr drizzles through my ears. He hasn't purred for me since he brought me back here. Now that he's purring, I realize how much of a difference it makes. It feels like it vibrates my very bones.

That purr dapples my mind with sunlit sparkles and any image that pops into my head takes on a rose-colored hue. Black bending me over the couch again. Black holding down my throat and railing me hard. Black kissing me roughly, his beard scratching my cheeks. All those images suddenly become bright and sweet inside my head when they're combined with that purr—like the sound pours sugar onto them or something.

I close my eyes and just revel in this change and how different it feels from the fighting and fury that's been going on for the past forty-eight hours.

More slick gathers at my entrance and my lower belly grows hotter than the Sahara. It's not a furious sort of warmth for once, it's a soft fluffy kind—like a blanket just yanked from a dryer.

I'm stunned and relieved and so utterly confused.

With one little noise, all my anger at him has evaporated and somehow, I suddenly want to cry and to hold him and have him hold me close as we curse our wolves for putting us in this terrible position. That purr makes me feel like he's just as trapped as I am by this situation. I fucking sympathize.

Black reaches the bottom of the steps and I tremble in place, chewing on my lower lip as I stare up at his handsome face and the beard I've ridden to pleasure more times than I can count right now. But then I notice a bruise on his cheek. His collar is creased oddly.

Has he been fighting? Is he alright?

Neither Black nor Matthew have given me any news about the outside world the past few days, so I have no idea what's going on. The only thing I could wrangle out of Matthew was that Jonah's okay. But I don't know where he is, or if Black exiled him, or anything. All I know is that Black made this deal with me and I have to keep my part of the bargain so that Jonah's protected.

Of course, the heat throws everything into a strange, confused spiral—but I know that Jonah and I were attacked by Dark Nights. I figured that out between the cycles. But are the Dark Nights causing Black other issues? Is he being attacked? Is he safe?

If Black's being attacked, how the hell can he hope to protect Jonah?

It takes every bit of willpower I have to hold back and not launch myself at Black with a million questions—demanding answers.

But my bitch of a heat derails me when he ratchets up his purr. My lust sweeps back over me full force and knocks away my thoughts like they were weak little cobwebs. Urges overtake me. I want to leap on him like I did earlier today and wrap my legs around his back while I sink down on his cock without any damned foreplay … but I don't.

I don't want to argue anymore and defying him will surely cause a new quarrel to erupt.

Fighting and fucking constantly has worn me thin and his purr has melted my spine enough for me to realize that I've been riding on adrenaline for days.

I'm bone-tired, so much so that I knelt for him like he wants—letting him play the king. I crane my neck to stare up at his massive form, backlit by the light on the stairwell, which is the only light on in the basement right now.

I decide I'm not going to challenge Black anymore. I don't know if the purr is messing with my thoughts or I'm just exhausted by the emotional tug-of-war that keeps happening, but I'm surrendering to him. I'll kneel. I'll call him "king" or "alpha" or fucking "master" if he wants because this heat has dragged me through hell and back.

Black has me on my knees because he wants me to realize our power imbalance. He wants me to stare up at him. He wants me to have to beg for it—which I have done at least two of the times he's come down here. If he tells me to plead right now to put his big thick cock in me, I'll do it, I decide. Only because I don't know how much longer this heat will last and I can't keep doing what I've been doing.

I'll burn out. If I'm not there already. I feel used up and hollow

My eyes travel wearily up his blue-gray slacks. They're his third pair today since I ripped one pair and got slick all over another when I humped his leg in a wild frenzy earlier while he sucked my tits.

These new pants fit him well, everywhere but the crotch, where his dick is thick and straining to get free and fill me up again.

I eye his black leather belt and lick my lips, remembering how he spanked me—just once—with it. It shouldn't have been hot. The sight of it should make me furious.

But my body's a complete traitor and I find myself staring as his hands slowly reach for his waistband and he untucks his white collared shirt.

Anticipation makes my fingers twitch but between his purr and his slow methodical movements, I'm hypnotized. I can't tear my eyes from him as he stares down at me, his chest rumbling as he unbuttons his shirt with agonizing slowness. God, I can't believe I mocked that sound before, that low growl that seeps into my skin and makes my thighs tremble. It's perfect. It's somehow both hot and comforting at once. I clench my legs together as Black's pace slows down, his fingers fumbling over the buttons.

Dammit. Is he doing that on purpose so that I'll jump him? I open my mouth to offer to help but then close it again. I want to fuck but undressing him seems … intimate suddenly.

It's silly; I've seen him naked dozens of times now and we've fucked in at least a dozen positions but some damn buttons make me feel shy.

So many wires between my head and body are crossed right now that I've stopped even trying to reconcile them.

I cast my eyes away from Black and try to get a handle on my swirling emotions as he finishes with his shirt and tosses it aside.

It's better if I don't speak anyway. I'm sure I'd say something to set him off and then I'd have to fire back, and we'd ramp back up to our full-on hate sex.

I just want an orgasm this time.

The metallic click and swish of his belt coming off sends my eyes flying back to him, though, drawn like magnets.

I watch as he slides that strip of leather out of every loop before letting it drop to the carpet.

Why the hell does my heart drop when he lets it go?

He kicks off his shoes, shucks his pants and underwear in one go, and I'm stuck staring at his thickness as he peels off his socks.

Finally.

My breathing speeds up as anticipation kicks in and I wait for him to grab me and have his way with my body until we're both melting.

But he doesn't reach for me. He doesn't even stroke his cock. He just stands there, this looming presence casting a shadow over me. My eyes creep upward, over his muscled thighs and his perfectly sculpted torso, up to the long hair that drapes around his face, hiding his expression from me.

My eyebrows lift in question.

"Princess," Black's voice is barely more than a whisper and I lean toward him so I can hear his orders. What's it going to be this time? Is he going to strap my hands up with the belt? Is he going to take me on the stairs and bruise my knees? What?

I clench my fingers as I wait to see just what he has in store for me, and my belly is full of moths. Not butterflies. Ugly, nervous, swirling moths. That's what I decide they must be because feeling butterflies around an alpha like Black is stupid. I'm just a sex doll to him and nothing more. I'm a bad pack member to punish. I don't mean anything, so there's no fucking reason for there to be butterflies flittering through my stomach right now.

"Princess," he repeats, and I find his eyes in the darkness. They suck me under, and I spin in his gaze as I forget to breathe.

"You're such a fucking good girl," he tells me, leaning forward and dragging a hand through my hair.

His praise makes my chest swell and I fight not to lean into his calloused palm as he traces the side of my neck and down my shoulder. It's the first nice thing he's said to me all day. And I'm shocked by how good his approval feels. I find myself relaxing in his grip as he traces his hand down my side, skimming just the very edge of my breast before tracing back up to my shoulder. He caresses me again and I emit a soft sigh of delight before I realize it.

My eyes widen and when I glance up, his eyes glow gold and his fingers dig into my shoulder. He grips it, hard, as if he's fighting with himself. But then—he snaps and the alpha I know comes out. "Jonah won you tonight. So you get one night with your beta. But I'm going to watch."

I feel like a bowling pin that's just been toppled.

What?

My brain doesn't even have time to compute the words Black just spoke, which seem like the cruelest thing he's ever said to me. Because surely, they can't be true.

But they are. Suddenly, there at the top of the stairs is a familiar silhouette.

Tears spring from my eyes and race down my cheeks as I struggle to get off my knees and run toward him, tripping over my own feet in a delirious haze.

"Jonah!" I cry, disbelief and delight painting my tone a bright, happy Day-Glo pink.

His arms wrap around me gently and draw me close and it's like coming home. The soft puff of his breath near my ear, the brush of his finger pads dragging along my naked spine. I whimper in relief and delight and utter and complete heartbreak. Somehow, Jonah won tonight, but what I want is forever.

I nestle into him, soaking up the now, taking what I can get, my heat tempered by the vast ocean of longing inside of me that's tethered to Jonah the same way the moon tugs the tides. The pulse beneath his chest taps against my cheek and I'm suddenly shaking, my body swept into overload by his very presence.

"I love you," I whisper, clutching him tightly, turning my body slightly so that the zipper on his cargo shorts doesn't scratch my naked thighs.

"I love you too," he responds softly and surely. I don't understand how his throat doesn't scratch and why I don't hear utter heartbreak in his tone. His words should be weighted like stones right now because we know this moment is finite. If Black's making deals with my beta, then things with the Dark Nights must be worse than I thought.

I reach up and caress his neck, his cheek. He's got stubble. "I don't let you have this much facial hair," I comment, deciding that if Jonah's going to pretend everything is alright, then I'll do the same. I don't want to waste a moment of our time together worrying.

He smiles down at me softly as he says, "I'm sorry, Elena. No razor."

"Hmm. Well fix it," I tell him, swallowing hard as I glance to the side and see Black. It unnerves me to know that he's watching. He's sitting in the recliner with one hand on his dick and staring at us like this is a porno.

Fuck him. I turn around so that I'm not facing him because I don't want to deal with him. I'm halfway tempted to drag Jonah to the bedroom, but I know that Black will just follow.

I point to the nest and ask Jonah, "Spoon me?"

We snuggle into the comforter on our sides, and he presses up against my back. He's hard, I can feel his boner through his shorts. But Jonah's always patient. Never pushy, unlike someone else.

I revel in the simple feel of his chest against my back. He's shirtless and so we're skin-to-skin and I soak in his closeness. "Touch me," I whisper, closing my eyes, pretending that we're back in Jonah's apartment, struggling to be quiet because his roommate's having a study session in the living room.

Jonah's fingertips skate up and down my torso, circling my belly button, teasing me. Eventually, he moves his thigh off my hip and pulls my left leg on top of his, opening me up for his touch.

I sigh in contentment as he gently tickles my thighs with a touch so soft it's barely there. Normally, I'd be impatient. I'd snap at him and shove his hand where I wanted it. But tonight, I let him tease. I let him trace letters on my skin once I realize that's what he's doing. I carefully follow his finger and make out the word he spells on my low belly: mate.

"Mate," I breathe softly, so that only he can hear. And that single word brings my heat smashing back through me with the force of a hammer. I writhe, reaching back and grabbing Jonah around the neck and hissing, "I need you now!"

Immediately, his hand seeks out my heat and he strokes up and down my slit. His touch feels so good that I'm shaking within moments. "Don't you dare stop," I gasp.

"Don't you want my mouth?" he whispers.

"In a second," I say as I start to gyrate against his hand, increasing the friction so that little ribbons of pleasure shoot through me. I buck against his hand as a shadow crosses the room and Black moves to stand in front of the bar so that he has a better view. My eyelashes flutter and I pant as he stops five feet away from me, that massive dick of his rising up against his belly.

I stare at his dick and that knot as I come all over Jonah's fingers.

When I'm finished, I reach down and make Jonah pause. I turn my head to my beta and kiss him, getting a double thrill from his kiss and from the fact that I'm deliberately ignoring Black.

My desire to fight with the alpha has apparently revived.

I feel Jonah smile against my lips before he opens for me and lets me deepen our kiss.

My tongue plunders Jonah's mouth and I sink into the moment, just reveling in our connection, eventually forgetting where I am, though my skin still buzzes with the awareness that we have an audience.

That's always been a little fantasy of mine—one I've forced Jonah to live out with me again and again—I love the idea of being watched.

I've pushed the limits in past, picking out areas where Jonah and I might get caught. But now, it's a reality that's so filthy and hot that I can't believe it.

Black's watching and that knowledge makes goose-bumps crawl up my arms as I drag Jonah's hand up to my nipple.

I feel power tipping in my direction as I see Black's teeth clench at the sight Jonah and I are making and I find I love that I'm driving the alpha crazy with lust.

Jonah's slick-soaked fingers pluck at my bud as I suck his tongue into my mouth and then release it. I yank back from the kiss and say roughly, "Jonah, eat me out."

I watch his blond head dip between my legs. He tosses one up onto his shoulder and then, with a blazing blue glance up at me, he dives in. I revel in the feel of his tongue, the sense of control and confidence he always gives me. And then, my eyes dart over to the alpha in the room.

He's stroking his cock, his hand sliding slowly up and down as his eyes swoop up and down my body, over the live sex show we're putting on.

Jonah works me up methodically, swiping faster and harder, and I let my hands stretch overhead, arching my back, putting my breasts on shameless display for Black—who starts to breathe heavily.

He reaches behind himself with the hand that isn't on his cock and grips a barstool like he might snap it in half.

God yes. I love this. I love the knowledge that he's going wild, the fact that Jonah's following my every command. It makes me feel like some heathen goddess and I moan, delirious with lust as slick drips from my folds.

From the side of the room, Black speaks in a low, rumbling tone. "Why don't you grab his head and ride him like you mean it, little wolf?"

"Don't tell me what to do." I say. But underneath my smartass retort, my chest is filled with a soft sense of surprise. I fully expected Black to toss Jonah aside. But he's not. He's keeping him in the room—involved with me. Black's letting me connect with my mate.

"I asked, didn't tell," he counters and my heart stutters to realize he's right. He did ask.

I start to think Black's gone soft and sweet when he adds, "I'd like to see his face slathered in your girl cum."

Fuck. That's so hot that it sends a tremor down my spine, and I can't help myself.

I reach for Jonah's head and hold him in place as I start to buck my hips, increasing the friction, shifting his head slightly so that it's just where I need it.

"Yes," I pant. "*Yes.*"

I'm wanton and dirty and completely unable to stop myself as heat flushes my cheeks and my thoughts scatter like marbles and feeling eclipses all else.

Jonah's tongue pierces my opening, and his fingers dig into my ass as I drag my clit up and down along his face until there—I get the perfect build-up and I fuck him until I'm there—at that point where I wouldn't care if a hundred people walked in. I wouldn't care if someone filmed this. I'm too far gone. I'm oblivious to consequences, the future, everything but this moment and this sensation.

When the feeling recedes, I realize just how hard my thighs are clenched around Jonah's face. I release him apologetically. "Thank you," I breathe.

He licks his lips and uses the back of his arm to wipe his cheeks and chin. Then he grins at me.

"Dick. Now." I command, in the next breath, not wanting to let this high retreat too much.

I want to ride this rollercoaster again and fall over and over with him. My hips gyrate even as I wait for him and my eyelashes flutter. I move to pluck my own nipples and let my heat wash over me.

Jonah quickly shucks his shorts, eager to do my bidding and eager for his own release. His dick is hard and long—he's ready for me.

He kneels back down in front of me, positioning himself at my entrance when suddenly Black surges forward and knocks him aside.

"I can't do it," he growls, as he brings his own thick dick toward my weeping pussy. "I can't stand there and watch him fuck you."

"We had a deal."

"If I don't interfere right now, my fucking wolf will," Black retorts, and his eyes flash gold, proving his words true.

I see Black's entire body stiffen and he shudders before he squeezes his eyes shut as he fights back his wolf. I'm honestly shocked he lasted this long without interfering.

When his eyes open, they're deep brown—he's in control again—and his gaze solidly connects with mine as he leans forward over me.

His hot length travels over my slit and taps my clit. I turn to stare at Jonah as my body responds, hungry—desperate for cock. My pussy doesn't discriminate; in fact, I've grown to love the thick stretch of Black's dick.

But Jonah's over to the side, looking so heartbroken that I can't stand it.

I lean up and shove on Black's chest. The alpha growls and traps my hands, thinking I'm trying to shove him off me. But I can't. I won't. I need to fuck so desperately right now, and I get it—Black's wolf is just as utterly stupid as my own.

"You get my pussy, but Jonah gets my mouth. Fucking lay down now."

"Don't tell me what to do," Black counters, using his grip on my arms to flip me over. He releases me as I spin and land on my stomach. Then he yanks at my hips, dragging my knees backward against the carpet and giving me rug burn. The alpha in him can't help it.

"You asshole!"

"What was that? You want my dick in your ass?" Black counters. "Murky, get over here and stick your dick in her mouth before I have to find another way to shut her up."

Fuck. Damn.

Is Black inviting Jonah back to play? Does he realize how much I need Jonah's softness to contrast his harshness?

The alpha's hand reaches underneath me and gently strokes my breasts as he whispers in my ear, "You want two dicks at once, don't you? You've thought about this before, haven't you, princess? Getting stuffed full and ridden hard?"

I whimper as his palms tease my nipples, barely stimulating them, making me arch my back in an attempt to force his touch beyond a tease.

"Yeah, you like this, don't you," Black says softly, nuzzling my ear before gently biting down on my earlobe as Jonah walks around me to stand a foot in front of my face.

I see the solid, swollen length of his dick.

"Maybe I won't just let him fuck your mouth, Elena. Maybe I'll let him fuck your ass."

I inhale, so turned on by his dirty talk, and maybe even the fact that I fully believe he'd do what he threatens.

He chuckles. "Yeah, that's what I'm gonna do, little wolf. If you're not good, I'll lay down and have you sit on my cock, and then I'll let Murky fuck that pretty little ass of yours." One of his hands reaches back from my waist and squeezes my butt cheek before he smacks it lightly.

"Fuck," is all I can manage to say.

I moan as he slowly pushes the head of his dick into me and I look up at Jonah, who slowly steps closer to my face. "Jonah," I moan, as Black pulls out, smacks my clit with the head of his cock, and slowly pushes back in.

"Is that what you want, love?" Jonah asks softly.

"Fuck yes, give it to me," I say before opening my mouth for his dick.

And suddenly, they're both inside me. Black shoves roughly and deeply into my cunt as Jonah presses his length slowly and carefully into my mouth. It's just like I imagined earlier in the day—pure fucking magic. My vision grows spangled, full of glossy little metallic flecks of glitter as two men murmur how good I make them feel.

Black starts to pump faster, shoving me deeper onto Jonah's dick. But at the same time, Black is careful not to knot me right away. He's learned not to do that until our last round, because he likes a lot of positions for rounds one through four. So he strokes in and out shallowly, teasing me with his fingers as I use my tongue to tease the underside of Jonah's dick.

My body belongs to Black, and Jonah's belongs to me.

Just having that thought makes my thighs start to quiver.

"You aren't allowed to come yet, little wolf," Black says. "Not unless you want Murky to take this sweet ass."

I pull off of Jonah and glare up at him, as if the very thought of him inside my ass is offensive, instead of exactly what I want. "You don't get to come until I get to come," I snarl.

Jonah nods.

Behind me, Black laughs and smacks my ass again. "You're a mean little mistress, aren't you, princess? That's fucking hot as hell." He leans down a little so that one of his hands can reach underneath me and stroke my clit as I move forward and swallow up Jonah again.

I try to focus on keeping a rhythm, on what my tongue is doing to Jonah, on the fact that he can't stop a little precum from oozing from his tip.

But Black won't let me escape him. He's a hunter by nature and a torturer by choice. He won't give up his pursuit and once he catches his prey, he's going to ensure the ending is long, drawn-out, and utterly inevitable.

Black's thumb and forefinger start to gently tug my swollen clit until I'm choking on Jonah's cock, unable to focus, unable to do anything as flashing lights swirl inside my body and my system screams out that a monster orgasm is approaching.

It creeps forward as shivers wrack my body and my breathing grows short and frantic. Black starts to fuck me at an angle, driving slightly to the left, where he knows his dick will drag against my g-spot. The sensation surrounds me and my vision flickers. When the orgasm grabs hold of me, I scream around Jonah's cock, bucking wildly, unable to hold back and uncaring that I can't.

I come with two cocks inside of me. And it's the rawest, most deliciously dirty thing I've ever done.

When I emerge from my daze, I realize that Jonah's removed his dick from my mouth.

Black slips from my pussy and then I'm being turned around. All I can do is blink like a doll as I see what's going on but don't really process it. Black lies back on the comforter of my makeshift nest and then pulls me forward so that I straddle him.

Black's grin is wild and darkly appealing as he says, "Naughty girl. Time for your punishment."

17

BLACK

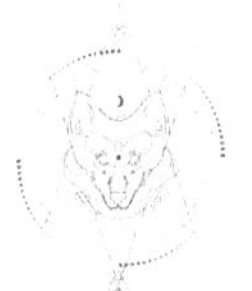

I'VE BEEN DOWN SOUTH in Woodsville, Alabama for two days of bullshit because Elena's heat broke after an intense night of threesome sex and my wolf was finally able to leave.

I'd never really imagined a threesome—definitely not with another guy—but she was wild and wanton.

She loved it when I dragged her up to her real nest in the attic and fucked her on the swing while Murky watched.

She loved when I was worn out enough that she got to ride his dick—and I discovered I didn't mind.

She took us both at the same time twice in that little attic room, until the space was a bouquet of sweat and sex.

Part of me is disappointed her heat broke because she'd collapsed with a contented sigh in between the two of us and I'd fallen asleep spooning her while she held hands with Jonah. I've never slept as soundly as I did that night—probably because I've never had such an intense marathon session before. My little wolf had been a completely feral princess.

I lick my lips at the memory of her gaping pussy dripping with my cum before snapping my attention back to the present and trying to focus on what the useless lawyer in front of me is saying. He's explaining why the asshole bankers I went to yesterday still haven't sorted out "Stone's estate."

The lawyer is an old man fighting baldness by plastering strips of long hair across his bare head with gel rather than just shave the whole thing. He looks like a molting zebra this way, and it's distracting as hell. He moves a stack of papers with his pudgy fingers nervously. Tim Hudgens—pack name, Barney Fife—is a beta if I ever saw one.

Beside me, one of my elites, Dewey Decimal, leans forward. A guy with dark brown hair and a Clark Kent sort of look, he's not your typical alpha. He's a book-smart guy who had to train like fuck once his wolf came in so he could fight his way into the lowest rung of the elites. At thirty, it took him over a decade to get there. He's only been one of my inner-circle for about a year. But he's pretty damned useful with legal crap.

"You're telling me that Stone didn't include a challenge clause in his will?" Dewey asks skeptically.

The fan overhead in this house-converted-to an office is the only sound in the room for a minute. It's off-center whir and the clack of its pull strings fill my ears as the Dark Night turned Lobo in front of me searches his massive legalese vocabulary for a lie. "We were not given one."

Barney starts sweating, and I could blame it on the Alabama heat, but I don't. I take full credit as I stand up and tower over the tiny-dicked motherfucker whose wife probably can't tell the difference between his cock and a pretzel stick. I lean over the desk, placing my hands on either side of his, getting right in his face.

"Oh, you weren't given one? How mightily convenient." I mock Barney's accent. "Luckily, all alphas have to submit a challenge clause to the others when they become the leader of their pack. If they die in an official fight against another alpha, their pack is absorbed into his."

I can see the lawyer's pulse throb in his neck as he tries to resist the urge to wheel his little office chair away from me.

"Dewey, pull up my online server, please. Search Stone's file. Legal documents." I stay put, enjoying the way the little southern man squirms.

Less than a minute later, Dewey plops a tablet on the desk, the document pulled up on it, screen screaming out that this lawyer is a fucking bottom-feeding liar.

Barney's hands shakily reach for the tablet and his face grows pale.

"Now, I'm going to forgive you this once," I tell him. "Because I'm going to assume Stone didn't give you what you need. But if you don't get this cleared up in say ..." I stand up and glance at my watch. "Oh, let's give it three hours. If you don't get this fixed by then, you won't like what happens to you."

The lawyer swallows. But then he shakes his head. His voice comes out low and strained as he says, "Thomas won't let me."

That does it. The civility inside me snaps and my wolf rises to the surface. I can feel my canines elongate though I stop my wolf from emerging any more than that. He growls at me for trying to control him. He wants to grab the neck of this stupid fucking lawyer in his teeth and shake a little, not enough to kill, but enough to ensure this slimy little turd knows who is in charge.

Instead of doing that, I lean forward so that my lips are right next to his ear and say, "Is Thomas your alpha?"

"You don't understand. Thomas is ... broken."

"That's not what I fucking asked." With a single blow, I sweep the papers and laptop off this fucker's desk. I would have swept away Dewey's tablet too, but the little worm in front of me has it clutched in his hands, holding it up like a shield. My eyes burn and I can feel them start to shift to wolf eyes—my animal is furious, snarling. I'm not far behind. Pack law is clear: Stone's wolves and all their assets belong to me now. But these stupid motherfuckers are tossing obstacles right and left because of some goddamned little princeling who thinks he should just inherit daddy's throne.

Barney shows me his neck and casts his eyes down. His voice comes out soft and breathy as he admits, "He won't just kill me. He'll torture my family first. I ... I have three sons."

I force my wolf to pull back as I straighten up because I can smell the sour fear on this guy. He's serious.

I snarl as I turn to Dewey, angry and frustrated at how Dark Night alphas have terrorized their betas. "Why don't you supervise this guy? Give him some motivation while Warcraft and I go check out their old pack house."

Dewey nods solemnly.

I turn back to Barney, who looks like he's about to puke all over his oak desk. "Thomas won't touch you. You and your family will fly back on the plane with me tomorrow. Finish this shit and pack up." I put my alpha tone into the order and Barney gives a trembling nod. I make eye contact with Dewey one last time, wishing we were in wolf form so I could tell him to play bodyguard via the pack link, but he gives me a chin nod that says he understands, so I leave it at that.

I jerk my head toward another of my elites. Warcraft, my third, follows me out, his polished shoes tapping a soothing rhythm on the wooden floor as we exit.

"You ready?"

He's going to assess the damage to the pack house and guesstimate what it would cost to rebuild. We agreed on the plane ride that making that many shifters travel all the way to Colorado for howls wouldn't work out. So, instead, I'll be out here in Alabama every Friday and Saturday, holding howls and taking care of business—once we can round up another batch of elites not loyal to the Stone fucks who can manage day-to-day operations during the week.

Warcraft works on his laptop as the driver we hired takes us half an hour out of town into a pretty area overgrown by trees I don't know the names of—a perfect spot for wolves to run. We end up on a dirt road that kicks up enough dust to coat the car in a thin layer before we finally reach a wide expanse that used to be the heart of the pack—now no more than a pile of charred bones.

I tour the smoking remains of the pack house—an old, once-beautifully mint-green antebellum mansion—as cicadas screech in the background, and northern cardinals *cheep*. The trees sag in the heat and I feel like doing the same, though I don't because we come across a few beta wolves cleaning up the mess, shoveling burnt rubble into the back of a truck to haul off.

Warcraft and I greet them and exchange Southern pleasantries, which means we spend at least a good ten minutes on small talk before I'm free to roam around.

"Those dudes aren't so bad," Warcraft comments.

"Most aren't."

"It's fucking hot as a cunt out here," he moans.

"Not nearly as fun as one though," I retort.

He chuckles and we separate to scan the house from opposite sides. I look over the still-smoking remains of the former Dark Night pack house. Based on what the betas told us, it used to be a three-story home. The bits of wall that are left look like burnt toast. The dirt that I walk through is speckled black and gray with ash, and more of it swirls through the air, tempting me to cough.

Right in front of the steps, I find a pile of rocks, just like the markers that human hikers leave in the woods to Hansel-and-Gretel their way out. Wolves don't need markers. We have noses. I wonder why it's there. Intuition tingling, I squat and pick up the top of the pile, a light brown limestone. I raise it to my nose and sniff.

I'm hit by the smell of blood, which normally, I'd scent straight away. The ash out here is covering the smell. I turn the rock over to see a brown smear on the underside, dried blood forming a capital letter *I* on it. I flip over the rest of the rocks, but nothing is on any of them.

Warcraft strolls over, squinting in the afternoon sun. "Ready to go?"

I stand up and slide the rock into the pocket of my suit jacket. "Yup." I don't tell him about the rock pile, because I have a feeling that Thomas Stone left them. Stone left me a stone. Yes, now I'm sure of it. The son of the former alpha who tried to shoot me up in a Kansas field is taunting me in a sick and psychotic way.

I'm not about to drag my elites into that; I fight my own battles. Especially those against spoiled southern shifters who think they can coast on their daddy's reputation and their own proclivity for being an asshole. My fingers trace over the stone in my pocket. Maybe, if I get lucky this trip, I'll sniff him out. If so, I'll use this little present he gave me to bash his skull in.

Trying to kill me? Forgivable. That's alpha nature.

Trying to scare me? My fingers tighten on the edges of the rock. Now, *that* is unacceptable.

I CALL ELENA THAT NIGHT, ONCE I'M BACK IN MY HOTEL room after three separate meetings with betas to go over the main pack laws for the Lobos—the laws that will now guide their lives. The meetings had been held in an old gymnasium, one of those turn-of-the-century brick school buildings that have been abandoned and swallowed up by strip mall merchants. Every space but the gym has been re-purposed.

Most of the betas at the meetings had been … betas. They'd ducked their heads and shown their necks, their eyes had skimmed over the list Dewey Decimal had given them. They'd nodded along as I spewed out a political spiel I'd written on the plane ride over about being so happy to be here and making things better than ever before.. I'd repeated my speech three times because there were quite a few more Dark Night betas than could fit into the gym itself.

After that had come meetings with alphas in smaller groups because filling a gym full of alphas was begging for a fight. But it had taken a long time and more glasses of sweet tea than I'd wanted to count before we were done. Predictably, not a single elite had shown. I wasn't certain if that meant they were working with Thomas the punk or if they just expected to have to fight to the death because that's how Stone ran things.

That's something to untangle tomorrow though.

Now, I just want to talk to my mate. I lean back against the wooden headboard and dial the number that I had Matthew program into my phone the day I met her and realized she was pack.

The phone rings. And rings. And rings again before I remember that Elena ditched her phone when she tried to run. That puts a sour taste in my mouth, one nearly as bad as a broken Tylenol capsule. I don't want to dwell on that, so I focus on alternative people to call instead.

I video call Matthew.

He answers on the fifth ring with a yawn. "Yes, Alpha Maddox?" His gray hair is ruffled and his eyes squint like he just turned on the light. What time is it? I glance over at the digital clock on the nightstand and realize that it's three in the morning my time, which means it's probably two for them.

"Sorry, I didn't realize the time," I say.

Matthew stares at me with dry amusement. "I'm well aware of the fact that you keep unusual hours. Is there anything I can help you with?"

I grind my teeth, suddenly feeling stupid. "I just … wanted to check on Elena."

Matthew gives a small smile then, his expression relaxing. "Well, her cooking hasn't improved, but her attitude is slowly getting better."

I nod stiffly, unable to force out the words for what I really want. My wolf appears in my line of sight, pacing at the edge of the bed. Hearing about Elena isn't quite what he or I expected. I'd intended to have Matthew bring the phone to her. But I didn't realize it was so late. I didn't realize that everyone else was sleeping.

By the time I focus back on Matthew's face on the screen of my phone, I realize his head is bobbing in the picture. He's moving.

"Matthew—"

"I'm bringing her the phone, Alpha Maddox."

A grin touches the edges of my lips. "She's going to be pissed at you for waking her up," I say, though I can't help the way my chest gives a little leap at the thought of seeing her.

"No. She'll be pissed at you for asking to see her."

"Technically—"

"We both know that you were about to," Matthew retorts drolly. "Besides, don't tell me that an alpha such as yourself is scared of a grumpy omega."

"You're lucky you're a glimmer."

Matthew just chuckles and knocks on the door of the attic. The sound travels through the phone and his body bobs in the frame. He opens the door and calls out up the steps, "I hope nobody's naked because Alpha Maddox is calling."

"Why would anyone be naked?" I growl, sitting straight up. That better be a goddamned joke.

Matthew turns on a side lamp using a switch near the door, crosses the room, hand shaking as he laughs and points the screen at his belly instead of his face. The fucker doesn't have the decency to flip the camera to the other side of the phone so I can see the room and find out whether or not Elena is in there sleeping naked next to that beta. My wolf gives a low growl, and while I don't voice it aloud, I'm in full agreement with him.

Murky better not have his beta paws all over our mate. Not unless we're ordering him to touch her.

Matthew hands the phone to Elena, whose hair is adorably rumpled and who looks pissed as fuck to be woken up. "What?" she barks.

"Are you naked?" I jump right to interrogation. That wasn't why I'd originally called, I'd just wanted to hear her voice, but Matthew's made me paranoid now—the fucker.

"No!" She sounds offended.

"Show me," I command.

That's when Murky's face pops into the side screen. He frowns at me, but the sight of him next to her just amplifies my wolf's need for control and dominance. He hates the fact that we left her behind even though I left her with Pluto because it was far safer for Elena to stay at home surrounded by our pack than down here with a wild wolf like Thomas Stone out for vengeance. I can handle him. My omega ... will never have to.

"You are such an ass," Elena hisses at me. But she pulls her hand away from her body so that I can see she's wearing a t-shirt. One of Murky's shirts.

A growl does erupt from me then. Women wear guy's shirts after they've— "Show me your pussy!"

"Alpha Maddox," Matthew's voice comes from off-screen.

"Leave, Matthew."

"But, that's my phone—"

"Buy a new one."

I hear Matthew's footsteps retreat and the attic door shut. My screen is facing Elena's chest, all I can see is the blue panel of fabric as I hear her and Murky arguing in whispered tones.

"Elena, you swore to do whatever I said," I tell her. I'm fully aware that I'm being an asshole, but the idea that she's fucking Murky while I'm gone makes me want to break every last thing in this room. I won't be able to sleep until I know.

The phone is wrenched out of her hand, and I see Murky's face. "She's a little grumpy tonight, Alpha Maddox. She's not good when people wake her. Just give her a minute."

"Motherfucker," I hear her curse me under her breath. But then I see the screen flip and the view change so that I'm looking at the sheets of the bed and the rises that make up their legs.

The beta—Jonah—I correct myself, is doing what I said.

I see Jonah's hand reach down and pull at the patterned sheets, dragging them down. Elena's knees come into view. They're locked tightly together, and her hands are tugging that shirt as far down as she can get it.

"Elena—" I start to warn her. She's taking too goddamned long. If she's fucked him, I'm gonna spank her ass so hard—

"You know you want to show Black your pretty pussy," Jonah speaks over me in a coaxing tone. It would annoy me if I didn't recognize the fact that he's trying to help. He's on my side. I forbade him to fuck her, so he's probably just as desperate as I am to see that snatch. He'd better be.

"I don't," Elena responds.

"You like the idea of people seeing you and staring at you. That's what he wants to do. He wants to jerk off to the sight of that sweet slit and remember how it felt to be inside of you." I see Elena's chest rise and fall more rapidly.

She's getting turned on.

I hadn't meant for things to go sideways like this, but the idea that she's getting worked up over me staring at her makes me start to get a little hard.

Jonah doesn't reach for her or pry her legs apart like I would have. He just keeps talking. "Remember how much he stretched you? Remember how I was able to get four fingers in you after that? And your sweet cunt felt so good and hot on my fingers."

Elena's death grip on Jonah's shirt loosens and it slides a few inches up her thighs, exposing her creamy skin.

"Yeah, you like the idea of both of us staring between your legs, don't you?" Jonah's voice gets lower, and Elena's knees start to part and fuck me—I'm hard as a diamond.

"You like being a dirty girl, Elena?" I ask.

At first, her knees stiffen, but then Jonah chimes in. "She likes it. She likes to fuck near windows. Outside. Elena likes knowing that her tight body might drive some random guy wild."

My wolf snarls internally at the fact that he knows things about her that I don't—but I swallow the sound because his possessiveness does not outrank the fact that our little mate's knees are slowly parting. Goddammit—I want to order Jonah to turn on more lights in the room so I can see better but Elena's already being so damn skittish, and I don't want her to retreat again.

"You touch yourself thinking about people watching you, don't you? Didn't you tell me that once?" Jonah whispers.

"Jonah!" Elena scolds, embarrassed.

"You want me to fuck you up against windows, princess?" I ask, encouraging her. No way I'm going to share the sight of my omega's body with anyone else. But if the thought gets her hot, then I'll talk about it all damn night. "Or what about on the balcony? You want to let your tits hang over the edge while I fuck you and Jonah stares up at you?"

Her knees slide farther apart. Oh, she likes that.

The camera dives between her lithe, muscular legs and all I can see for a moment is shadow. Then Jonah must flick on the phone flashlight because it gets bright and then I can see it. She isn't wearing panties and she's bare. I see all of her. I drink in the sight as I reach down into my boxers and fist my cock.

"Have you been a good girl, princess?"

"I'm not a dog!" she retorts.

"I think he just wants to know if you've been dirty," Jonah mediates.

"I haven't touched myself," she admits bitterly.

"Good. But I want you to right now."

I lift my hips and slide down my boxers so that I can grip myself more easily. And then, with Jonah and I both whispering dirty words at her, I watch my mate touch her pussy until she's trembling. Her folds are gleaming and her clit so swollen. I want to suck on it so badly that I grind my teeth together.

"Don't come!" I warn her. "Not yet."

"You're a dick."

"Yes. I am. Jonah, start jerking off. I want you to come all over her stomach. I want to see it. Elena, yank that shirt up over your head so I can see your tits. Now!" I order them.

I grin when the camera shifts clumsily as they both hurry to comply, too turned on to argue. Maybe I just need to keep my omega in a constant state of arousal to keep her from mouthing off. That doesn't sound like such a bad idea.

Soon, I get a glimpse of Elena from above, her creamy breasts exposed, her nipples hard. One hand twists a nipple while her other hand circles her clit. I see Jonah's dick slide into the screen once or twice, but my eyes are focused on Elena's body as I stroke my own cock. I want to time my orgasm with hers.

It means I wait, somewhat agonizingly, because I'm furious that I'm not there to actually touch her, so I keep ordering everyone to stop. Once. Twice. On the third time, Elena moans and isn't able to pull back.

"Jonah, you'd better come!" I tell him as I erupt onto the hotel sheets.

God-fucking-damn.

I used to mock phone sex. But that … that was hot. Not as hot as sliding inside my mate, but it will do. I yawn and kick the sheets off the bed. It's too hot in Alabama anyway. Who needs sheets? I fix my boxers and sit back against the headrest.

"Give Elena the phone," I tell Jonah.

When he does, I get a little thrill from seeing her post-orgasm dazed look, instead of the sour one she normally gives me.

"Prop the phone up on the pillow next to you so I can watch you while you sleep."

She rolls her eyes and says, "What? Don't have a nanny cam installed in here?"

"Nope. But now that you've given me the idea …"

She props me up against a fuzzy pink pillow that invades the right side of the screen.

"Now go to sleep."

"I haven't gotten to clean up."

"Jonah, go get a rag and clean her up. Elena, lie down."

"Yes, sir, evil overlord, sir." She mocks.

But then she gives me a little smile that shows she's teasing. And I'll be damned if that doesn't squeeze my heart a bit.

She yawns and lays back down. I recline on my back, propping the phone up on my abs, just staring at her.

She blinks heavily back at me as all sorts of unspoken emotions drift back and forth between us.

Jonah cleans her up, but then he lays down and his breathing grows steady long before hers does.

Is she fighting sleep just like I am? Trying to hold onto this moment a little bit longer?

When my eyelids feel like anvils, I murmur, "Go to sleep."

My mate tucks a hand underneath her cheek and closes her eyes compliantly. She looks like an angel, and her peaceful expression is the last thing I see before I peacefully fall asleep.

I wake up sweating with a start in the middle of the night. I furrow my brow, wondering what the hell is wrong as I sit up in bed. Maybe the damned A.C. broke. That would be the logical explanation. But my intuition tingles and the hair on the back of my neck stands up. I don't really think that's it.

My wolf comes into view, hackles up. He doesn't think we woke for no reason either.

My eyes dart around as I lean forward on the bed and scan my hotel room, sweating profusely and scenting something different—lilac? Do they have an air freshener in here?

Or...is someone in here? It doesn't smell like a wolf's scent—it's too manufactured. I glance over at the windows, but they're closed. I look over at the door and the stupid little chain is still attached.

But my nerves don't settle, so I sit up and look around anyway, glancing at the clock. It's 4:30 and all looks quiet on the western front. But looks can be deceiving. I pick up the rock on the table and realize that one of the drawers in my dresser is cracked open.

I didn't leave it that way.

I let instinct guide me and I shift to monster form, sprouting up so tall that my wolf-head nearly brushes the ceiling. I turn toward the only spots someone could hide in a hotel room: the bathroom and the closet. My heart dashes ahead of my feet, pounding like a hammer driving in a nail. I smash open the bathroom door, letting it smack into the wall. Nothing. No one.

I turn to the closet, which is a small affair with one of those sliding doors. I raise the claw clutching the rock, reading to bash in someone's skull. Then I reach out slowly and drag the door back.

Nothing.

Fuck! I want to roar—but this is a human hotel and animal sounds will get me kicked out.

I look back over at the bed and that's when I realize … my phone is gone. I fell asleep with my phone on my stomach.

That sends a shiver up my spine, especially when I scent a human underneath the overpowering flowery smell that's pervading my room.

In werewolf form, I lurch around the bed and my claws clumsily sift through the sheets I tossed on the floor. Where's my phone? Did someone come in here while I slept and take it? Even though I scent a human, this bullshit reeks of Thomas.

I should shift back to human form to make my search easier, but instinct is telling me there's danger, so I don't. If Thomas is involved, I don't want to be caught in human form. Adrenaline rattles my veins as I claw the sheets to ribbons, searching. I don't find it. I stare around the room in frustration, but the only other thing amiss is that drawer. That person could have bumped it when they came in. Or … maybe they cracked it open on purpose.

I stride over to the dresser, heading straight for that drawer.

When I yank it out, I find my phone inside. Next to it are four stones and a potpourri satchel—that's what

I've been smelling. I flip the stones over one by one to reveal the letters *W-I-L-L.*

I howl in fury. I can't stop it. I tremble, wanting to destroy things.

He had someone break in here while I was fucking *sleeping*—

But Stone wants me unhinged. He wants me furious.

My wolf rears back, wanting to howl at the moon goddess and go hunting. I tell him no and force a shift back to human as I grab my phone.

An alpha on a rampage makes mistakes.

I haven't lived this long by going on rampages.

I swipe to unlock my phone and see the background's changed to a photo of Thomas's smiling face.

This psycho is asking for war. Well—he's got it.

18

ELENA

SOMETHING'S FUCKING wrong with me. My heat is over, but I still keep thinking about Black. That last night of the heat—with him and Jonah together—that was literally the hottest thing I've ever experienced. Not only that, but Black, even though he was dominating … was actually a little bit … I don't even know … human? Likable? Mischievous? Underneath that dark-as-pitch persona, he came across as a little bit playful. He ordered me around but there wasn't a sense of expectation with it; his orders felt more like dares that night. Instead of hating him for them, I'd felt a gleaming bit of pride at each one I completed … especially when it made him purr. Moon goddess, that purr.

It almost felt like we formed some kind of connection that night. But that can't be right. He hates me and Jonah. And everything about him and his insane life is ruled by shifter instincts, which I firmly and fiercely loathe.

That phone call last night … Black was back to his bossy, thoughtless self, calling at an ungodly hour and waking us all up for his convenience. Although, the fact that he called Jonah by name like he recognized him as a human being … no, I'm overthinking things. Names don't mean anything. Neither did the fact that he wanted to watch me sleep. *Creepy, Elena. Creepy. Not cute.* The sad thing is I have to argue with myself about that because this foolish part of me really does think it was adorable.

It's all just wishful thinking. My mind is tricking me, trying to justify all the filthy sex we had by associating it with emotions. That has to be it.

Oh! I know! It's Stockholm Syndrome, I tell myself as I stretch, climb out of bed, and yank off my nightshirt—aka Jonah's t-shirt—in the early morning light. I'm up in the attic room in my nest. I've slept here for three nights now, and I have to say it's glorious. It's cozy and warm but not hot, and there's a pillow to squeeze for every mood I'm in. Black didn't force me to return to the basement, even though I was expecting it.

He left me up here and let me wear clothes again. I haven't had to crawl around naked. I still have to cook shit every day, though honestly, I've found that better than sitting around. I just don't understand why he's keeping me under house arrest but being so damned decent about it.

Ugh, there I go again with prisoner mentality. Well, it's been worse than this, so this isn't actually so bad. Hello, Elena, he hasn't let you go back to school! You're off the track team! You still haven't spoken to your mother. That last one isn't much of an argument though, because I'm certain she's heard about what happened through the shifter gossip chain. She's probably preening to be associated with the head alpha now.

Still. I don't understand Black at all.

I glance across the room at my beta, whose back muscles gleam golden in the light drifting in from the window. My eyes catch on his mate mark and my heart gives a possessive throb just before he yanks a white shirt over his head. I'm still mystified by the fact that Alpha Black has let me sleep up here with Jonah since that night, especially since the big brute flew out of town the second my heat broke to deal with Dark Night shit.

Of course, he gave us strict orders before he left.

He'd grabbed Jonah by the shirt collar and said, "If you put your dick in her while I'm gone, you lose it." His alpha tone had filled the room with vibrations that sank all the way to my toes.

Jonah had nodded fiercely, his head whipping up and down so quickly that I'd thought he might hurt his neck. He hasn't done more than cuddle me since even though I've slept nude underneath his t-shirts each night trying to tempt him by rubbing my bare legs against his. Jonah hasn't buckled.

But then last night's phone call threw everything for a loop. Jonah came all over my stomach. Does that mean the order still stands? Or are we allowed to play now? Or is Black just trying to test us?

Bastard pack alpha, I mentally curse Black as I grab a lacy orange bra and panty set. But something is wrong with it, even though it's brand new. The panties are all wadded up and gross, like someone spilled glue on them. Or something else … "Jonah?" I ask, turning to him topless, the lacy orange tangle dangling from my fingers, front and back panels stuck together. "Did you do this?" He's been up here since Black dragged us back to the Lobos, so my options are either him or Matthew. I really fucking hope this is Jonah-cum.

He glances over at the panties and then gives an embarrassed shrug. "Something for you to remember me by if you know ..."

I roll my eyes. "Super romantic."

"You hate romantic."

"True. Also hate ruined underwear." I wad it up and throw it at him.

He catches it easily. "Hey! Can't you at least return the favor before you give them to me?"

I glare at him. "Maybe if you'd help me come, I would."

He holds up his hands, the panties dangling from his middle finger. "First off, I totally helped you come last night. You're welcome. Secondly, if you're talking about right now, without him, *no way*. Now that I don't think Black is actually gonna kill me, I'd rather not die."

I flash him an irritated look but the wound that's been scarring over inside my chest the last few days rips open at his words—the very thought of Jonah dying cuts into me and leaves a jagged sort of pain that makes it hard to breathe. I stop arguing, even playfully, because I can't handle the thought. I'd rather Jonah not die either. I don't want him to die *ever*.

That brings all the fear right back up into my throat, irritating it like bile. My stomach lurches because this shit with Black still isn't ironed out. We fucked—me smashed between the two of them like a goddamned pincushion that night—and I loved it. Then last night was ... last night was ... I circle right back to the dilemma I woke up with, this strange, confused emptiness, almost like I'm longing for Black to come home.

I find a set of navy-blue panties that hasn't been defiled and slide them on, pairing them with the orange bra as I finally voice the worries that have been stewing in my stomach for the past few days. "Jonah, what do you think he's doing with us? Is this some kind of game?"

Jonah sighs. "No." He stops buttoning up the coveralls he's putting on so that he can go outside and work on cars for free again. "I don't know what it is. I talked to my mom about it yesterday—"

"Wait. He let you see your parents?" I ask, shocked rage flaring up across my cheeks. I mean—I don't really want to talk to my mother, I can only imagine how annoying her reaction to my wolf and Black's mate mark will be. And I definitely don't want to face her knowing she outranks me right now. That riles me up. But the fact that I wasn't even offered the opportunity to contact her rubs me the wrong way. The fact that he offered it to Jonah also riles me up. Because why the hell would Black do something nice like that? It just doesn't compute.

"Hey, I can see what you're thinking. It's not that. I told Matthew they'd be worried, and he let me call. It wasn't strictly forbidden so, technically, it's not against the rules."

I let out a sigh and some of the tension filling my shoulders escapes. Jonah and Matthew went behind Black's back. That makes so much more sense than the idea that Black would *let* Jonah do anything. "I don't think Black will give a shit that he *technically* didn't prohibit it—he's going to be pissed."

"Matthew's a glimmer, so at least Black can't off him." He shrugs. "You can always ask him to let you talk to your mom if you want."

I shake my head. "No thanks." Even though I still lived at home before this mess, it isn't like Mom and I are besties. I avoided her more than I saw her. Now, avoiding her is just a little easier.

Jonah walks closer and slides his hands down my arms, grabbing onto my hands and then resting my palms gently on top of his. "Honestly? I think Black's as confused about this whole mate thing as you are."

I give him a sarcastic 'yeah right' head tilt, the same one actresses who play mothers on television use all over the world. "He's *not* confused."

"He is. I think he feels something for you," Jonah lifts my hands up to his heart. "I think you might feel something too, Elena."

I pull away from Jonah then, outrage sparking through me. "He feels possessive of *his toys*." I walk off, shaking a shiver from my spine at the idea that I might feel something too. That's not true. Anything I feel is a result of this warped little game he's playing with me. Black's pulling my strings and that isn't the same as real emotions. It isn't the same at all. "I feel nothing for that bastard."

Jonah shakes his head and when I glance back at him, his expression is solemnly disbelieving. "He could have been so much worse to both of us. We both know I should be dead right now. But you marked me. And killing me would—"

"I'd never forgive him," I growl.

"Exactly."

"Don't make him into a good guy because he's not as much of an asshole as we expected!" I retort angrily, turning from Jonah and striding over toward the dresser on the right-hand side of the room. I viciously yank open one of the drawers. There are a limited number of clothes in this room, most of them slutty costumes. But I have found a couple skirts and crop tops I can live with. I've been too proud to ask Matthew about other clothes. Or not even proud. I just literally did not think that was an option for prisoners. I would never have thought about asking Matthew for permission to call my mother. Who asks the prison guard for help?

Jonah, that's who.

Little Mr. Brightside. Little Mr. Delusional. Little Mr. Let-Me-Tell-You-How-You- Feel.

I blow out a breath, realizing I'm getting riled up about this. I force myself to close my eyes and just calm down for a moment. None of this is Jonah's fault. My sweet beta has done nothing but help me. "Sorry," I apologize and then nearly tear up, a sob clogging my throat before I'm able to swallow it down.

I just … I just don't know how to handle everything I'm feeling right now. I don't want to miss Black. I don't want him here barking orders at me. At least, the human part of me doesn't. But maybe the omega part of me has infiltrated my head because my throat tightens at the knowledge that Black flew off into dangerous territory—surrounded by shifters who hate him—but he left me behind. And he let me and Jonah be together.

Gah.

It's like a whirlpool. I keep getting sucked under into this twisting spiral of feelings that make no sense. They spin me until I can't breathe and I feel like I'm about to drown. A lone tear escapes as I toss on a red plaid skirt that makes me look like a naughty schoolgirl. Then I swipe away the stupid teardrop, annoyed with myself. I don't cry over alphas. I swore to myself I never would.

"Don't be sorry. This is confusing as fuck," Jonah replies with a sigh as he grabs a pair of work boots. I glance over as he sits down on a sex bench to lace them up and I have to shove back images of Black bending me over the bench and spanking my ass while Jonah knelt in front, kneading my breasts and sucking on my nipples.

Dammit.

Maybe that's why Black's letting me stay up here. He's trying to fuck with my mind. He knows the scent of all our sex will keep my brain muddled and my wolf instincts will overpower my common sense.

That has to be it. It has to be. Well, fuck him. Maybe I'll drag Jonah into a spare room tonight—since apparently Matthew is handing out prisoner favors like lollipops. A spare room without all these stupid scents will let me sleep with a clear head and see things as they really are.

I come to that conclusion and the frenzied little tornado inside my stomach stops swirling. Life starts to make sense again. Because Black is a total and complete asshole and anything else just doesn't make sense.

I CRACK MY NECK IN BLACK'S MASSIVE MARBLE kitchen, a black apron tied around my waist. I work at the island in the middle of the huge room, with dark cabinets and marble everything surrounding me. Amber-colored afternoon sunlight filters into the room and I curse as I nearly cut my finger.

"Dammit!"

"You alright?" Matthew asks from his spot beside me. He has perfect posture, a clean white apron over his tuxedo suit, and cuts everything absolutely evenly.

I glance over at his perfectly sliced onions, which didn't make him cry at all. "I retract every good thing I've ever thought about you."

He chuckles. "Why is that?"

"Because right now it's annoying how good you are at that."

"Practice makes perfect, Luna," the butler responds with pedantic inflection.

"Oh, go join an after-school special. And I'm not your luna. You aren't even a Lobo."

"Honorary member."

"Says who?"

"Gave myself the title. Got it printed up and put it on my office door to see if he'd notice. Alpha Maddox can sometimes be a bit slow about that sort of thing."

I laugh and then turn back to the green peppers I'm cutting up. "Has he seen it yet?" I admire Matthew's ballsy approach to his boss. I wish like hell the same techniques worked for me.

"Not yet."

Today I'm supposed to be cooking some kind of jambalaya for a meeting of the elites. It's a big deal, because Black's getting back home and they're going to go over everything he's done on his trip. My stomach wriggles nervously as I wonder what Black will be like when he gets back. Did the trip go well? Horribly? He hasn't called since last night, even though Matthew told me that the phone we used last night is now officially my new number and I need to keep it on me at all times. That's why the little black rectangle is sitting a few feet down on the countertop.

I haven't asked Matthew how the trip went, even though the butler is sporting a new cell phone and clearly knows Black's itinerary. I don't have any clue whether I should expect the big alpha to stomp inside angrily or if he'll be so fucking happy that he'll sweep in and grab me, dip me, and kiss me like a conquering hero.

Oh fuck. I need mental help. I literally just pictured Black as the cover model in one of those period romances my mother reads. Bodice rippers, she calls them. He popped into my head in a white shirt that's sliding down his arms, his massive torso exposed, that long curly hair of his tossed back by the wind. I clench the knife in my hand and squeeze my eyes shut, trying to erase the image.

"When does he get back again?" I ask Matthew, who has moved on to de-veining shrimp with an efficiency I could never hope to master.

Matthew glances up at the digital clock above the stove. "In about an hour. Exactly three minutes less than last time you asked."

I huff out a sigh and separate off a stupid stem, but I don't cut down the pepper far enough so I end up having to fish dozens of tiny seeds out of the stupid vegetable. "I did not ask three minutes ago."

"I would almost think you're anxious for him to get back."

"No. I'm counting down, savoring the last little bit of my freedom," I retort.

"Mmm." He makes a sound of agreement, but his tone is pure skepticism.

"Fuck you."

"I don't think Alpha Maddox would approve of that, though I am flattered," Matthew quips.

I can't help but laugh. "You've got some sass. I'm surprised he hasn't fired you."

"Yes. Well, contrary to popular belief, Alpha Maddox does appreciate people who are straight with him. He's got enough ass kissers."

"That's the truth," I roll my eyes in agreement, thinking about two betas who dropped by early to set up for the meeting. They hadn't had anything but glowing things to say about Black. Delusional. Of course, maybe if I'd joined the pack normally instead of being kidnapped by the giant fucker, maybe I wouldn't hate him quite so much.

If my wolf wasn't an omega, of course, that wouldn't have happened either. I search for her avatar form as I scan the room, but she's disappeared again. Typical. She'll probably show back up the second Black returns so that I run up to him and make a fool of myself.

You'd better not, I mentally threaten her, just in case she's considering it.

The back door opens, and I nearly jump out of my skin, thinking it's Black. My knife clatters to the floor as I see Pluto stride inside.

Goddammit, Elena! I'm embarrassed as fuck as I carefully squat, all too aware of my short skirt, and pick up the chef's knife.

Matthew's grinning at me, so I shoot him a glare as I straighten, and turn to look at Pluto instead, who's glancing at me in curiosity. He's wearing a crisp black suit and is freshly shaven, the epitome of a middle-aged player who knows how good he looks. It makes me want to roll my eyes. He's got the same arrogant swagger as Black, though he can't pull it off with nearly the same grace as the true alpha.

No.

Did I really just think that?

Pluto's eyebrows lift when he sees me. "Shouldn't you be trying to run away?" he asks.

I flip him off as I walk over to the sink to wash my knife, knowing better than to start shit with him. Pluto's been trying to get under my skin since Black flew out. He still hasn't forgiven me for "putting the pack alpha in danger" as Matthew explained it to me. But guess fucking what? I hadn't wanted Black to come play Superman and rescue me. I'd have been happier if those Dark Nights had just done us in.

My wolf pops up then, her avatar form landing on top of the faucet in front of me. Her expression is skeptical. She knows I'm lying.

Shut the hell up, I say, turning away from her avatar and focusing on chopping my peppers, a frown marring my features when I realize that Pluto's right. I haven't actually tried to leave again even though Black's been out of town, and I've had the perfect opportunity to run. Why is that? Is it because Jonah's still here? But we could run together.

What happened last time hits me in the lower spine and turns the back of my knees to jelly. Maybe trauma-induced fear is keeping me here … because I saw the expressions on those Dark Nights inside that farmhouse. They weren't just going to take me and put me in a storage closet in the basement. Cruelty was brimming in their eyes, about to overflow.

I have to set down my knife because the memory makes my hand tremble and I nearly cut myself.

Yeah. I'm afraid of running. But why haven't I even really thought about it? I've been busy all day every day with cooking eighteen different things but still … is it because I've softened toward Black?

I search inside myself and though I try to rouse all the anger I've had for him, I can't really do it. Jonah's words from this morning circle back to me. He thinks Black has true feelings for me.

My wolf trots into my line of sight and stares at me hard.

Mates are love, she says, flashing me images of two wolves nuzzling.

My throat gets dry as a corn husk in the fall. *It's not love. It's sex,* I argue, though I'm not able to put as much force into the argument this afternoon as I did this morning.

It's just really hot, threesome sex, I repeat. Though he and Jonah never crossed swords, I know for a fact that Black got off on watching me dominate Jonah. He got off on the sight of the two of them splattering my breasts with their cum. He got off on a lot of things we did together. So did I.

He's as dirty and perverted as I am. But after what he did to me—how could I ever feel love for someone who just claimed my body but took me for granted?

My wolf shakes her head, frustrated with me, but I turn away from her back to my knife, ignoring Pluto and Matthew as they converse about the upcoming meeting in low tones.

Black is a hot fuck. And an alpha asshole. I'm not into that dickhead.

My wolf straight up snorts derisively and shoots me a mental image of his dick. She thinks I'm very into it. I ignore her as I continue my train of thought.

But that begs the question: if he's hot and a good lay, why is a hot alpha his age still single? What skeletons lurk in his closet? Besides those from the Dark Nights, of course. He could have any woman he wanted but he lived like a monk from what I can tell. Or maybe I can't tell …

Based on the gossip and the looks from the betas wandering in and out of this place lately, coming in to report on the new shifter-only pool being built, asking about the next pack howl, trying to get Matthew to hire them for this or that task. Everyone looks at me like I'm some strange freak of nature. And it could be because I'm an omega. Or could it be because Black's crazy and they pity me and they know something that I don't?

I mean, I know he's crazy to a certain extent. He's an alpha. He's an arrogant jerk who expects everyone to kiss his ass and say they like the taste. And just like my mother, he's possessive and wild.

But I haven't seen him get violent with me. Yet.

My mind drifts back to my parents as Matthew puts a huge pot on the stove and starts dumping ingredients in and I chop ever-so-slowly. My mom never was violent with my dad in front of me. I'd only ever saw the aftermath. He'd go to the store and come home. Mom would send me up to my room and they'd argue in the kitchen while I played on the butterfly-shaped rug on my bedroom floor with Barbies, trying to talk loudly enough to cover up the sound of their raised voices. By the time I was called down to dinner, Dad's face would already be swollen, and Mom would be silently fuming.

I swore I'd never let that be my future.

What am I doing?

Why am I not running?

Why am I here in an alpha's kitchen cooking his dinner?

I set down the knife and back away from the counter, staring off into space as fear mounts me and digs in its spurs. I need to get Jonah and leave before Black gets back.

"Matthew, I need to make a phone call," I say.

Both Matthew and Pluto look over at me, curious. I turn off the sink and slowly dry my hands on a towel, trying to work my face into the proper expression for a lie. "I haven't talked to my mom yet. With the heat and everything ..."

Matthew nods. Pluto jerks his head. "You can use the dining room."

I nod, grabbing the phone and trying to walk slowly, not run. Even though goosebumps are forming on my arms, I try to breathe deliberately and slowly so that they don't see how nervous I am. I try to force myself to think about ridiculous things like pinwheels or the disastrous time I tried the high jump.

When I make it out of the kitchen into the dining room and close the door, I slump against it in relief. My heart slams into my skin, trying to break free. I spend a minute panting against the door before I realize that Pluto might be listening. I'm going to actually have to call my mother.

While I let her prattle on, I'll figure out how to get Jonah and me out of here for good. I dial with shaking fingers.

She answers on the first ring. "Hello." Her voice is crisp, without an ounce of friendliness.

"Mom?" I ask.

"Elena?" Her tone immediately changes to surprised shock then outrage. "It's been nearly a week!"

She immediately brings out the little girl in me, the one who wants to please her mother and keep the peace. "I'm sorry. I shifted. Then Alpha Black found me—

"Alpha Maddox," she corrects.

I don't bother stating his name because his name isn't the point. I move toward the tall, arched windows on the side of the dining room, pushing back the sheer curtains and studying the locks. They look like old-school windows, the kind that swings open like a door if you crank the handle. Perfect.

"Elena! Elena! Why haven't you called?" I realize I just stopped talking to Mom and now she's pissed.

"I … went into heat." I cringe as I say it. Those are not words I ever wanted to utter in my mother's presence and as soon as they leave my lips, I wish I could cram them back in.

"You didn't sleep with anyone, did you? You didn't mate-mark anyone?" Mom's voice comes through the line high and frantic, surprising me enough that I stop trying to shove at the old-school crank for a moment.

"Why?"

"FUCK!" Mom's fury explodes through the phone line, her alpha tone coloring her voice and making the hair on the back of my neck curl up. I find my shoulders hunching reactively.

"Who did you mark, honey? Who? Don't tell me it's that beta bitch boy you've been seeing on the sly. Don't think I don't know about that!"

I hang up on her and stand as my entire body grows red hot. I want to punch something but settle for squeezing one of the fancy chair backs until my fingers ache. How dare she fucking judge me! How dare she! And Jonah's not a goddamned bitch! He's my soul mate. Fuck her. Fuck her and fuck Black. And fuck this entire shifter life. Jonah and I are going to make it to New York this time because my heat just ended so it's literally goddamned fucking impossible for me to have another one so soon. We're leaving.

I move again toward the window.

But then the dining-room door swings open. I turn and watch in shock as Black comes strolling in, wearing a crisp white shirt, gray slacks, and a sultry grin. His beard is perfectly groomed, and his long hair meticulously combed back from his face. He looks like an alpha, radiates energy, and his scent crashes over me, making me inhale so hard I nearly snort and humiliate myself.

Oh god.

"You're back early," I state the obvious.

"Caught a tailwind. Just landed.

"Could have called ahead."

Black ignores that and marches right over to me. "Wanted to surprise my mate."

I freeze because suddenly, I'm unable to breathe. I don't know if it's those words, his scent, or the look in his dark brown eyes, but suddenly, I can't move, can't think. Black strides right up to me and I find myself backed up against the table, trapped between his thighs.

Just like *that,* my chance to escape again is gone.

19

BLACK

I SCRUB a hand across my face.

I want nothing more than to claim Elena's mouth, to kiss her possessively and bruise her lips so that she thinks of me all evening—every time she takes a sip of water or says something snarky or sarcastic. For the past three days, I've imagined coming home to her and sweeping her into my arms so I can ravage her mouth.

But I don't.

There's something in her eyes that stops me. I'm not certain what it is—sadness or confusion or fear. But her expression doesn't swirl with happiness to see me, and I'm immediately smacked down by how different my mind and reality are, as I hold her elbows and stare down into her pale, un-made-up face. She looks even more beautiful without makeup.

Gorgeously unhappy.

I step back, stomach sinking as disappointment sweeps over me. I'd thought that last night of her heat that we'd broken through a barrier and connected. I thought she'd seen who I really am.

But of course, I had to leave.

She's had days to build back up that wall. Fucking hell. I can see it in her eyes, she's shutting me out. She's standing there in a nearly sheer white blouse and a skirt that hardly covers her ass, looking like a naughty schoolgirl wet dream—but I might as well be an actual goddamned teacher. She feels so fucking unattainable right now. I wonder for the eightieth time if our dirty phone call was a mistake. Maybe I should have simply called and had her put the phone by her pillow. Maybe I should have been gentle around her. Jonah said she wanted betas and betas are gentle.

Gentle's not in my nature though—not anymore. I had to burn all the gentle away to get where I am. I study those gray eyes of hers and those long lashes. My eyes drift over her pale cheeks and full lips, down to my mark at her throat. It looks beautiful there, stirring something up inside of me that I haven't felt in a long time, so long I can't even put a name to it.

The moon goddess has never made things easy for me. I've had to fight for everything I've ever had. It doesn't look like things with my mate will be any different.

I swallow hard and step away from Elena, not wanting to do anything that sets off the starting gun and makes her race away from me. "We'll talk later, okay?"

She chews her lip and gives me a stiff nod, her eyes glancing to the side as if she'd rather be anywhere else. That glance away—it feels like someone ripped duct tape off my arms. It hurts.

My natural instinct is to force her to submit, to crowd her, to claim her again until she's as wild and mindless and ecstatic as she was that night, sandwiched between me and Jonah, screaming filthy things.

But I can't do that.

Her beta knows her. That galls me, but it's the truth—a truth I've been arguing about with my wolf the entire flight home. Elena hates alphas. Fears them. And if I want to win her over someday … I can't force her into a corner.

The epic line from *Dirty Dancing* flashes through my head. "Nobody puts Baby in a corner." I wonder if Elena's even heard of that movie. Probably not.

I step back from my mate, fighting every wolf instinct I have, holding back even the urge to hug her and tell her I missed her, thought about her, dreamed about her, craved her scent. "I have to go to a meeting."

She nods, still refusing me those gorgeous gray eyes.

I curl my fingers so I don't grab her chin and force her to look at me. "I'm glad you're safe. Stay inside … alright?" I tack the question onto the order as an afterthought. I'm trying but it feels unnatural, like trying to button a shirt with all the buttons sewn on the opposite side.

But the question gets her attention. She turns her face to me, looking puzzled.

"Stone's son is not taking this transition well." I make the understatement of the year. But Elena doesn't need to worry because I'm going to take care of it. My hand lifts to touch her cheek but I stop myself. "He's one of the guys who went after you that night. So I want you inside and safe."

"What about Jonah?" Of course, she immediately thinks of the beta.

I cringe, not only for the fact that I didn't think about him, but that now I look like an ass for leaving him working outside on cars when I'm telling her to stay in. "I'll tell Matthew to send him in."

She nods and her lips part, almost like she wants to ask something else. But she closes them again.

I don't know if she's stopping herself from saying something sarcastic or saying thanks.

We stand there for a long moment staring at her and there's a pinch inside my chest like longing—a pinch I haven't felt in nearly two decades. I give her a small smile, not my normal grin. And then I stride from the room cursing wolves and emotions and women and the way they snarl you up inside.

"Bring Jonah in," I tell Matthew once I reach the kitchen. The glimmer turns to me from where he's dumping shrimp into a big soup pot, the kitchen fragrant with the smell of spices and seafood. He gives me a quick nod. I turn to leave but pivot on my heel to look him in the eye a second time as something occurs to me. "And order Elena some goddamned clothes that cover her ass." My luna's been walking around this house in clothes like that for two days and Matthew didn't even think to tell me? Who the hell saw her in that?

My butler gives a disappointed sigh.

"Dirty old man."

He shrugs, unrepentant. "Looking doesn't hurt."

I point a finger in his direction. "It will if you keep doing it. Get her covered up. Now."

"One convent robe incoming."

I flip him off then jerk my head at Pluto to follow me as I lead the way to the front hall and the stairwell, suddenly irritated by everything.

“Bad trip?” Pluto asks.

“You could say that.”

"Stone Jr. is cutting off his nose to spite his face," I tell Pluto. I've given him basic updates while I've been gone and he's been manning the fort, but he doesn't know the full details because who knows if those fuckers tried to tap my phone.

"How so?" Pluto asks as we ascend the stairs to a meeting room on the second floor. Elena's scent lingers in the stairway and I glance sideways at Pluto, wondering how he's dealing with it.

"You smell that?" I ask.

He rolls his eyes. "Vicks on the nostrils. I'm not an idiot. None of us are going to start in-fighting right now when we need all our focus to be on bringing as many Dark Nights into the fold as possible. I swabbed down every elite's nose myself. We need to keep our heads clear for this shit."

"Yeah, we do." I shake my head and sigh as we turn left, away from the wing with bedrooms and toward the meeting rooms that have been used for at least three generations of Lobos. "Thomas Stone is seriously fucked up. The shifters down there are terrified of him. Oh, that reminds me. I brought home an attorney and his family. Can you find somewhere to put them up?"

"Sure thing." Pluto nods. "How was the alpha's mansion?"

"Didn't even go there," I respond. "We went to the fucked up pack house, but not the mansion. Too much other shit to take care of. Legal, banking … those should all be untangled in a few days. Then I'll go back."

"Why not just stay?"

I glance back at him. "You know why."

"Her."

"That … and I have an idea for dealing with Thomas."

Pluto gives a long-suffering sigh and stops on the Persian rug set in front of a portrait of a Lobo alpha from a few hundred years ago. The oil painting looks smugly down at us and for a second, I can see why Elena is irritated by alphas. The guy in the portrait looks full of himself. I'll have to make sure I don't look like that.

Pluto clears his throat and says, "Look, you know I'm not saying this to challenge you. But you can't let a mate interfere with your pack leadership."

"I'm not."

Pluto gives me a look that says otherwise, and I growl at him, taking a step closer.

My wolf is ticked—white hackles raised—but I look at him and then I look at Pluto ... and I tell my wolf, *Simmer down.*

Pluto glances down the hall and says thoughtfully, "I've always admired George Washington. Decent human. Smart. A bit vicious. But what he did for this country—refusing kingship, now that's practically a fucking miracle. Changed the world."

"God, am I in for a recitation of your Master's thesis?"

"Fuck off. This is important." His eyes turn back to me and lock into mine as he says, "I've always wondered if Washington's choices would have been different if he'd had children of his own. What if he'd had a son? What if his dick hadn't been you know ... broken? If he'd had a son, Washington might have chosen to be a king because attachment does things to people. It changes them. Their priorities shift." Pluto looks back at me. "Where are your priorities right now?"

Elena's face flashes in front of my eyes and my chest tightens. Now that I've claimed her ... I'm attached.

Even if she hates me until her dying breath, I'm bound to protect her. Cherish her.

Fuck. Pluto's right. I'm getting sentimental, and that's the last thing I need right now.

It's yet another chink in the armor that will give Thomas Stone an inroad to defeating me.

As fucked up as things are with Elena right now, if I focus on fixing them, then I'll lose sight of this psychopath. And what good is that for the pack?

I stare back at Pluto and harden my resolve. "You're right." I grab the door handle and yank open the door to the meeting room. "It's time to focus. Because Thomas Stone's one fucked up little pup. And we need to drown him."

20

ELENA

I SIT down at the long dining table, pushing back the satin table runner and tracing my nail along the wood grain on the edge. Tears fill my eyes and spill over. Before I know what's happening, my head is tucked onto my arms on the tabletop and I'm sobbing my eyes out—because my hope of running is gone, because those Dark Nights who chased me are clearly still out there, because my mother insulted Jonah, because my feelings for Black are this awful thicket full of thorns. It seems no matter where I step, no matter what I do, I get pricked.

I cry because I'm trapped by this wolf, this pack, this life I stumbled into that I didn't even get to choose.

I know, deep down, that I'm a brat for crying over that. Not many people get to choose their lives. They're stuck with things they never wanted—illness, abusive parents, and a million other awful things. Stuck. Stuck. Stuck.

But I'm not in their shoes. I'm in my own. And I can feel myself sinking like I'm in quicksand.

I know—now I truly know—how my dad felt about things. How life can make you feel like you can't even breathe. I look around and hardly recognize anything about myself. I've gone from human to shifter, from Elena to omega … and I don't know what to do.

Part of me wishes Black had hugged me, purred, given me some kind of reassurance before he just walked off, and then another part of me is upset that I even wanted that. I just feel too many things all at once.

My skull pounds as I cry but I can't stop, not even when I give myself hiccups and feel like I can't catch a breath.

I sob until my throat is raw, not even caring that Matthew can probably hear all of it. I couldn't hold these tears in if I tried. I cry until exhaustion overtakes me and I'm simply hollowed out inside. My eyes drift shut under lashes that are heavy with tears.

I wake to a hand on my shoulder.

I blink fuzzily, only to see Matthew standing near me, the walls behind him painted orange by the sunset. There's a crick in my neck as I straighten up and swipe at my lips to check for drool. Thankfully, I don't find any.

Matthew has a glass of water in his hand, which he holds out to me. I take it gratefully and then rub a palm over my eyes, which have gotten crusty from all the tears I didn't bother to wipe away earlier. I'm sure my skin is blotchy and I'm an utter mess, but I don't bother feeling self-conscious because crying is probably the least embarrassing thing I've done in this house. I just gulp down the water, hoping Matthew will pull a smooth butler move and slip silently from the room.

He doesn't.

He pulls out a chair next to me and sits down sideways so he's facing me head-on. "We should talk."

"We should?" I ask, and find my voice is froggy. I clear my throat and take another sip of water, staring at the table runner and the elaborate candelabra full of pale white candlesticks.

"Yes."

"Okay …" I let the word trail long because I have no idea what Matthew could possibly want to say to me.

"First of all, I need to know about your fashion, because I've been ordered to buy you … and I quote … 'some stuff that covers her ass.'"

I chuckle and nod, grateful, especially after that knife incident this afternoon. "Um ... how about ... go with ... if it's black, it's good." I figure that's easy enough for an older man, right? That way he won't buy me some pastel flowery crap that looks like it's from some bygone era.

He laughs and pulls a new phone out of his jacket. "I told Alpha Maddox you'd want a nun's outfit. Called it."

"You did." I can't help but crack a smile.

"Okay, well I'll order one of those. We'll save it for one of those days he's in a good mood and can take a joke."

"He has those?"

"Occasionally. Alright. What else?"

Matthew and I spend a good half-hour picking out and ordering clothes for rush delivery from a boutique in town—fancier stuff than I've ever bought in my life. I mean the yoga pants alone were over a hundred bucks. The girly part of me is thrilled and I can't wait to get my hands on some of the cute jean shorts and dresses. Also, new running shoes. I haven't run since this entire mess went down, though I've snuck in exercises the past few days. My body is aching for a nice long run, but the hooker heels up in the attic won't cut it. I can't wait to slide on a fresh new pair of running shoes and I almost clap my hands at the thought.

But Matthew wipes away my excitement when he says, "Alright, now we need to talk about Alpha Maddox."

My spine immediately stiffens because Black is the last person I want to talk about—especially with his butler. I think I'd rather call my mother again. "We don't."

"We do. You need to know some things."

Matthew puts a gentle hand on top of mine. "Look. There are things he won't talk about, and I doubt any wolf would because they're afraid—"

"Of getting their literal head bitten off?"

He nods. "But … a long time ago, in a galaxy far away … Alpha Maddox fell in love."

Why does it feel like someone just dropped an anvil on me? Heat spreads across my body and my wolf appears, striding across the edge of the table, a whole two inches tall to my eyes. Her hackles rise and she stares threateningly at Matthew. I try not to show anything on my face, because my reaction is just confusion. It's just the mate mark aching on my shoulder. *There isn't an ache any lower than that,* I tell myself.

Matthew gives me a sympathetic grin. "He was in his early twenties. Like you. Her name was Violet."

My wolf starts to growl, viciousness tearing from her throat. Underneath Matthew's hand my fingers tense.

"She died, Elena. She had chronic health issues—I don't know the full details, but I know she was in and out of the hospital and passed away at twenty-four."

My hand goes limp, and my wolf goes silent as everything inside of me catapults into regret and sympathy. Immediately, I picture Black in the hospital at her bedside, holding her hand and weeping. "Oh, goddess." My eyes drift to the door of the dining room, wondering if that's part of why Black is so hard now, so utterly *alpha* and emotionally stinted. It makes so much sense why he wants to be in control. He lost control in the most terrifying and tragic way.

My view of him shifts and changes, like a camera racking focus and moving in for a close-up. So many pieces fall into place.

Matthew nods. "I don't know if that was harder on him or if what her best friend did was worse."

His words bring my gaze darting back to his face. "What?" What could possibly be worse than that? What could possibly be worse than having the person you love die? My dad's passing was absolutely the most defining moment of my life. It changed everything about me and the entire future I saw for myself. What's worse than losing your happy future?

Matthew sits back in his chair, his hand retreating from mine as he hunches his shoulders, as if telling this bit of Black's history weighs him down. "Violet's best friend was named Carolyn. She was a low-ranking beta and supposedly a real looker, though I speak from gossip—I've never met her. She and Black grieved Violet together, and as it sometimes happens, people bond over grief. They started seeing each other."

My chest tightens again, partially from resistance to the idea of Black dating and partially from anticipation because I know this story doesn't end well.

"I think Black was a middling alpha then, he hadn't fought his way into the elites yet. Anyway, one day, he supposedly came home to find Carolyn cheating with an elite."

The bottom of my stomach drops out and my mind immediately starts shouting, *There! That right there is why alphas are assholes. That other guy felt entitled—* I tell that part of me to shut up. Because I can only imagine the jagged hole that ripped through Black's soul the moment he found out the girl he loved ... didn't love him enough to just leave him. Didn't respect him enough to tell him things weren't working. As much as my parents' relationship has scarred and formed me, I can only imagine how these things changed Black. I witnessed an abusive relationship, but Black was in one.

What Carolyn did—cheating—told him he wasn't good enough.

Not just that he didn't get a happily-ever-after because of fate … but that he didn't deserve one.

What's worse than losing your happy future? I have my answer.

My chest pulses as I immediately put myself in Black's shoes and imagine someone doing that to me. I think of what I'd do. And then I recognize … his arrogance and dominance—they're shields.

My thoughts wander to Black's interactions with me. I left him without officially breaking it off. I chose Jonah without telling Black I'd never chosen him to begin with.

Shit.

I wonder how many nightmarish memories I brought back.

I didn't know all this of course but guilt seeps into my bones despite that fact.

He thinks I'm like Carolyn.

He thinks I'm a selfish bitch like her. I'm not sure if I blame him.

My wolf howls. I don't know why. I don't know if she's protesting our mourning or what. All I know is that I feel horribly, terribly sad. My eyes brim with regret and my hand travels up to my neck. "Why the hell did he mark me then?"

Matthew tilts his head to the side. "I don't know."

My fingers feel the raised little scars from Black's bite. He's tied to me by these scars, I know that much about the shifter world. Mate marks can't be undone. He marked me even though he knew I hated him. Even though I'd run away, and he thought we were engaged. I'd thought his bite was an attempt to dominate me.

Maybe it was.

But was it also a twisted, warped thing he did because he's given up on the idea of someone ever wanting him?

I chew on my lip and then take a sip of water.

"You know … life throws us all a lot of curveballs. And sometimes they suck. But you can waste a lot of energy on hatred. Or you can figure out how to play the hand you were given."

Matthew leaves me alone with my thoughts after that—which is perhaps the most dangerous thing he could do.

Because suddenly, I don't see Black as evil. I see him as broken.

What the hell am I supposed to do about that?

21

BLACK

I AVOID Elena for the next two days, diving into work and plans for the southern annex, as the elites and I have started calling Dark Night territory. We have to erase the term Dark Night from our vocabulary if we want other shifters to do the same. I've also had to field phone calls from the other pack alphas. The Dead Rabbits alpha is not pleased about this turn of events and isn't a fan of the fact that his territory is now minuscule. I tell the dick he's welcome to challenge me if he wants to take on the administrative headache.

"No way. But if work gets to be too much, I'll take that little omega off your hands. I have plenty of free time—"

I hang up on him.

Work becomes my life. I hardly leave my office except to shower and occasionally nap. I even work out in my office, making a couple betas drag my treadmill and a few free weights in here so I can be in phone conferences while I exercise.

Matthew empties my trash of energy drinks and then I fill it right back up again.

All the paperwork for the southern annex is slowly coming together—the official side of things. But I've sent two elites on the jet back down there midweek to deal with the fact that Thomas Stone and his gang of fuckheads ran a bus into Barney Fife's law office, destroying it.

Warcraft texted me a photo this morning showing that they desecrated the office with spray-painted dead wolf heads like they're a bunch of adolescent boys. That just reiterates what I've been able to research on Thomas, whose pack name (which I refuse to call him) is Pain.

Thomas, like many cowards, operates off the basis of fear and supposed unpredictability.

But dicks like that have an M.O. They don't typically do the dirty work themselves. Thomas didn't come into my hotel room. He sent a human. If he'd come, his alpha wolf wouldn't have been able to resist attacking me. And he knows he'd lose in a direct fight. That's why he does these cowardly things.

I glance at my phone and pull up the calendar because I can't remember what day it is. Tuesday. Only a few more days, and then I'll fly back down to take care of Thomas once and for all.

A knock on the door of my office startles me because Matthew and Pluto have taken to just walking in. "Yes?"

I'm surprised to hear Elena's voice through the door. "Can I come in?"

"Yes." I stand up at my desk, my hand reaching for my unkempt beard. I can't remember the last time I brushed my hair or combed my beard. I think I showered. But suddenly, I feel slightly self-conscious of the mess in here. I grab an empty energy drink and toss it into the trash.

Elena walks in wearing a black sports bra and yoga pants, her hair tossed up into a ponytail. I'm immediately thrown back to my middle school days before I could get my hands on actual porn magazines and jerked off under the covers to my mother's fitness mags. Of course, Elena puts those models to shame.

She stands in the door, hesitantly, gaze darting around like she's not sure she should be here.

I wonder what she wants, what she needs to ask me for that Matthew can't give her. My dick has some ideas, but I tell him to calm the fuck down. Elena's not in heat right now, so she doesn't want anything from me. When she goes back into heat ... maybe she will. I'll only give it to her if she asks—I've promised myself that much. I won't push her again because my short naps are full of the image of her closed-off expression. It happens every single time I close my eyes.

I hate that face she made. I'd come back from a trip, from dealing with a psychopath and she hadn't even wanted me to touch her. I've done such a good job fucking up my mate that she didn't even miss me—didn't even want to scent mark me when I returned.

I curse my wolf again for tying us together, though my heart's not really full of anger. I just have this longing because...I wish it all went down differently.

But it didn't and crying about it won't do any good. Until she goes back into her heat or wants something to do with me, I've got to focus on this merger. I must focus on this pack and what's best for them. My wants or needs are secondary, no matter how my wolf or stupid heart protest that.

"I ... haven't seen you."

"What do you want, Elena?"

Her head immediately drops to her feet, and I realize my tone came out harsh. I sigh. "Look. I'm sorry. I'm under the gun here. Our pack has just doubled in size, there's a shit-ton to do—"

"Can I help?" her question takes me completely off guard.

"What?"

She repeats her question, though she gets a little bit sassy, over-enunciating each word like I'm an idiot. "Can. I. Help?"

"I don't think—"

"I don't know everything, but I can pay bills or something. Get the basics off your plate."

I narrow my eyes, tilting my head, trying to understand why she's coming to me out of the blue.

"Look, Matthew wants to cook some French onion soup today and I hate the smell of onions and I just—"

"Sure," I nod toward the meeting table and watch her walk over and pull out one of the new chairs Matthew ordered after I broke the last table and a few of the chairs. The back of the seat is so big that it makes her look tiny in comparison. I can't hold back a smile or stop the way that the tension in my chest deflates a little at the fact that she's not afraid to spend time with me.

This was not how I expected to spend the day. But suddenly, it's looking a little less grim and dull.

I grab a stack of southern annex bills that Barney Fife, the attorney, has been forwarding to me and bring them over to her. Then I grab a backup laptop out of one of the cabinets beneath my bookshelf. I set it down on the table in front of her and lean over her right shoulder to log in. As I do, I inhale her white chocolate and wildflower scent and every muscle in my body relaxes. Having her here doesn't just calm me though, it energizes me, and I fight against the urge to check her out.

But that's not why she's here, I remind myself. *She's just avoiding the smells in the kitchen. She didn't actually come for you.*

I force myself not to check out the way her sports bra lets her nipples pebble as I straighten. "Double check those bills against the credit card I logged into to see what's been paid. If it hasn't been paid, put it in a stack. Once you're through them all, I'll give you the card number and you can pay whatever's left in the stack … please." I tack on the please but then want to kick myself because it sounds stupid.

"Got it." Elena immediately gets to work, and I head back to my desk. But I'm so distracted by her presence now that I can't think straight.

The wild game distributions I'm working on take a backseat to the way her hair trails down her back or the way the sunlight turns her arm golden. When she turns to me and asks for the credit card an hour later, I realize I've gotten basically nothing done.

I hand over the card and move my laptop to the side so that I have to turn my chair and can hardly see her. I still only work at half speed, because I keep glancing over. But a smile drifts across my face as the morning wears on. Gradually, I slip back into the zone, but not quite the same frantic zone I've been in trying to balance the needs of my current pack with the fact that I need to hold fights for new elites without having a damned pack house to host them. I slide into a space where my mind is buzzing with my to-do list in a productive way instead of a harried and stressed one.

Elena's presence soothes my animal or something and once I'm used to her being here, it feels sort of nice to have someone working beside me.

At noon, Matthew comes in with a tray that already has plates. Of course it does, because the sly old bastard doesn't miss anything. "Here you are, Alpha and Luna."

I stiffen at his words as he sets the tray down, my eyes flying to Elena to see how she'll react. I expect her to spit fire at him, but she merely flips him off as she grabs her sandwich and takes a bite. "Mmm." She closes her eyes and moans in bliss. Matthew's chicken salad sandwiches are pretty amazing, but still, I wait for her to blow up—I tense, ready to snap back at her and defend my butler's needling statement.

When she doesn't, I turn to Matthew.

He looks smug, the bastard. Why can he get away with saying shit when I feel like I walk on eggshells now?

He turns and walks out, leaving me alone with my utterly confusing omega.

She didn't protest being called luna? Was that because she knew I'd say something? Maybe she doesn't want to end this fragile peace between us any more than I do. I know there's no way she thinks of herself as my luna. She still thinks she's a prisoner. I sigh. That's a conversation I need to have with her. But if I do, will she just run?

My wolf bristles and growls. He won't let her run. And that is the problem. I don't want her to feel like a captive any longer … but at the base of things, she is because I can't let her go.

"An alpha will always have to be the asshole," My dad's words come back to me. "The thing that nobody likes to acknowledge is the world needs assholes to keep them safe."

I've always agreed with that statement. Still do. But right now, I wish someone else could be the asshole and deal with all this shit and I could just be … me.

My stomach grumbles and I set my paperwork aside, rising from my seat, annoyed that Matthew left my plate at the table with Elena instead of putting it on my desk. My options are asking her to bring it to me or sitting with her. I'm not feeling equipped to do either nicely since I'm going on nearly sixty hours of sleep deprivation. I'm bound to fuck this up and say something that leaves her twice as pissed at me as before. I don't want to go back to stony silence or have her spewing fire. Not when I know we can have this sort of peaceful camaraderie. Not quite friendship. But not quite enemies either.

I reach over and grab my plate, picking it up silently, intending to walk back over to my desk and eat.

But Elena's voice hesitantly asks, "Would you mind … telling me about shifter stuff?"

Those gray eyes flash up to look at me and I find my ass in the chair beside her before I know what's happening. "Sure."

Her hands gesture at the bills. "I just paid all these and realized how little I know. I mean, why do shifters need to buy twenty tons of corn feed?" She holds up a bill I had Matthew print up.

I take a carrot stick from my plate and jab it in the direction of the bill before taking a bite. "Those are the farm bills."

"Farms?" She shakes her head.

I realize that she's never gone through orientation, and I feel like an idiot. "Quick history lesson. Packs used to be small and local. World War I changed shit. We realized how much humans could mess things up, supply chains, and whatnot. And shifters have ... specific needs." I pick up the farm bill and hold it aloft. "We have farms that raise game animals. Lots of them."

Her brow furrows. "But, why?"

"As an omega, this need is less pressing from your wolf ... but alphas have to hunt. We don't have a choice. It's part of our nature. We hunt, we protect, we provide. We have to."

She nods. "Okay, so you raise the game animals so the alphas have animals to hunt?"

I nod. "We raise them so we can set them out during pack howls. Most of the wolves go for the run, but alphas are required to hunt at least once a month to keep their bloodlust in check."

Her eyes widen and she leans back in her seat. "It's that bad?" She shakes her head skeptically. "But my mom—"

"We are very good about making sure our alphas have what they need. Fights for rank. Hunts. Good jobs in shifter-owned companies: oil and gas, tech, some in finance. If we can help alphas succeed, they feel fulfilled and take care of their packs." I grab my sandwich and take a bite while Elena mulls this over.

"But World War I?" she eventually asks.

"Wolves didn't have their own industries. They didn't have as many resources so, across Europe, supplies ran short, and … well …" I trail off because I don't like to think about what happened.

"And what?" Elena asks, making me realize how utterly naive my mate still is about our world.

"They shifted to werewolves."

She still doesn't get it.

"When an alpha can't find prey amongst animals, he finds it amongst the humans, Elena."

Her eyes grow wide as I nod and confirm her worst fear.

"I work so hard to keep order among the packs because I'm taming wild beasts."

I watch Elena's pulse throb as she stares at me and sees me for what I really am—a monster.

She doesn't run. I'm surprised by that. Given her hatred of alphas and the fact that I just confirmed that we're inherently evil, I fully expected her to run to Jonah if not all the way to the gate.

I wouldn't have been able to let her leave, of course, but I fully expected it. She surprises me when she stares down at her plate, breathing hard for a moment as she takes it all in.

"Is it hard?" she asks, head still downcast.

"What?"

"The bloodlust. Is it hard to control?"

"Depends on the day. It's part of why I host howls here every week. That way alphas with a greater need can come by more often."

"How many do?"

"A lot."

She nods too quickly as she nervously processes. But she doesn't speak again, and I find myself volunteering more information, which I'm not sure is a good or a bad thing.

"The southern annex, where the Dark Nights were, only held howls once a month," I tell her with a disbelieving shake of my head.

"That's not enough?" she guesses.

“Not nearly. They don’t have enough farms down there either. My guess is that’s part of why the elites and the head alpha down there were … more violent.” I try to soften the reality for her. She doesn’t need to know the twisted punishments I heard about during my meetings with the southern betas.

“So, you’re going to fix it, right?” she looks up and those gray eyes hold nothing but confidence.

Fuck. That look shoots right through my heart. I want to see that look again and again and again. It’s better than porn, better than an orgasm, better than a successful hunt—the look of the woman you want believing in you. It’s goddamned everything.

I nod, and that nod is as good as any oath a human ever made with their hand atop a Bible. “I’m going to fix it.”

“Good.” She gives me a smile and I tell my mind to save this moment so I can savor the memory again and again.

“What can I help with after we’re done?” Elena asks.

And I’m not sure what happens … but somehow, she ends up in my office the next day. And the day after that. Suddenly, it’s Thursday and it feels like she’s worked with me for years. I hand her assignments every few hours and we work without speaking until she needs something. We eat together and I answer her questions about pack life. We work some more. At some point each evening, Jonah comes in from fixing old junkers outside and she goes off with him.

I offer to stop having old cars brought in, but he declines.

"As long as I get to eat here, I don't really need the money. And a lot of these wolves … they really need the car, Black. It's the difference between having a job and not for them."

I nod and let him keep doing what he's doing. Only Jonah could take something that was supposed to be a punishment and find a noble cause in it.

Fucker.

No wonder she loves him.

But I can't even begrudge him because he's too damn nice. And even though she sleeps next to him, she spends her waking hours with me.

Within a few days of getting back from Alabama my entire world is flipped on its head—and I really fucking like it.

I have no idea what I've done to deserve it. In fact, I'm pretty sure I don't deserve it, but I soak it up like it's sunshine and I've been stuck in the dark.

Pluto grumbles a bit here and there about having my omega in my office—until he sits down and works beside Elena in silence for a couple hours. Then he grudgingly tells me, "I'm glad she's helpful. Just don't let it turn into a distraction."

"I won't fuck her while you're in the room."

"Is that what you're doing while I'm gone?"

"Relax. You're fine. Everything's fine." I don't tell him I haven't touched Elena since the day I returned. I hand her papers, but I don't let my fingers brush hers. I inhale her scent like it's fucking cocaine, but I don't touch her. Because she hasn't asked me to and for some damn reason, that's my new goal in life. I want her to ask me to touch her before she goes into heat next month. Ask me of her own volition.

I even dream about it, during the few hours a night that I sleep.

I'm getting more done with Elena there each day, but there's always more work. There're a dozen problems a day to solve for the Lobos, and Dewey keeps calling me with more down south.

A shifter neighborhood had a fire. Thomas Stone is the suspected arsonist.

A shifter bar had a brawl. Elites who are with Thomas are thought to have started it.

I need to wrap up things here so that I can get back down south and straighten everything out.

I rub my forehead early Thursday morning as I stare out the window, bidding goodbye to the moon goddess and hello to a new day. I've moved the Lobo howl up this week so that I can fly out tomorrow. I hope that means everything will go well. My eyes glaze as I glance back at my computer screen and think of the twenty other things I need to get done today.

A knock sounds at my door and Elena walks in wearing black running shorts and a sports bra. "Hey you," she says.

That almost sounded casual. I give her the smile I can manage, which isn't much of one.

"You look like you're about to keel over."

"Nope. Just need more coffee."

"How about a run instead?" she asks.

I blink, nonplussed. Did she just ask me to go do something with her? Something fun?

I glance between her and the desk, Pluto's warning echoing dully. "I …"

"A dead alpha can't protect me. You trying to kill yourself?" she snaps, her tone suddenly fiery.

"I'm doing my job—"

"No. You're avoiding shit. Me." My eyes snap up to see her plant her hands on her hips. "You think I haven't noticed?"

"I'm working, Elena."

"You're hiding behind work. And I want to know why."

I give a bitter, broken laugh. "You don't even know—"

"Guess what? You're going to tell me. On our run. Come on asshole. If I beat you, I'm gonna spank your ass in front of Jonah." She's out the door a second later, sprinting across the hall.

My wolf tears through my skin and I shift, bones melting and fur erupting from my skin as I dart after her. How dare she threaten to spank me! She's a fucking omega! My omega! Though he's furious, I'm over the moon. Elena's being playful. She initiated something. It's not what I was expecting but goddamn if my heart doesn't rise into the sky like a hot air balloon.

I dart through the front door and barrel past her on the front patio, making sure my fur swipes against her legs and startles her as I scramble around Jonah and the junker he's fixing. I head for the trees behind the pool.

"Fuck! No! I didn't say wolf form!" she shouts as she scrambles after me.

I chuckle and find myself energized by the fire in her tone and by the fact that I found a loophole. She didn't say shifted or unshifted run. She didn't technically forbid it. I hear her scream in outrage behind me and then suddenly, she's inside my head.

You goddamned motherfucking cheater! Elena snarls.

Decided to shift too? I ask pleasantly, thoroughly amused.

You know I had to.

You didn't have to. You could have jogged behind me, picturing how I'm going to spread your legs wide before I spank your ass.

I hear the moan in her head before she can cut it off. Yeah, she likes that.

Maybe this not touching her thing has worked out.

What not touching me thing?

Dammit. I hadn't meant to thought-project that. I try to think of something to say that plays it off, but I wait too long, and the pause becomes serious.

Why haven't you been touching me? Elena repeats. *Do you regret the mate mark?*

Her tone takes a turn. It almost sounds sad, which can't be right. But I can't help myself reacting to that perception of sadness. *I was ... trying to respect your boundaries. Fuck that sounds lame.*

She doesn't speak to me for a long time. *Black, that's not lame. It's nice. No. Not nice, it's normal. That is what a normal, non-alpha, respectful guy would do. Who body-snatched you?*

I dart around a tree and curse the groundskeepers who make this place immaculate. I can't lose her in brush and later act like it was an accident.

Hey! Hey! I'm sorry. I'm a bitch. I'm not trying to mock you. Well, honestly, I was because this is just totally unexpected. Why do you care now?

I keep running until I reach the brick wall that fences in the grounds and then I turn sharply, keeping it on my right side.

Hey! Hey! Come on, Black. Tell me what's going on.

What do I tell her? I don't even know what to say. I didn't like the way she looked at me? Or do I tell her I know things I probably shouldn't about her family because Jonah was trying to get me to see things another way?

Black! Her tone turns pleading. Needy.

The alpha in me can't resist that. We aren't supposed to leave our mates begging. Not for something real.

Trepidation army-crawls through my chest as I search for the right words, words that won't throw Jonah under the bus but will let Elena know I understand where she's coming from, and I respect it.

Look. I heard about why you don't like alphas.

What?

She's going to make me say it. Dammit.

I heard about your dad. I don't want you to think ... I don't want you to ever think of me that way. I know the chances aren't good. I just ... that isn't what I intended. I didn't know about all that. And I'm trying. Okay?

Too many words. I'm saying too much and she's saying nothing. No response. She hates that I know. She hates what I'm saying. She hates me.

Elena stops running completely and I turn to look at her. Her tiny black wolf is frozen on the grass. I dig my claws into the dirt and circle back to her. My wolf whines, not liking how she's sitting so stiff and frozen. *I'm sorry.*

It's a lame apology. It's not enough. But I'm at a complete loss and she's shutting me out. And I'm pretty certain that whatever sort of tepid peace we've had going is shattered and I'll be alone again.

That hurts.

But it's what I deserve.

I sit and wait for her to rail at me for looking into her history because there's zero chance I'm outing Jonah. She needs him. I wait for her to berate me for all the assumptions I made when we first met; first about her pack and then about how she felt.

She shakes her head like she's coming out of a trance and her moon-gray eyes meet mine. Her nose quivers. *No. It's okay. I umm ... I should probably tell you I know about Violet and Carolyn.*

Those names hit me like bullets. It's been years since I've thought about them but mentioning them catapults me back in time to a dark, lonely place.

Oh. That's all I manage.

We sit there in wolf form, both of us about to drown in memories we'd rather forget.

Mate, my wolf reminds me, shoving me to my feet. And before I know it, my muzzle is in her neck and I'm giving her the wolf equivalent of a hug, breaking all my rules, touching her without her coming to me first.

I'm pissed at him, but he doesn't give a shit. He sees her sadness and can't stand it.

When I pull back, Elena stares at me for a moment before she darts away through the manicured trees. My heart falls as I realize I touched her without invitation again, breaking my own rule.

But then Elena snarkily calls out, *Can't wait to spank you, Black.*

I scramble to my feet and chase after the little minx. *On a cold day in hell, omega.*

And my heart lifts as I chase after my mate, and she runs like the wind.

22

JONAH

I DON'T KNOW what's happening or how or why it's happening but Black and Elena are getting along. And part of me is grateful because I know this is what she needs. But then, underneath that, I'm also viciously jealous.

I don't scent sex on her when she emerges from his office night after night, but I almost wish I did because I know she's spending every daylight hour with him. If they aren't fucking, and I don't hear fighting whenever I come inside to cool down or take a bathroom break, then that means they're getting along.

Which means I'm losing her.

Her heart was mine…but she's come out of that office the past three nights with a soft, contented smile. And that's ripping me up.

I was going to give him to her. But I thought I'd be dead. I didn't think I'd be around to see it.

Watching the person you love fall for someone else—I don't know if Black could have picked a worse punishment.

Is he doing this on purpose? Is that why I'm still here? I don't fucking understand. He asked me about the car thing, he offered to stop sending vehicles up here—but he's never mentioned letting me and Elena go back to our lives.

Last night Elena came up to me and said, "He works himself to death."

I had shrugged. "He also gets all the perks of being a pack alpha."

"Does he really though?"

I'd gestured around at the attic room filled with every sex toy known to man. "I mean…kinda."

She'd stared at me pityingly and walked away.

I'd wanted to tell her that he got her too—but I didn't want to start a fight. I pushed her toward him because he'd keep her safe from all the monsters out there who want her for what she is.

But now I'm bitter and feeling selfish as I stand outside in my coveralls, the warm morning light hitting my shoulders as the scent of a sprinkler-wet lawn drifts across my nose.

It should be great. I should be happy.

I'm not scrambling to pick up extra shifts to make rent like I am most months. I'm not struggling through classes because stupid rules at the shop want a degree if you ever hope to become a shop manager. I'm doing what I love and I'm actually helping people.

I fully recognize that Black did that for me.

But I don't know if I like the price of this worry-free life now—not if the price is Elena.

My stomach twists strangely as I wheel my tool chest outside and unlock it, pulling out tools to prep for the day.

The pale blue Pontiac I'm supposed to fix is parked in the drive, instead of outside the gate.

I'm in the middle of reading through a note the car owner left on the driver's seat about how the steering wheel keeps tugging right when the front door slams open.

I turn to see Elena there with a brilliant smile on her face.

I start to smile back, but then I realize she's not smiling at me. She giggles as she runs down the steps. Then a pure white wolf comes darting after her, sideswiping her on the drive.

Her humor contorts to fury as she yells after him that he's a cheater and I realize, with a sinking heart, that they're flirting.

She shifts without a second glance in my direction and then they're off around the house.

I'm completely forgotten.

I freeze. Part of me desperately wants to shift and find out what's going on, but what if I tap into the mind link and hear something I don't want to know…

I snatch the phone out of my coveralls pocket and call the one woman guaranteed to love me no matter what.

She answers on the first ring. "Jonah! How are you sweetie?"

Just her voice soothes me the way nothing else in the world can. It wraps me up like a warm blanket.

"Hey, Mom."

"What's going on sweetheart? I heard that you fixed Mr. Brenley's car a few days ago. He told me to tell you thanks."

"Oh. Good. Yeah. Tell him he's welcome and stuff."

"Jonah. Tell me."

"What?" I ask, squinting down at a pair of robins hopping through the grass.

"I can tell something's up. Tell your momma."

The awkward story spills out…even the part where Elena mate marked me and Black mate marked her, though I spare her the details.

"Well, that's unusual."

I snort derisively. "You think?"

"Unusual. But honestly…it might be a good thing, honey."

"A good thing?"

"Well, a pack alpha is busy. An omega—needs attention."

"But also protection."

"But also attention."

"I heard you. Why are you repeating that?"

She laughs. "Jonah. Where is she gonna get attention when he's busy?"

Oh. "But you're basically saying I'm backup? Mom, who wants to be their mate's backup option?"

"Maybe it's more complicated than that."

"Yeah. Well, it is. Because she hated him two days ago

and today they're all fucking—"

"Language," her tone isn't harsh but stern as she reminds me.

"Sorry. But today they're flirting. He just claimed her without asking. And she ran from him. And now… It just…doesn't make sense."

"Not everything does, honey."

"Not helpful," I tell her.

"Sweetheart, it's true. The heart is funny and it can take over your head."

"But how can she forgive him?"

"Who said she has?" Mom sighs and says, "Remember your cousin and her boyfriend? It didn't make any sense that he left. But shifter life doesn't always make sense."

Chills course down my spine. How could she bring that up? How could she bring my worst fucking nightmare up? Of course, I remember. "I thought that shit, finding a mate and abandoning the people you love, was like a one percent chance?" Is that what my mom thinks is happening? That Black is Elena's true mate but her human side was fighting it? Or maybe…did Elena mate mark me just because she wanted to escape Black?

I know she has been fighting against her wolf tooth and nail. The best moment of my life suddenly becomes warped by paranoia and I can't help but think that maybe Elena forced her wolf to bite me even if I'm not her true mate.

I have trouble breathing and it takes me a second to realize that Mom's been trying to get my attention because I honestly forgot I was on the phone.

"Honey, relax. Please. I can hear you panicking. I'm not saying it's—"

"I've got to go. Someone's here," I lie and hang up on my mom because she's absolutely zero help. Bringing up my worst nightmare and undermining my mate mark means she scores a zero on the mom test. Not fucking comforting.

I pace around the car, dragging a hand along it, eyeing it just in case someone is watching so I don't look like a crazy person. But I don't see a single thing on the vehicle because my mind is racing over the same questions again and again.

Can Elena really fall for Black after everything just because his wolf marked her?

Can she fall this quickly? It took her a year to admit her feelings to me.

Or are her feelings for Black stronger?

Mouse appears in my vision, pacing and staring plaintively in the direction the alpha and omega disappeared. He desperately wants to join them. But we weren't invited because two's company. Three's a crowd.

Fuck.

I try deep breathing, but panic is welling up. I need to do something to quell it.

I shove my phone and the note from the owner in my pocket and grab some tools. But then I end up blanking out again—glaring at the trees and just wondering…are they fucking out there right now?

Are they wolves or humans?

Is he whispering how beautiful she is in her ear?

I torture myself with questions.

I glance down, surprised to find a wrench in my hand. I stare at it, and for a split-second, I consider doing Black's job for him. But I'd probably just knock myself out. That would be my luck. Then Elena will think I'm some kind of clumsy idiot.

Something moves in my peripheral vision and I see Elena streak toward me in wolf form, a tiny black bundle of fur.

Just behind her, Black emerges from the trees, his huge white wolf nearly double her size. She nearly flies, her feet hardly touch the ground. But his bulk provides a huge advantage. I watch as he steadily grows closer. He could easily overtake her, but he nips at her heels with his teeth instead and then chortles.

They're playing.

Flirting.

I grit my teeth and turn away, not wanting to watch, but Elena makes that impossible when she leaps up onto the hood of the Pontiac I'm fixing for an elderly beta. She dives across it, heading for the front door.

Black is right on her heels. His huge paws put divots into the hood as he launches five feet into the air and lands right in front of her—cutting her off before he dashes up to the front door. He shifts at the last second and smacks the door with his hand—completely unashamed of his nudity.

His grin is wide and arrogant as he says, "Beat you."

Elena shifts then, her gorgeous body erupting from her wolf, her fist rising so that she can punch him in the chest. "You held back."

He shrugs, eyes sparkling with humor. "Maybe."

"No holding back!"

"Oh, I won't. Not with that spanking I'm about to give you."

I turn away, unable to watch any more. My chest is twanging oddly, like a guitar that's out-of-tune.

I stare down at the car in front of me dully, not even sure what issues it's having any more. I can't remember. My brain is floating off somewhere else.

I wish I was somewhere else.

Something brushes against my sleeve and I turn to see Elena staring up at me.

Her eyes are full of mischief as she stands naked in front of me and yanks the wrench from my grip.

I'm frozen as I watch her toss it to the ground and it bounces with a rough clank.

"Come on, Jonah. You need to watch," her voice is breathy and seductive and suddenly, I scent her arousal. "You need to watch Black punish me."

She yanks my arm toward the front door and I follow in a daze, my feet automatically complying with her demand even though my mind is shouting, *No! Hell no! Fuck no!*

My wolf howls in delight. He loves sex and he's about to be included.

But I'm sure that's not what's going on. My human mind is pretty certain that I'm about to be dragged inside to watch Elena fall apart as Black fucks her and she forgets me.

Elena leads me to the office they've been working in day after day and when she giggles, my chest rattles like a catalytic converter that's gone bad.

We walk all the way inside but Black isn't at his desk.

The door slams behind us and Elena jumps. I jerk in surprise.

I hear the lock click.

Turning, I see Black—still naked—with a dark, intent look on his face as he strides forward and grabs Elena by the shoulder. He leads her over to the front of his wide wooden desk and then places her hands on the middle of it, so that she's bent forward.

"Spread your legs, little wolf," he orders.

Elena gives a sharp inhale and complies, letting . "Yes, alpha," she breathes in a sultry tone—like she's enjoying this.

"Whose mate mark is on you?" Black asks as he backs away from her.

"Yours."

Third-wheel syndrome kicks in hard. I'm pretty certain that they've both forgotten I'm in the room as Elena growls, "Spank me, Black."

"Not yet. I want you to think about what you did first. Tell me why you were a bad girl."

"I wasn't!"

"You challenged your alpha. You thought you could beat me."

"If we'd run as humans, I could have!"

"Uh-oh. That doesn't sound very apologetic. Should I add extra strikes?"

I glance outside at the birds fluttering through the trees. I pretend I'm somewhere else. I don't hear Elena's response, but I do hear Black's next command.

"I'm not touching you until you beg for it."

That makes Elena whirl around in disbelief, and I can't help how my eyes are drawn to her. Her face transforms from outrage to understanding and then…to tenderness.

I shouldn't have looked. My eyes drop to my feet as she turns back around. I hear the shuffle of papers as she plants her hands back on the desk. Somewhere in the distance, I hear the air conditioner compressor kick

I walk over in a daze and kneel down behind Elena, my fingertips lightly caressing the smooth skin of her gorgeous peach-shaped ass as I watch Black line his cock up with her mouth.

Maybe…maybe that night in the attic wasn't a one time thing. God, I fucking hope it wasn't.

Maybe my mom—no, not thinking about her.

I shut my brain the fuck off as I lean forward and plant kisses along the middle of Elena's right ass cheek. Then I swipe my tongue under the curve of her butt, pulling back when I reach her inner thigh. I repeat the process on the other side. By the time I finish, she's moaning around Black's cock, thrusting her ass out so that my tongue swipes closer to her folds.

I change positions. I duck under her legs and spin so that I'm sitting with my back against the front of the desk. This way I can lick her better and use my nose to nuzzle her.

My mate mark tingles as I use my hands to spread her pussy open only to see she's soaking wet. Her little pink clit is so swollen I can see it poking out of her hood, begging for me.

The sight makes my dick grow hard as I realize that Elena really liked those spankings.

But she's going to like what I do to her more.

A competitive streak flashes through me and I dive back toward my mate's cunt with one purpose, to make her come so hard she bites Black's dick.

I let my tongue drag over her clit, finding the little bud and teasing it by licking in slow circles all around it. I also bring my hands up and slide them up and down Elena's pussy lips, just inside, where I know she's sensitive.

She bucks, nearly lifting off my face. I have to sacrifice one hand so I can wrap it around one of her legs, fingers digging into her ass as I hold her in place.

I pull my head back enough to threaten, "Elena, you'd better be good or Black's gonna have to pinch those nipples while I kiss you better."

I hear a desperate little moan come from her mouth and I know she likes that idea.

Elena bucks again. On purpose.

Black growls and I can feel her entire body tense when he puts a hand on her shoulders. "No biting, little wolf."

I chuckle and dive back down, intent on giving her pleasure now that Black's going to punish her.

"Yes. Fuck. God. Fuck. Yes!" Elena screeches before I hear her gag as Black fills her mouth again with his cock.

Her pussy grows twice as wet and as I lap at the sweetest cunt imaginable, I think that maybe there's a reason Elena waited to tell me she wanted me. Maybe it wasn't about me not being enough. Maybe…it was because she has two mates, not just one.

I mean, that's unheard of—but so are omegas.

And what could be better for a girl whose human side clashes with her wolf side? Why doesn't she deserve the best of both worlds? Someone to protect her and someone else to worship her?

I hear Black groan his release. Elena sputters and swallows and then she screams as I insert one finger and pump it into her. She reaches down and grabs onto my hair, smashing my head back against the front of the desk as she rides my face.

"Goddamnit Jonah! I fucking love you!"

She screams it.

To Black.

To the world.

To me.

23

ELENA

I ARGUE with Black until I'm blue in the face that afternoon because I want to go to my first goddamned howl and he wants me to stay home.

"You're safer here," he grunts.

"Fuck that! I'm a wolf. I need to be initiated."

"Not around other alphas, you don't." He gets all growly and controlling, which—instead of infuriating me—makes me hot as hell.

"Scared I'll like them more?" I challenge, stepping up to the hulking brute and getting in his space. Of course, all that really does is put me in the midst of his woodsmoke and caramel scent, which dazzles me a little and makes it hard to think straight.

"You're about to earn yourself another spanking."

"Promises, promises."

He snarls, his teeth elongating, his eyes flashing gold.

But that only makes me smile, because I realize I'm not scared of him anymore. He wants to control me because he's the one who's scared. But he's made an effort not to command me because he cares. And somehow—that effort makes a difference.

I step even closer, and rub my cheek against his collared shirt, scent-marking him. "Please, Alpha Black? What if I beg?"

"Fuck!" He roars and steps away from me then, chest heaving as he rounds his desk and seeks to put some space between us. "You're going to make me fucking late."

I feel drunk on power, on the fact that his dick is straining against his pants. Part of me hopes he'll throw me on the desk, lift the skirt of the black mini dress I've worn (after our session with Jonah this morning), shove my panties to the side, and fuck me wildly. I lick my lips in anticipation.

But Black grabs his laptop and closes it with a snap, then shoves it into a briefcase. He refuses to look at me. "Cut that shit out. We have to host the howl tonight. I fly out tomorrow."

"Please. You don't have to initiate me tonight then. Just let me see."

He shoots me a dark-eyed glare as he heads around the opposite side of his desk, as far as he can get from me, and marches toward the door. "Fine. But grab Jonah. He's going to babysit you. And if you so much as shake a single alpha hand and I smell it on you—"

"Challenge accepted, Alpha. I'll make sure to keep count of how many hands I shake so that you know how many spankings to give me."

His parting growl makes me giddy.

Jonah and I arrive at the pack house early in the afternoon.

As we pull up, I stare up at it in wonder. It's better than I imagined. If log cabins could be called mansions, this would be one. The packhouse is a three story collection of logs and gleaming windows set in the middle of the Colorado mountains on a huge swathe of wild and unkempt land accessible by only one road.

I admire the stone chimney that emerges from the roof before taking in rows of picnic tables set out in the front yard. Black's already here somewhere with Pluto so they can set up.

After we climb out of the car, I get excited about touring the place and figuring out even more about shifter life, which is still largely a mystery to me. But before Jonah and I can even walk inside, a truck rumbles up behind us. The back bed of the vehicle is full of animals in cages.

I watch the shifter herdsmen, farmers, livestock producers—I'm not sure what to call them—deliver deer, rabbits, and an antelope they've raised for the hunt tonight.

Black walks out of the cabin and steals my breath for a moment with how utterly composed and dominant he seems.

He shakes hands with the farmers and makes small talk for a minute before he points out where the animals should be released. To my surprise, they're all sent in separate directions.

"Why different directions?" I tilt my head and ask Jonah, standing close to him.

"It keeps down aggression against betas," Jonah explains as we watch an adorable little deer blink in surprise when it's cage is set on the grass and opened. A second later, the creature scampers off. "Alphas will fight other alphas over the chance to get a kill, but they'll really get angry if a beta shows them up. Rank, status, egg-on-their-face. You get it."

"Sounds like high school bully shit to me."

"See? You *do* get it."

I laugh easily and after the animals are gone and the truck pulls away, Black nods at us. "Why don't you give her a tour, Jonah? But lather her up in some sunscreen or something first to dampen her scent." Black's gaze drifts possessively down to my legs, which are exposed in the short skirt of this dress. "Maybe some sweats too."

"It's ninety degrees out."

"And a parka. Maybe a balaclava so it muffles that smart mouth of hers."

"Just wait," I threaten, pointing a finger at him.

But Black's already turning and sprinting up the steps of the pack house in his fancy-ass suit.

Next to me, Jonah says wonderingly, "I still find it hard to believe he's okay leaving me alone with you."

"Me too. But I'm not going to look a gift-horse in the mouth. Let's find that sunscreen so you can touch me all over." I grin naughtily.

Jonah shakes his head. "We are not doing what you're thinking. There's no way any alpha tonight could resist your scent if your cum is in the air. Unless you're into gang bangs with pot-bellied alphas who peaked ten years ago—"

I shudder and hold up my hands at that visual. "Okay. Get the damned lotion and make it PG. Ugh. Gross."

Jonah gives me an innocent shrug, as if he doesn't know I might not be able to look a single alpha in the eye now.

Then he darts away.

After my utterly boring lube up with coconut-scented sunscreen, which Jonah says effectively ruins my smell, we tour the grounds.

Jonah walks me over to the Drop and we climb up on a huge boulder near the edge and stare down at the vast canyon below.

The rock layers colorize the canyon in all sorts of shades of brown, some layers hinting at orange, others at red. The sheerness of the drop is fascinating too, as is the way that small, defiant little trees cling here and there to breaks in the cliff face. A tiny, glittering stream snakes through the bottom. I stare down at it as a harsh wind backhands my cheeks. A storm is brewing somewhere in the distance and the sky is getting ready for a deadly fight between the clouds.

"Hard to imagine something so small has the power to carve out cliffsides," I say, staring at the little ribbon of water.

"Yeah. True."

"I find small things are unexpectedly dangerous," Black's voice comes from behind us and we turn to see him standing on the ground just below us. "Especially when they're quick, stubborn, volatile, wet and slippery..."

I hop down from the rock and then jab him in the side but he only laughs and jerks his head toward the building in the background. "Come on. People are about to start arriving."

"This early? The sun hasn't even set."

"There's a hospitality committee. They're going to cook. And every single one of them is going to want to meet you."

"Oh." A sudden onset of nerves makes me bite my lip and I follow him, making a panicked face at Jonah as I do.

"It'll be fine, luna."

"Don't call me that," I hiss.

But Black and Jonah share a look and I swallow hard. "Everyone's going to call me that, aren't they?"

"Yup."

"Nevermind, I don't want to go to this howl. Jonah, drive me back—"

"Too late now, the staff already knows you're here."

With an overwhelming sense of trepidation, I follow Black up the back steps toward the kitchen area, where I can already smell burgers and hot dogs…and maybe even baked beans. My wolf appears in my line of sight, tilting her head at me—as if she doesn't understand why I'm nervous.

Can she not understand the idea that people might call me luna nearly gives me a fucking panic attack?

Mates, she replies, her head swiveling between Black and Jonah. As if having them here at my side makes any of that irrelevant.

Mates. Plural. How the fuck am I supposed to explain that?

We go through a back door and enter an industrial kitchen that's full of more stainless steel than I've ever seen in my life. There are stainless steel tables, a giant walk-in freezer with a steel door, several ovens, a fridge. My eyes travel over the appliances, trying to avoid eye contact as every head in the room swivels in my direction.

"Everyone, this is Elena, my mate," Black just tosses that term out there. In public.

I mean, it's true—he marked me. But..announcing it feels fucking final.

And what about Jonah? I glance hesitantly at him, trying to gauge his reaction.

He's stone-faced, determinedly neutral, though I can see a pink flush creeping up his cheeks.

I'm pissed at Black for claiming me in front of everyone, though given the gossip among shifters—realistically, they probably already knew. Still. This is one of those things he should have fucking talked to me about.

I put my hands behind my back so that all these strangers can't see me curl them into fists as I give a fake smile.

The woman closest to me walks over. She's a redhead, probably late twenties, early thirties. Gorgeous. She's wearing crimson lipstick on in a shade that—under normal circumstances—I'd love to ask about. These aren't normal circumstances, so I just widen my smile and hope she doesn't notice I'm gritting my teeth.

She holds out a hand. "Elena! So nice to meet you! I'm Abby."

"Hi. Nice to meet you too." I shake an outstretched hand and smile up at the beta who's about three inches taller than me. I'm not sure how I know she's a beta, I just do. She doesn't give off the air that my mom does, that sort of high-intensity energy. And she doesn't emit a sense of total dominance like Black. Abby bats her falsies and I wonder why the hell she wore them when she's about to shift at the howl tonight. Won't they fall off or rip like clothes? I add it to my list of things to ask Black and Jonah about shifter life.

"I heard you and Alpha Maddox are engaged. Congrats. Have you set a date?"

I freeze in panic. Fuck. I forgot about that.

My eyes flee this conversation, running toward Black, and I wish my feet could do the same because I want to hide behind him. Two seconds into meeting my first shifter...I am not equipped handle this.

Marriage.

The very word makes my throat go dry.

No.

I can't think about that.

Honestly, since I gave him back his ring, I kind of assumed the engagement was off. What has he been telling people?

Jonah puts a hand on my shoulder and saves the day like a fucking superhero.

"They're enjoying their time together right now. There's no rush."

The redhead's brow furrows. "But I thought you had a heat. Aren't you pregnant?"

Oh god, I'm going to hurl.

I turn and sprint from the room, ignoring the gasps that go up behind me. I race back out the back door, realizing that the clouds threatening a storm in the distance are starting to roll in, casting their ugly shadows on the ground.

I don't know where I'm running, only that I'm going away. I end up on the path back to the Drop, only stopping short when I spot a nude man with golden curls crouched near the cliffs, a dead deer at his side. The deer's eyes are glassy, its neck torn open.

The man's right arm is doused in red and he's drawing on the boulder that Jonah and I climbed earlier.

The letters T-A-K are already visible, written in blood.

The sight is so bizarrely grotesque that I freeze. Pinpricks travel up my arms.

What the fuck?

My wolf appears in my line of sight, her avatar panicked. Her shoulders hunch and whines. Shivers creep down my spine and I take a step backward. But I stumble on one of the stones in the dirt and fall to my ass, making the stranger whirl around.

My heart thumps rapidly as he stares before a slow, unhinged smile crosses his face.

I try to scramble to my feet, but he shifts…into a monster.

I scream as I turn and try to sprint. I try to shift—but my wolf has disappeared! The fucking bitch has left me just when I need her most!

My feet stutter and stumble as panic laces my veins with clumsiness. I pump my arms and try to move faster, but then I feel the scrape of his claw along my spine—

Smash.

I'm thrown to the side, my shoulder striking the dirt and pain slicing through me as a bush attacks my face with branches. Despite an ache that warns me my bone might be cracked, I shove myself up out of the bush so that I can watch as Black's pure white monster roars at the stranger.

When did he get here?

The other werewolf quickly pivots and runs in the opposite direction, into the woods.

That fucking coward, attacking a woman. An omega.

Black darts after him as I shove up to my feet, cradling that shoulder and realizing that my arm burns all the way from neck to fingertip.

My alpha doesn't go far. He circles quickly back to me, still in werewolf form, one monstrous arm wrapping protectively around my shoulders, his claw resting over my heart as he sniffs the air, trying to scent more danger.

My heart thrums as my weak human eyes and nose search for clues too.

But I can't tell. I can't fucking tell because Fluffy's abandoned me.

Gradually, Black's muscles relax, which means the threat must be gone.

Thank goodness, because my knees feel like they're about to give out.

My eyes grow glassy and I stare up at Black, ready to say thank you, but I find his gaze glued to the boulder and the letters on it. I turn back to the boulder and ask, "What is it?"

Black steps back, shifts to human, and then pulls me back into his arms. "A message. From Thomas Stone."

"What?"

"That was him, the cowardly fuck. He left these for me in Alabama. Little love notes."

I grab onto Black's arm, yanking it. "Are you fucking serious? And you didn't tell me?"

"I didn't want you to worry. You were safe at my place."

Oh, I want to punch him. My fear and pain morph into fury that he's kept me in the dark about this. "So... what? You were going to handle this shit all on your own?"

"Yes." His tone is matter-of-fact. He doesn't even recognize what an arrogant, better-than-thou ass he's being.

"Really? How?"

"I have a plan—" Black's sentence is cut off as an explosion rocks through the forest.

A shockwave and then a massive blanket of heat roll over us. The scent of smoke is everywhere. Debris clouds the air.

I blink, ears ringing, eyes unsure what they're seeing.

At first, I can't make out what Black is saying. His lips move but my ears don't work. I watch him say the same thing twice, until I'm able to piece it together by reading his lips.

"The pack house."

I turn—heart fleeing my body—as I barrel back toward the pack house. "Jonah!"

24

JONAH

Minutes Before...

WHEN THAT WOMAN asks Elena about marriage, my balls fly up inside my body and smash into my stomach. I think I might puke.

The three of us are still working out what the hell this crazy dynamic is. But with one stupid question, this red-headed bitch shatters all of it.

My face pales.

So does Elena's.

I glance up at Black's expression, but the alpha is unreadable, as always.

Is this wedding still a thing? Is it still on?

I stare at him wanting answers, but my mate doesn't wait for any.

I awkwardly try to interject. Words spill out of my mouth. I'm not even sure what I'm saying. I just keep a manic smile on my face as I mentally beg someone to change the subject.

It doesn't work.

Elena turns tail and runs out the back door, the creak of the hinges and smack of the wood against the wall setting off an eruption of gasps all around us as the other shifters in the pack are scandalized.

I'm frozen.

Part of me wants to go after Elena but another part of me wants to hear what the hell Black's going to say to everyone.

Is he going to claim her and cut me out publicly? Is he going to tell the truth? What is the truth from his perspective?

My gaze moves from the door back to him and I'm surprised to find him looking at me. His dark eyes stare down at me and my wolf urges me to bare my neck and avert my eyes.

But if I do that, I'll basically give him a free pass to claim Elena in front of these people. My heart cracks at just the thought of letting him publicly erase the connection between my mate and me.

I don't bow my head.

I stare straight at my pack alpha and dare him to be an asshole.

A liar.

He grits his teeth and I see his throat bob as he swallows.

The moment draws on. It feels like an eternity because I swear my heart puts out a year's worth of beats during our stare off.

Then he turns, and without a word, strides out the back door after our mate.

As soon as he's gone, I let out a breath I didn't even know I was holding.

Fuck.

My hand comes up to my chest in a futile attempt to calm my heart rate.

All around me, gossip erupts. But I can't make out any actual words because my body is finally catching up with what just happened and my knees feel like Jello. I can't believe I just did that.

I take a shaky step toward the back door to follow them, when Pluto barks out my pack name.

"Murky! Where's Black?" I turn to see the cocky alpha coming into the kitchen from an interior door, a phone in his hand.

"Out back," I say, embarrassed by how breathy my voice comes out.

Pluto quirks a brow as he strides over. "What's wrong with you?"

I shrug.

He heads right for the back door. He must have something urgent to tell Black.

I follow him, intending to go find Elena, but he stops me just outside.

"Nope. Wait inside. Dangerous fucker's been spotted in the area."

That only makes me take another step onto the grass. "Elena's out there—"

My sentence is cut off as all around me the world erupts into a black cloud. At first, I'm confused by why I can't see but, a split second later, I realize what's happening and I'm filled with regret for the fact that I didn't go after Elena sooner.

Her face flickers through my mind and I think, *I should have given her one last kiss,* before my nerves are shredded by searing heat and ungodly pain.

DEPRAVED: THE FERAL PRINCESS BOOK 3 - PREORDER NOW

Preorder Book 3 on Amazon Now!

AFTERWORD

Thank you times a bazillion for reading!

I hope I made your day just a little bit naughtier and more exciting. Thank you from the bottom of my heart for supporting my dream of corrupting minds like yours with book boyfriends who are better than reality.

If you want to laugh some more, and maybe cry a little, check out Magical Academy for Delinquents #MAD. It's reverse harem, but the harem all gets together to pull off a magical heist and it's pretty much kickass fun if I do say so myself.

If you'd rather read kinky fantasy, then check out Knightfall. In this enemies to lover RH, a reluctant princess has to win back the knights she jilted in order to save her sister and the kingdom. Lots of BDSM vibes here.

I have lots of other book babies too, and they all love to be picked up and cuddle close to your heart.

Please consider reviewing this lil read before you go so that other people can come in forewarned about how evil I am. I mean, you have a duty to your fellow readers, right?

Kisses,

Ann

ACKNOWLEDGMENTS

Thanks to RK, Khali, Kira, Jenni, and Lysanne, Thank you to Dom. Thanks to the hubs for helping me during my daily battles with technology. Thanks to Laura at Covers by Aura for the gorgeous covers that inspired this story.

Is it weird to thank your parents at the back of a book they won't read? It's not, right? I want to thank them for supporting all my artsy and awkward phases so that I eventually turned into this smut-writing gem.

ALSO BY ANN DENTON

Tangled Crowns Series
(Completed Trilogy)

A medium-burn, medieval fantasy reverse harem romance with an enemies to lovers story.

Knightfall - Book 1

MidKnight - Book 2

Knight's End - Book 3

Depths - Book 4

Surfaces - Book 5

Pinnacle Series

(Completed Duet)

A medium-burn paranormal heist reverse harem with a badass main character.

Magical Academy for Delinquents #MAD - Book 1

Delinquents Turned Fugitives #DTF - Book 2

Darkest Flame Series

A co-write series with Katie May with medium-burn reverse harem paranormal romance containing psychotic, alpha males, student/teacher relationships, strong language and steamy situations.

Demon Kissed - Book 1

Demon Loved - Book 2

Demon Sworn - Book 3

Mage Shifter War Series

(Completed Duet)

A medium-burn paranormal mafia reverse harem with shifters and fae. Kidnapping and enemy themes. Co-written with Elle Middaugh.

Fae Captive - Book 1

Fae Unchained - Book 2

THE STORY OF A DARK MAFIA PRINCESS

(Standalone)

A romantic satire I wrote for April Fools. They both have their problems, but sex conquers all.

The Story of a Dark Mafia Princess

Hammer Time
(Standalone)

A medium-burn paranormal comedy reverse harem featuring lots of ancient deities and potty humor. Co-written with MJ Marstens.

Hammer Time

Lotto Love Series

(Completed Duet)

A medium-burn, contemporary romantic comedy reverse harem about winning the lotto and doing whatever the hell you want with it.

Lotto Men - Book 1

Lotto Trouble - Book 2

Ruby - Jewels Cafe Series

(Standalone)

A medium-burn, fated mates reverse harem with angels, demons, and Christmas miracles.

Ruby - Available Here

The Lyon Fox Mysteries

An urban fantasy / cozy mystery series with a magicless fae, a lot of laughs, and a dash of romance.

Magical Murder - Book 1

Enchanted Execution - Book 2

Supernatural Sleep - Book 3

Hexed Hit - Book 4

Timebend Series

A post-apocalyptic fantasy thriller series. Whoo that's a mouthful. Can you tell this was my first series? Haha.

ALSO BY ANN DENTON

Melt - Book 1

Burn - Book 2

CONNECT AND GET SNEAK PEEKS

Do you want to read exclusive point of views from different characters, make predictions and claim your book boyfriends with other readers, see my inspiration for these books, and hang with fellow romance lovers? Then join my Facebook Reader Group! I promise you'll love it!

Join Ann Denton's Reader Group

Facebook.com/groups/AnnDentonReaderGroup

ABOUT ME

I'm a shy lady who has always been obsessed with reading and travel and live theater. I've lived in four states and currently reside in Oklahoma, hence the nickname from my writer friends: Annie Okie.

I have two of the world's cutest children, a crazy dog, and an amazing husband that I drive somewhat insane when I stop in the middle of the hallway, halfway through putting laundry away, picturing a scene.

Made in the USA
Coppell, TX
18 August 2021